THE DEATH OF LIGHT

A Scolaris Mystery Book 2

LOU COLLINS

BOLDFACE PRESS LTD

Published in 2023 by Boldface Press Ltd

Copyright © by Boldface Press Ltd, 2023

First published in 2023 by Boldface Press Ltd

The moral right of Lou Collins to be identified as the author of this publication has been asserted by them in accordance with the Copyright, Designs and Patent Act 1988.

This is a work of fiction. Names, characters, places and incidents, other than those clearly in the public domain, are either the product of the author's imagination or are used fictitiously. Any resemblance to actual persons, living or dead, businesses, companies, events, or locales is entirely coincidental.

All rights reserved. No portion of this book may be reproduced, stored in a retrieval system, or transmitted in any form or by any means, electronically, mechanical, photocopying, recording or otherwise, without the prior permission of the copyright owners and the publishers.

Cover design by GetCovers

For stardust and wither ♥

Acknowledgments

Huge thanks to my VIP readers for their time and words of encouragement. I couldn't have done it without you!

Liz W, Sandi T

And to my husband, who bravely endures my endless plot ramblings and laptop addiction, thank you for being my rock. Your love and patience are truly unmatched ♥

Black chaos comes, and
the fettered gods of the
earth say,
Let there be light

Thomas Hardy, The Return of the Native

Chapter One

Quill - 6 weeks to the ceremony

Instead of the usual excitement that accompanied the start of a new training cycle, Quill felt numb. She peered through the wooden balustrade of the balcony, a tin of polish and a yellow duster drooping from her hand. The Compendium Room lay below, book-lined walls and cherry-wood desks gleaming in the weeping-willow light. But no amount of polish could shake Quill's melancholy, or the intuition that something was deeply wrong. Even the plush, plum-coloured carpet beneath her feet seemed garish, too bright for the gloom that had settled over her.

While she took the rickety stairs, Scolaris hummed with the pulse of human enterprise. In the Science district, labs belched plumes of multi-coloured discovery. Physicians treated patients behind clinical white walls, while Engineers and Architects designed intricate contraptions and practical spaces. While in Law and Order, truth and lies blurred into insignificance in the face of expediency. In a city where knowledge was the most valuable currency, Quill was an insignificant cog in a giant machine, her own dreams and ambitions dwarfed by the vastness of it all.

The citrus scent of lemon beeswax filled the room as Quill attacked each surface, settling into a monotonous rhythm. A fingertip gouged into the thick wax. Each sticky blob worked into the grain and rubbing in ever-increasing circles until her arms ached. As soon as her grim reflection stared back at her, it was time to move to the next section and start the process again.

Not that she minded the work. The satisfaction which came from completing the task, then admiring the gleam, was immense. It was the broken promise the room represented that she struggled to accept. A few weeks ago, her master had taken her into his confidence and offered to train her as a scholar.

Why had he bothered? Clearly, he had no intention of doing so.

His cruelty smarted, dangling her dream in front of her, then snatching it away. Only one explanation made sense—she lacked the intellect to succeed, and the quicker she accepted the truth, the better.

"Ah, marvellous, you're here and the room is spotless. Wonderful to be back, eh?" Master Wittgenstein appeared in the doorway as the clock chimed ten.

"I can hardly contain myself," she said, left eyebrow raised as she stared at him decked out in the brand new robe she'd laid out last night. But he'd already moved on to distributing the first day's teaching materials, and the barbed comment missed its mark.

"What we need now are the scholars. Oh, and water. Studying is thirsty work. Fetch the jugs will you, then you can serve and listen."

"I'll get the drinks, but I'm not staying." Quill's nostrils flared as she gripped the polishing cloth so hard between both fists that it tore in half.

"Good grief, whatever has got into you? I thought you'd be excited, grateful even. Young people today, I just don't understand them," he said, tutting and shrugging his shoulders as he fussed over the arrangement of each pile of papers.

Infuriated by his total lack of awareness, Quill tensed, her slim body ramrod straight as she hissed through pursed lips, searching for the words to express herself. "Don't worry, I know my place. I'll get the drinks." Then she hurried to the kitchen before the scholar could reply.

🐾 🐾 🐾 🐾 🐾 🐾 🐾

Ever since the master shared the secret garden, Quill found it almost impossible not to slip outside whenever she got the chance. The haven hid behind a blue and green tapestry which disguised a stone door at the rear of the tiny kitchen. The sense of freedom she experienced from tilting her head skyward, the breeze stinging her marked complexion, was exhilarating. So too was the skin-tingling excitement whenever she bent the truth to protect the secret. Still, she didn't plan to lose sleep over the deception because it was for a noble cause.

An oppressive heat took her breath away as she stepped outside in the master's old boots. A pair donated to her despite being at least double the size needed for her dainty feet. Sapped of energy, the green tops of potato plants, leeks, and carrots wilted. An echo of Quill's sudden need to seek shade and a refreshing drink.

Why was it so hot?

Though summer was still weeks away, she couldn't remember a brutal atmosphere like it. The library stayed cool inside its thick stone walls, ancient texts preserved for future generations within its vast collections. Thoughts of books provoked unwanted emotions—disappointment, anger, and fear. The master's betrayal consumed every waking moment, that there was no-one to share her troubles compounded the problem.

I wish I could speak to Kai.

Since solving Professor Hawkin's murder, their paths hadn't crossed. Sweat collected around her hairline and trickled into tiny cinnamon-brown waves, plastering them to the pale skin around her earlobes. The stout trunk of a mighty oak could have provided much needed shade. Yet nothing but dwarf trees grew behind the stone-walled perimeter. Any hint of vegetation risked exposing the secret sanctuary to the unsuspecting city.

Relaxed on the wrought-iron bench among the raised beds, her face and bare arms sizzled, tingling in the heat of the sun. The raucous alarm call of a magnificent male Lilith startled Quill, and she cupped a hand around her eyes, hunting for the cause of the commotion. As the bird's black tail feather passed across her line of sight, she spotted a yellow-green flash of light. The rate of her pulse increased as she bolted upright, over-blinking, searching the sky. With suspicions she'd unwittingly looked at the sun, the light vanished, and she slumped against the metal rungs, returning to a glum stupor. Almost at once, the coloured light returned, this time persisting. Glowing and shimmering, the object was visible despite the sun's glare.

Struck like lightning by a momentous truth, Quill knew what it was and what it meant.

Despite their differences, there was no time to lose. She had to share this discovery with the master.

※ ※ ※ ※ ※ ※ ※

Held at arm's length, water sloshed over the sides of two huge copper jugs as Quill trotted along the narrow, dark corridor between the library and the Compendium Room. While hoping that no-one had arrived yet, she groaned at the murmur of voices beyond the solid oak door. She paused, took a deep breath and plastered on a smile, then pushed inside with her left hip.

A sea of earnest, youthful faces greeted Quill's somewhat damp arrival, though nobody paid her any attention besides Master Wittgenstein, who hissed at her through gritted teeth. "Where have you been? Did you get lost?"

"Of course not. There's something important I need to tell you," she said, hiding her words behind the metal pitcher.

"Save it for later. Pour the water so we can get started."

"It can't wait. You should hear this now," she said, much louder than intended. Instantly the hum of conversation ceased, and she sensed at least a dozen pairs of eyes examining her as she slopped the refreshment into the glasses provided.

"Ahem, may we begin?" The ancient scholar spread his arms wide in a gesture designed to encourage the new students to take their seats. As everyone obliged, forgetting Quill's interruption, it gave her an opportunity to examine the group. It was no surprise that the demographic was all male and in their late teens or early twenties. Seated in pairs, desks arranged in a semi-circle facing the master's lectern, they appraised their wizened teacher. All that is except one, a black-haired, tall fellow with a striking aquiline nose and square chin, who stared instead at her. An unreadable twist formed on his ripe lips. Quill shrank under the intensity of his gaze and hugged her chest with her slender arms as she turned toward the front. But even as the lesson began, her mind whirring with her failure to deliver the message, the sensation of being examined millimetre by millimetre refused to leave her.

The first morning's tuition passed in a blur. The itinerary remained unchanged over decades, and Quill hadn't missed a day since beginning her service. Master's warm, husky tone filled the space as he delivered the introductory lessons on the library's history and the role of the scholars who studied there. The flawless performance delivered a wealth of information as he shared decades of experience with the enthralled audience. While she longed to savour the lesson, never tiring of the details, her resentment simmered as a finger click or nod summoned her to refill glasses and provide fresh paper.

I should be with them—a scholar, not a defecto.

Her frustration threatened to boil over into rage. As novices, the group wore the floor-length scholars' robes but in brown. All were keen to graduate to the standard grey robe once they completed initial training. Few would ever wear the white garment like her master, though they each desired it, Quill included.

Aside from the black-haired novice who reminded her of a Lilith bird, those remaining paid her no attention. As she served, the lesson progressed and Quill observed the new group of hopefuls. Cecil Sheppard and Prosper Foley sat at the desk to her far right. Cecil was shorter than her and stick thin—burgeoning on malnourished—with huge protruding eyes. Prosper was the exact opposite. Tall and overweight, his complexion was a permanent shade of angry, a damp collar of sweat around the neckline of his robe. His breathing was audible, like rocks knocking together in his rib cage. To her far left, Arthur and Aric Leitch were difficult to tell apart. Carbon copies right down to their mannerisms, including their awkward pen grip which utilised every finger.

Ouch, how is that comfortable?

Quill made a mental note of a dark black mole on the back of scholar Aric's neck, the lone way to distinguish the two.

The black-haired gentleman who continued to study her was Bran Harland. She recognised the family name as the master often mentioned his father, Harland senior. A protector who handled innovation in the Architects' District, including the development of new building methods and materials.

Why is the son of a prominent citizen becoming a scholar?

While scholarship was an important role within Scolaris society, it came with a life of duty and self-sacrifice. A prospect far removed from the trappings of power and success enjoyed by Bran's father. It was an odd choice.

Bran's companion, who was older than everybody else, already looked the part. An auburn mop stretched from his crown to the middle of his back. Round glasses perched on the end of his nose, the lenses of which were so small, Quill doubted they were fit for their purpose. Jacob Dowling peered over them rather than through them. There were additional students, but they faded into the background like dust balls on a skirting board. They appeared attentive, like all the young men passing through training toward a studious life. Quill couldn't tell how or why, but there appeared to be an automatic hierarchy among them and she wondered if they'd met before. Those who vanished into the surroundings languished at the bottom, desperate to join their peers. Most resembled younger versions of the ancient scholars who graced the library every day. Juvenile copies who possessed more hair and less fat than their geriatric predecessors but were otherwise identical. The nameless, faceless students were subordinate to Cecil and Prosper, followed by Dowling, then the twins. And high above the rest stood Bran, oozing confidence, a swagger about him which Quill found disarming. That they were all male reminded her that not only her rank but also her gender thwarted her ambitions.

The entire group was now the proud owner of a large stack of scrawl, which included the basic rules and expectations of scholarship. Next, the topic turned to the initiation ceremony–an official welcome scheduled to take place in six weeks. Quill stifled a chuckle at the image crowding her mind. A troop of students who completed their training then spawned into grey-haired, myopic versions of themselves. Phenomena no doubt caused by the hours spent in the myriad of library corridors. Her attempt to hide the hilarity proved fruitless, as she met the master's unequivocal scowl. Worse still, it garnered a raised eyebrow from Bran Harland who, much to her embarrassment, examined her like an oddity. Not to mention that breaching the studious silence announced her presence to the others. Their disapproving faces left no doubt they didn't appreciate the interruption. Insidious whispering followed as heat fanned from the pit of Quill's stomach. Warmth filled her chest until it broke over her face like molten wax, to which she instinctively lifted a hand to hide her cheek.

Old habits are tough to break.

The insecurity of her marked complexion reared its familiar, if unwanted, head.

Time dragged as sounds echoed and reverberated around her skull as if she were in a tunnel. A splash of black shot across her peripheral vision, causing further confusion as she struggled to recalibrate her senses. After what seemed an age, she emerged from chaos to the sound of indignant voices. Aric Leitch, his diction clipped and precise, launched from his seat. "Look what you're doing, stupid girl."

Still disoriented, Quill spotted a dark patch of black growing in all directions from the boy's midriff like mould. Then it hit her. She'd been so caught up in her own thoughts she'd lost focus and knocked over an inkwell, washing Aric's work and his brand new robe in a black rinse. The reason these men insisted on using ink pots was a mystery. She was about to offer an apology when the master's abrasive tone interrupted. "Quill, get this mess cleaned up immediately, and for once in your life, stop daydreaming and concentrate on your duties." Pausing, he scratched his lined head with gnarled fingers, muttering as he leafed through the papers piled high on the lectern in front of him. "Now, where were we before we were so rudely interrupted?"

"Too right," said Aric, his voice muted, a twisted grin of satisfaction on his lips. "Focus on your duties, defect-*oh*." He smirked, the childish insult to her social class cruel and deliberate.

Quill gripped the edges of her tunic, stretched them to each side and slow curtsied, an obvious forced smile across her lips. "I'm so, so sorry. Please forgive me." As she batted her eyelids like a naughty child, Aric glared, fists clenched at his sides as she turned on her heels and stomped away to the soundtrack of full-bodied laughter. A surprising noise which emanated from Bran Harland, who winked at her, sending her scurrying away to find a new robe.

Chapter Two

Red

To say the job of Chief of the City Guard had complicated Red's life was the understatement of the century. After the hiatus following the discovery of Professor Hawkin's body and those of the six missing defectos—who didn't officially exist—the previous fortnight had flown by in a disastrous sequence of deadly discoveries. One death soon turned into two. Indeed, the rate of corpses appearing across the districts was exploding into an unprecedented tragedy whose timing couldn't have been worse. As the youngest chief in living memory, Red was trying to navigate his new role, which came with many unexpected challenges. Now the City Guard also faced the arduous task of solving mounting numbers of unexplained deaths. The murders of the professor and his poor unfortunate victims had opened the floodgates to an unusual era in Scolaris history. Rumours circulated through headquarters. Superstitious nonsense which linked his promotion to the rising body count. He suspected that disgruntled guardsmen fuelled the office gossip, colleagues who were jealous of his appointment and eager to engineer his downfall. Though anyone could work out that the accusation was ridiculous. Still, he could do without the complications.

Stood with Dr Virgil Fox, the forensic pathologist, they conducted a cursory examination of the most recent victim. Red exhaled. It was hard to face the dead man's ecstatic expression, the same as the grin etched on Hawkin's features, those of the mistreated and expendable defectos, and Ivy Penrose—the woman who'd confessed to Hawkin's murder. A frozen rapturous stare repeated over and over as the body count ticked higher.

"It's another one, then?" Red massaged the dull throb pulsating in his forehead as he did his best to avoid inhaling the intense, sickly sweetness which filled the air.

Dr Fox scribbled away on his clipboard as he paced around the corpse like a caged animal. Tutting, he frowned and continued writing. "You know I can't speculate until after the full autopsy. My biggest concern is how soon I can get to it. Cases are mounting and at this rate I'm going to need an assistant. I'm sure I don't need to remind you that processing bodies promptly is the best way to preserve evidence and pinpoint the cause of death. There's only so many hours in a day, and I've been working non-stop."

"Haven't we all? It's been a rough couple of weeks and I appreciate all the extra time you've been putting in, Doc. If you need personnel, find some."

"I wish it were that simple. Before Hawkin, I'd never dealt with a murder investigation. All my technical knowledge comes from books. I'm simply a doctor with a passion for forensic science who volunteered to perform autopsies. Whether there's anyone else who shares that interest is an unknown quantity. I don't know how to find someone suitable. There's not even a formal training program for the job."

"Unbelievable. Sometimes I wonder if we're living in the dark ages."

"You're not alone. Autopsies are rare. Most often physicians certify the deaths of their patients and that's the end of the formalities. Unless you die unexpectedly in a hospital, no-one checks the circumstances. The system needs an overhaul."

"Good luck with that."

Crestfallen, dark circles surrounding his focused, intense eyes, Fox returned to the clipboard and his note taking. "Okay, so I'm logging him into the system as number ten." He pointed his pen toward the latest victim, who lay in an untidy heap beneath a hedgerow, an unwelcome addition to the tranquil surroundings of the Physicians' District. The dog walker who'd reported the discovery appeared more concerned with the trauma suffered by the pet than the fate of the unidentified male. "And now I need to complete the full examination of number one."

Ten unexplained deaths in the last fortnight. It bore all the hallmarks of an epidemic. "How long will the tox results on one take?" asked Red, eager to drive progress.

"On the basis I'm doing every single thing, how long's a mathematical equation? Hopefully, in the next seventy-two hours on bodies one to three. I've collected samples from each as a priority, to ensure nothing degrades even if I'm delayed examining the remains themselves. I hope to have something on the first set of specimens later today, so I'll let you know asap."

"Okay Doc, setting aside your disapproval of speculation, off the record, what do you think? What are the odds it's the same toxin that killed Hawkin?"

"I'm not a betting man. I'm a scientist. The tests won't lie, be patient."

Fox's response was frustrating, but expected. Red might have bet a lot of money on the outcome. His instinct grew stronger with each new victim. The question he needed to answer to halt the grisly tide was straightforward–where was the drug coming from?

Apart from the vial found in Theo Penrose's office, neither he nor Quill had discovered any more. The samples at Professor Hawkin's had been destroyed during the adulterer's demise and there were none with the defectos hidden in the old pavilion. The select few privy to the murders assumed the toxin had vanished into obscurity, along with Hawkin and his unconscionable experiment. Assumptions had a way of backfiring, which now appeared to be the case. Somehow, someone had this narcotic, Red was sure of it. And to make matters worse, whoever they were, they were sharing it.

"Have you identified anyone yet?" asked Fox, interrupting Red's chain of thought.

"Not so far. None of them were carrying any personal effects. Unsurprising, considering they're all missing their clothes."

"I don't think they're defectos."

"What makes you say that?"

Fox lowered his voice. "Well, no-one's malnourished, nor do they show signs of the wear and tear I'd expect from a life of service."

Red grimaced, searching the vicinity for unwanted eavesdroppers, relieved to find none. "So if this mess relates to Hawkin's work, the experimental phase is over. Does this chemical have a name?"

"Not officially, no. We can hypothesise that Professor Hawkin extracted what he needed from the Asterian Marble—a rare butterfly indeed—then he harnessed its power in the laboratory. Whether he intended to create something so deadly, we'll never know. I'd categorise the chemical as a stimulant and a depressant. The substance works on the zones of the brain responsible for creative thinking and perception. An unfortunate side-effect slows the nervous system, which for specific individuals causes heart failure."

"So that look on their faces is because they're intoxicated?"

"Again, don't quote me. I can only guess, unless I take the drug myself, which unsurprisingly I'm not about to do. Whatever they're seeing or thinking, they've paid the ultimate price for a few moments of pleasure."

"It's difficult to comprehend ten deaths and not a single report of anyone missing. Perhaps none of them have relatives to miss them?"

"Interesting theory. Their demographic is similar, male aged between forty and fifty. Even if there's no family, wouldn't someone notice their absence at work?"

"I considered that, but so many people work freelance it's possible no-one would miss them immediately."

"Do the locations of the bodies help?"

"Not so far. Take this one. There's not much activity nearby. Unless you count the neighbours." Red peered over the hedge and took in the sombre view of ancient tombstones which stretched into the bleak cemetery like rows of crooked teeth. "We've discovered them in each district, though not in the defecto quarters. House-to-house enquiries in the immediate vicinity all proved a waste of time. Short of knocking on every door to ask if anyone's mislaid a family member, the current course of action is to hope that someone comes forward. If I had my way, we'd be making a public appeal for information. But it turns out that the office of Chief of the Guard is ninety-per-cent political. I should've paid closer attention to Jim Ross's warning. I can't move for bureaucracy. Everything has to pass through the Law and Order subcommittee, and being honest, they have no teeth. The real decision-maker sits right at the top."

"Novack?" asked Fox as he crouched to examine every millimetre of skin through a magnifying glass.

"Yeah, have you met him?"

"Hmm," said the scientist, distracted as he peered behind the dead man's earlobe, "once. Barely spoke to him, though. You should see this."

Red's pulse quickened as he strode forward, the footfall of his shiny boots deadened by the lush verge. As he stooped toward the deceased's bald head, Fox stepped aside, tucking the magnifying glass into the front pocket of his overalls. Magnification wasn't necessary as Red spotted a familiar, distinctive tattoo–a black swirling G symbol. Returned to his full height, he turned to face his father's old friend. "Here we go again. I need those toxicology results."

"Leave it with me. Bearing in mind the delicate nature of the investigation, for identification, I'll be referring to the toxin as M."

Red nodded his approval and headed down the leafy lane, birdsong filling his head.

It could be worse. At least I'm in the fresh air and not in the mortuary beneath all that rock and earth.

The familiar grip of anxiety twisting his gut was never far away. He was almost out of earshot when Fox called to him. "When you speak to Novack, ask him to appoint a junior pathologist immediately. If we proceed via the committee, they'll tie us in knots for weeks. Direct access to the top man has to mean some benefits."

"I'll see what I can do," said Red, waving in Virgil's direction.

"Oh, and send your mother my respects."

Red cringed, a rictus grin deforming his features. He wasn't ready to admit they still weren't talking, so bolted instead.

Chapter Three

Kai

Kai had grown accustomed to a level of self-confidence which belied his age and experience. Unfortunately, the move from Serenity Gardens to 1, Courtyard Place, had a detrimental effect on this state of affairs. The relief at finding a new position so soon after Dr Cooper's spectacular fall from favour didn't last as he grappled with the practicalities of his fresh surroundings. Although his stint with the physician had been short-lived, he missed his old room and the tranquillity of the Physicians' District. While no-one could forget how Cooper facilitated Professor Hawkin experimenting on defenceless defectos, the medic only ever treated him with kindness and understanding. Most of all, he missed Jed, who reminded him of his late mother. His former home, which comprised the traditional house and its shiny new clinic, was simple to navigate. Despite the limitations of his sight, it had proved straightforward enough to memorise its narrow corridors and distinct rooms. The same was not true for the apartment's sleek expanse. An absence of doors and partitioning walls caused confusion, not to mention the hazardous split levels and an open fireplace set into the floor, an instant death trap for people with low vision. Even with his faithful cane, he couldn't shed the twinge of anxiety as he moved from the lab to the living quarters and back again. There was something else he'd discovered. Buildings often gave off vibrations, nothing tangible, emotions almost. Serenity Gardens felt like a warm hug. The place had absorbed the loving care doled out to the practice patients over the years, then radiated it through its surfaces. But not here. Courtyard Place was soulless, an empty vessel crying to be filled. The apartment made him shudder.

Professor Moore, his new boss, proved difficult to read. The scientist rarely spoke, but that wasn't the only puzzle. Doctor Cooper had only stipulated his private living room as off-limits. The rest of the house, its grounds, and clinic were open to the public. Moore's approach was precisely the opposite. The major thrust of their encounters centred around his repeated strict instructions never to set foot in the laboratory or the bedroom. A rule which meant that carrying out the full range of serving duties was problematic. But the fellow prioritised his privacy, which, of course, was his prerogative.

"Boy. Coffee. Newspaper." The sandpaper voice startled him. This appeared to be Moore's favoured method of communication. Single. Word. Commands. It was actually rather funny, but Kai knew how to suppress that feeling. Fading into the environment was a skill you learned early as a defecto.

After taking a deep breath, cane tip-tapping in front of him, he headed to the kitchen and prepared breakfast. The scientist expected high standards, and Kai focused on each minute detail.

Coffee, thick and black and sweet. Two slices of bread—barely toasted—buttered to the edges and drizzled with honey.

There was an art to perfect toast production that involved hovering over the toaster, waiting for the faint aroma of burnt wood, which signalled the precise moment to press eject. It hadn't taken him long to perfect the process.

As Kai laid out the meal on the fine porcelain, enjoying the smooth, chilled surfaces at his fingertips, he called to Professor Moore that the breakfast was ready. The thud, thunk of the fellow's dual walking sticks echoed like a faltering heartbeat. A slow and steady sound which signposted his approach.

Does the poor man find it hard to live here, like me?

Despite never getting close to Moore long enough to piece together the shapes and shadows that were the limits of his sight, Kai formed an image of the fellow. The knowledge his master relied on sticks in each hand combined with the sound of each painful shuffle conjured a hunched, aged, and arthritic figure. Though his thick wool coat felt long and roomy so he couldn't be precise about the scientist's size. Because he left emergency pairs of spectacles scattered around the apartment, Kai pictured intense, inquisitive eyes peering through thick, square lenses. Although the command, *glasses*, was a firm favourite, Moore still hadn't worked out why his defecto couldn't immediately produce a pair.

Maybe the professor's a closet sadist?

Mealtimes were brisk affairs. Moore finished almost before he'd begun, then hobbled toward the lab. Despite being a workaholic, even Doctor Cooper enjoyed talking about the day ahead. A recap of the patients he expected to see and an occasional check on staff welfare. Professor Moore wasn't rude exactly. But nothing resembling a *please* or *thank you* had emanated from his lips, and small talk was not part of his repertoire.

The odd expression of thanks wasn't too much to ask, was it? Maybe I should be thankful since I have a job and a place to stay.

As the echo of Moore's footsteps faded, the man's last command rang around the kitchen as Kai lowered the crockery and cutlery into the hot, soapy water. "Garden," was the instruction, followed by, "stay out of my room."

Moore loved the terrace. That had been obvious from the outset. Kai spent most of his time outdoors, and while it had taken him time to adapt, he could detect the difference between the soft pine bark, solid wood boards, and slate paths to find his way. Which, together with the powerful minty aroma of evergreen shrubs, enabled him to keep the lawn neat and clipped and manage the borders. Jed maintained the grounds at Serenity Gardens. He wished he could ask her how to tackle technical aspects like pruning and propagating, as these were skills he didn't have. Still, the sun shone as spring morphed into summer, and Kai enjoyed the heat tingling his cheeks through the glass walls. As he recognised there were worse ways to spend the day, his major regret was not having seen Quill since his arrival. He'd hoped their friendship might grow now that they lived near to one another, but so far, their paths hadn't crossed. Perhaps assuming they'd often see each other was a mistake.

Dishes washed, dried, and returned to the sleek cupboards. The nagging tone raised the same question which had plagued him for weeks.

Why is Moore so insistent that I stay out of his room? The scientist's in the lab, his mobility restricted. What's stopping me from exploring?

An alternate voice followed this rebellious thought—the loyal, conscientious, and rational one. The one reminding him he was a servant, and the professor's status entitled him to privacy. After all, it was a bedroom.

What could Moore be hiding?

With that question percolating, Kai walked from the kitchen to the manicured garden through the sliding doors.

Chapter Four

12 hours earlier...

Dr Sterling Novack had questioned his eyesight, then his well-being, when he spotted a yellow-green flash in the midnight sky. But as night wore on, the object grew brighter, overshadowing the moon and the constellations. He knew he was witnessing a moment of history.

The guest star first appeared in the heavens south of the city of Scolaris in early May. With scintillating, radiating light, the orb announced its auspicious arrival. That it remained visible even as dawn approached, the sun creeping above the horizon like a plump cherry, confirmed Novack's suspicions. They should bring the ceremony forward without delay.

"Come on, Luna. Time to go. We've got a lot of work to do." He ruffled the soft black pelt at the top of the Cavalier King Charles's head while she slept, curled up on his boots beneath the bench. His loyal companion did not stir, and the reassuring warmth of her petite body made him loathe to leave. But the heat of the day rose like a swarm of vermin, closing around them and making beads of sweat form under his green wool suit. "Sorry, girl. Sleep time's over. We need to move before we fry," he said as he levered himself from the hilltop seat behind his house. As he stretched the stiffness from his tired arms and legs, pins and needles made his feet seem like they didn't belong to him.

Luna belatedly stirred, staring up at him with enormous, sorrowful eyes. The young dog yawned, licking her lips and panting in the sweltering heat as she rose on her front paws, a move which revealed a perfect circle of white fur on her breastbone against a black-and-tan coat—the spherical inspiration for her celestial name.

As Novack headed through the trees to the garden, his mind whirred with the crucial arrangements. The Protectorate should meet to confirm the guest star's existence and ratify advancing the ceremony. Then the scholars could be told. An enigmatic smile pulled at his lips when he realised he would be at the heart of the excitement to follow.

Even though the sun struggled to penetrate the huge domed crowns of the beech tree canopy stretching over forty metres above his white-haired head, the heat was almost unbearable. Luna circled, forged ahead, then trotted faithfully back to sniff his brown leather boots, which attracted damp leaves and beech masts like magnets. Relieved, the doctor glimpsed the teal wooden door into the garden.

Why isn't the gate locked exactly as I left it on the way up late last evening?

Luna's sudden low growl followed by her dashing away as if hunting rabbits startled him into giving chase. He was afraid the gardener wouldn't return if she ransacked the beds again. "Luna, Loona," he called, without success, as he reached the gap in the gateway and stepped onto the gravel track at the top of the garden.

The path wound under a rose-covered arch, through the flower beds and shrubs, and sloped down to the rear of the house. At first glance, Novack thought the dog had vanished. A vein in his left temple throbbed as he mopped the sweat from his forehead with a cream satin pocket square. Then, to his right, a ripple of movement through a mass of two metre blue delphinium spikes caught his attention. "Luna, come back here, you naughty girl. You'll get me hanged." Aggravated, he stepped off the path and onto the border. Vibrant pink and purple hollyhocks and tubular white foxgloves saturated the air with their soft floral scent. Bees buzzed between blooms ripe with sweet nectar.

Overpowered by a fit of sneezing caused by the sudden influx of pollen, Novack rubbed watery, itchy eyes. Disoriented, he turned left and right in the towering foliage, desperate to get his bearings. As he stumbled, heading deeper into the border in the direction he'd seen the last hint of movement, something snagged at his feet. Gravity took hold of his body, throwing him forward, his hands grappling the flower stalks to break his fall. That he didn't snap his neck was a minor miracle, but the excruciating pain throbbing from his right ankle to his hip as he lay face down in the dirt was enough to trigger a reaction. "Ow!" he howled, clutching his pulsing, bootless foot as it doubled in size in seconds. "Help! Hello, Yulia! Anybody? Help! I need help!"

But nobody came.

The sun rose higher, burning his despairing angular features, ignorant of his plight. Startled by a rustle in the undergrowth, Novack wondered if he'd passed out from the heat and the pain. With blurred vision and parched lips, he tried to home in on the sound.

Where is that noise coming from?

"Luna, is that you, girl?" he asked, his voice thin and hoarse. "Come here. Come on. I've got your favourite treat." He fought to keep his tone light despite the humiliation of lying horizontal in a flower bed while pursuing a wayward pet. The hissing, snuffling sound grew louder and louder, creeping nearer and nearer to his prone body, and he braced himself for an onslaught of leathery licks.

Life had a funny way of throwing up unfortunate coincidences. Had it not been for the mischievous dog, Dr Sterling Novack might have paid more attention to the telltale signs—the whooshing of blood in his ears, feather-like hairs erect at the nape of his neck, and beads of cool sweat forming on his clean-shaven lips.

Then the world turned black, swallowed by fear and pain. Everything pointed to one simple fact. Something had stalked him from the bushes—something dangerous that walked on two legs, not four.

Chapter Five

As Quill balanced an awkward pile of fresh brown robes, cleaning cloths and tubs of polish, she failed to spot the disgruntled mob funnelling into the corridor. With her line of sight obstructed, she barrelled straight into the figure at the front of the pack—Aric, already enraged by her clumsy mishap with the black ink.

"What is wrong with you?" he said, while cleaning equipment and clothes rained down as if he were the eye of a domestic storm. Surrounded now by the group of young men, Quill avoided articulating the reply in her head. Words sharper than the meek response she dug up from somewhere deep within her. "Sorry. I didn't notice you behind all this stuff. I have clean robes. Wasn't sure of the size, so I brought a selection." With her gaze glued to the floor, Quill retrieved the spilled items from the carpeted corridor, relieved to have a reason not to make eye contact. All she could see ahead were pairs of feet and pressed brown linen hems.

"Sorry. Is that the best you can do? It's going to take more than sorry. When you've cleared up this mess, you can take the robes to my defecto. We're taking a break. It's so demanding this study, not to mention boring. The old man certainly enjoys the sound of his own voice." Aric's comment prompted nervous laughter from the rest of the group and mutterings of agreement.

The childish mob mentality pushed each of Quill's buttons, something that wasn't hard to do in her already fragile state of mind. "Don't speak about the master that way." Rage simmered millimetres below the surface as she fought to keep her tone even and measured. "You'll never be half the man he is, even if you live to a hundred and fifty. And if you think becoming a scholar is boring, then you aren't worthy to wear these robes. Perhaps you don't have the intellect?"

Her concluding barbed comment sent Aric Leitch tumbling over a cliff of self-composure, a fall from which there was no return. Quill recognised it in the hunch of his shoulders and sensed it in the hush. Each of the group performed a synchronised intake of breath as they waited for the eruption.

Then Arthur leaned in close, breaking the tension for a second. "Are you planning to let her get away with that?" A fraternal glare of utter contempt met his pointed question, to which Arthur mouthed, "Sorry," as he stepped backward toward the safety in numbers of the group.

Returned upright, clothes and cleaning equipment retrieved and re-stacked in her arms, Quill faced the boy's black-eyed hatred head-on. Aric's raised arm came out of nowhere, and with lightning reflexes she covered her face with her outstretched palms, jettisoning the precarious load once again. With her eyelids clamped shut, recoiling, she waited for the attack, but a disembodied, thick, masculine tone intervened. "No. Aric, stop. Not here. Play nice."

As Quill peeped between her fingers, Aric's bony hand hovered millimetres from her cheek. The owner of the voice held the wrist firm, then strong-armed the offending appendage back to Aric's flank. "Did you hear what she said to me?" said the aggressive youth, spit flying from the corners of his mouth.

"I don't care. Let's get some air. Now." Like lost sheep, they followed the command of their shepherd, Bran Harland. With bowed heads, they filed past Quill, making their way to the main building, on route to the outer courtyard.

Relieved to have escaped her encounter with Aric physically unscathed, Quill pushed aside thoughts of the potential long-term repercussions of challenging his authority. Supplies gathered, she returned to the training room to find a buzz of activity. Master Wittgenstein was absent, probably making use of the tuition break to work on one of his many projects. In the students' absence, their servants set up a line of wooden trestle tables along the back, covering them with a set of pure white cotton cloths left out for the purpose. Then they laid out an enticing selection of dishes in readiness for lunch. There might be at least two more hours of tuition before anyone ate, but the freshly baked aroma of bread would drive them all mad with hunger in the meantime. None of the defectos would sample the spread.

They served and slipped into the shadows—that was their lot in life. Despite her frustrated ambitions, Quill recognised that in many respects her life was easier than her peers.

Rustic round cobs, flour-dusted white bloomers with cracked crusts nestled among corn flat-breads and dense, dark slices of rye. A cornucopia of comfort accompanied by slabs of cheese, ranging from crumbly cream to deep waxy orange, and everything in between. Not forgetting the array of pickles which competed for a coveted space on someone's plate. Earthy brown onions, cabbage and beetroot, tomato medleys, eggs, and walnuts transformed into tangy relish, perfect to cut through the rich, fatty cheese.

With her stomach growling, salivating, Quill diverted her attention away from the tempting spread. The servants hadn't noticed her arrival as they played a familiar game of pickle one-upmanship, surreptitiously moving each other's offerings to secure the most prominent spot for their home-made delicacy.

She saw new people solely during the annual round of student scholarship. In the past she had stuck to sideways glances while she worked, uncomfortable with the awkward stares the feather-like brown birthmark on her right cheek always provoked. Knowing she had to deliver clean robes to Aric's servant, whoever that was, she cleared her throat and told herself the day could only get better. "Good morning. I need to speak to Aric Leitch's defecto." None of the brown tunics reacted, so wondering if she needed to speak louder, Quill stepped closer.

"Hello, I know you're all busy, and it looks delicious, but I need to give these to Aric's servant. Can you help me?"

The women turned together with two men, leaving the rest to ignore her. The smallest of the female contingent, who was little more than a child, smiled at Quill. As the girl fiddled with the front of her tunic, which hung from her slender frame like an oversized sack, her cheeks flushed crimson. Though she opened her mouth to speak, the withering glare of the short, squat mature lady hovering at the child's shoulder struck the girl silent. The youngster shrank into her uniform, wisps of blonde, almost white hair falling into her eyes as she spun toward the table and continued her work. Quill felt a twinge of guilt, knowing that her question had caused the scrawny youngster discomfort. "That's me," said a haughty voice from among the servers, who didn't turn. The effect of those words on the group was instantaneous, as everyone hurried back to their duties as if their lives depended on it. Deliberate and slow, the tallest of the men turned to face her, an emotionless blank expression on his angular features. Coincidentally, this man had a mountainous black mole in the centre of his chin. It could have been a match for the one on the rear of Aric's neck. Understanding what it was like to have such a striking facial feature, she did her best not to stare.

"So you're the clumsy girl who ruined Master Aric's robe. I'll never get that stain out. You'd do well to stay out of his way, and mine. Now give me the robes," he said, arms outstretched.

If she'd expected to make new friends, this obnoxious man suggested otherwise.

These folks are nothing like Kai.

The realisation added to her sense of loneliness and isolation. Handing over the pressed garments, Quill said, "It was an accident, and I apologised."

"Ha, I can imagine Aric's response. In my experience, forgiveness is not in his nature."

"You know him well, the brute. Had it not been for Master Bran, he might have hit me."

"That's a shame. It might've knocked some sense into you and taught you your place."

"My place? What do you mean?"

"We've heard all about you. Quill, Master Wittgenstein's defecto, the girl with ideas above her station, who thinks she's better than the rest of us because she lives in the library. A young woman caught up in the murder of six missing defectos."

"You make it sound as if I had something to do with their deaths. I'd never hurt anyone and I don't believe in violence, unlike you." The revelation that word had spread of her involvement in the investigation of Professor Hawkin and the missing servants came as an enormous shock. She could imagine the extent of the lurid tale passing from person to person, the details changing at every iteration. Far from being applauded, the opposite was true, and the court of public opinion had judged her guilty of an unimaginable crime. Evidently, that placed her in no-man's-land. Held in contempt and brutalised by the new scholars who she dreamed of joining and worse still, reviled by her peers based on rumour and innuendo.

Resigned to the fact that the conversation was a lost cause, Quill cleaned the ink from the wooden tabletop. "Hi," said a soft voice, like a puff of air to her neck. "I'm Zara. Don't take any notice of Norris. He's a bully, like Aric. If I didn't know better, I'd think they were family." The young defecto helped herself to a cloth from Quill's supply and lent a hand in trying to erase the black stain from the wood grain, although both were wasting their time.

"It's okay. I can take care of myself, but thanks. Are people talking about me?" Quill grimaced as soon as she asked, unsure whether she wanted an answer.

Zara's blue eyes darted around as she increased her efforts, rubbing at the ink with the momentum of her juvenile body, and continued in hushed tones. "Yeah, that bit's true. I mean, they're all chatting about it," she said, with a faint flick of her head toward those working. "They've got nothing else to talk about. We don't get much chance to chat. Can you really read?" The girl stopped scrubbing with her freckled pale face millimetres from Quills. Her innocence radiated a search for hope and unknown possibilities, but it was impossible at that moment to take on such a heavy burden of responsibility. Embarrassed, Quill nodded, scrabbling in her mind for small talk to change the subject without sounding too lame, when Norris interrupted. "Zara, get back to work. They'll be here in a minute. There's no time for gossiping, and if you know what's best, stay away from this one." The man's tone was hard to ignore and made the girl flinch, dropping the cleaning materials and scuttling toward the buffet table. Norris drew closer as he invaded the space between them. So close that Quill could smell the pickling vinegar on the man's breath, which made her stomach lurch. With her body arching to escape, bent almost double at the waist, she found herself pinned against the desk by the unpleasant man and his rancid odour.

"A message from Master Aric," he said, shoving a ream of ink stained paper against her chest, forcing her even further backwards. "Rewrite these by tomorrow or you'll regret it. The right word in the right ear, it's easy to get a defecto reassigned, especially a troublemaker."

Quill longed to tell the insufferable man what she thought of him, but the last thing she needed was more trouble, particularly as her good standing with Wittgenstein was in doubt. A few weeks ago, she'd believed the master would defend her without question. Since then, her confidence had waned. While chewing her bottom lip, desperate not to give him any satisfaction, Quill nodded, sliding her body along the edge of the desk to escape his clutches. It might mean working late to get the job done, but if it got Aric off her back, it would be worth the sacrifice.

A hum of voices signalled the return to study, for which she was eternally grateful. As the master appeared in the door, Quill shoved the pile of papers behind her trouser waistband and plastered on her best smile. His wiry, white eyebrows furrowed in response, a quizzical look that she knew well as he strode toward her. Uncomfortable, swallowing hard, Quill rubbed at her arms to eradicate the goosebumps. As the ancient fellow reached the first row of desks, Master Godwin's liver-spotted bald head popped up in the doorway. "Master, forgive me for interrupting. There's a letter," he said, holding a blue envelope in his outstretched hand.

Wittgenstein stopped, rotated one hundred and eighty degrees, and retraced his steps. As he took the note from Godwin, he shooed him away with a flick of his bony fingers. The custodian's voice filled the room as he opened the envelope, strolling to the lectern. "Settle down, settle down. There's a lot to get through before lunch, so let's begin." As he retrieved the contents of the mail, his emerald green eyes flitted across the paper, his pallor turning a deathly shade. Then his body sagged, folding at the knees and hips, deflating like an old cushion. As he gripped the rostrum, his knuckles went white, and he fumbled for a glass of water, gaze locked onto the page.

Quill darted forward, the sound of her pulse drumming in her ears. "Master, what is it? Let me help you."

As she crossed the distance between them, he took a large slug of drink, replaced the letter in its envelope, and stuffed it into the pocket of his robe. With the back of his hand, he wiped his brow, smoothing and straightening his unkempt hair. "The Ortus. Let's talk about the Ortus." As the words escaped his mouth, as if by magic, the Compendium room filled with light. Intense and blinding, it flooded in from every angle, a total surprise which forced them to shield their eyes behind cupped hands or forearms.

"Quill, child, quick, pull the cord before we're blinded."

Still squinting, a kaleidoscope of coloured dots flashing across her vision, Quill stumbled across the room, groping for the long tasselled cords that operated the drapes. Hand over hand, she tugged. The *click-clack* of the track mechanism pulling the thick damson cloth was a welcome sound as the curtains banished the dazzling glare.

"Is everybody in one piece?" asked the master, tremulous as Quill fumbled in the darkness for the lamps, grunting and groaning students in the background. "Quill, is that what I think it is?"

"I believe so."

"What, what is?" asked Arthur, rising from his seat. "What's happening?"

"I tried to tell you." Quill fixated on the ancient scholar's wrinkled face, acutely aware that she had an audience.

"Well, you didn't try hard enough. Child, this changes everything. Class dismissed. Reconvene tomorrow, early. Be here at seven, sharp."

With that stern announcement, the master gathered his lecture notes and scurried away, beckoning as he slipped through the door. "Quill, my study. Now!"

Chapter Six

With the scholars bemused, chattering over each other as they tried to make sense of the morning's bizarre events, Quill cast a last longing look at the delectable lunch. Resigned to the knowledge she wouldn't be sneaking any under her tunic to eat later, she hurried toward the exit in pursuit of Wittgenstein. She'd almost escaped when the tall figure of Bran Harland filled the doorway.

Now that she was close to him, the natural leader of the pack towered over her petite figure. Even though Bran was lean, he occupied the space with the force of his personality—a confidence which seeped from every pore. It was difficult to tally this imposing presence with the relaxed way he leant his forearms against either side of the door frame. Long black hair kissed the top of his shoulders. Gentle waves swept back from a high forehead framed his intense angular features, as his fearless sable eyes bored into her.

"Excuse me," she said, her voice cracking under the pressure of his intrusive gaze.

He lounged from left to right to block her clumsy attempts to squeeze through the tiny gap beneath either armpit. "Tell me, what's going on?"

The question sounded like a command, and the twinge of disappointment that followed took her by surprise.

You're just a servant.

She reminded herself that it was natural he'd treat her like one. Almost at once, he continued. "Please."

As she sensed the flush rising on her cheeks, she knew her face betrayed her thoughts. "It's not my place to say anything before speaking with the master. Sorry."

Bran stared at her like an eagle waiting to pounce. "Loyalty is commendable, but I suspect yours is misplaced. It's obvious you and the old man don't see eye to eye."

"How do you know that?" The words spilled from her mouth unchecked. "Um, I mean, that's not true. What gave you that idea?"

A wry grin signalled that her feeble attempt to cover up the all-too-candid remarks had been an epic fail. To make matters worse, Bran dismissed her protestations as if he were swatting a lazy fly. "Whatever you say. I believe you, thousands wouldn't. Fill me in on the secret later, and in return, maybe I can keep Aric off your back."

With that bargain dangled, Harland dropped his long limbs to his sides and sauntered toward his lunch.

For once, the master's study did not resemble a rubbish dump. In the weeks since Professor Hawkin's death, Quill had made it her mission to seek every scrap of hidden detritus lingering among the stacks of books, pamphlets and scrolls. What began as a token of appreciation for her mentor's promise to train her soon morphed into a war. Her personal crusade against mouldy crusts, moth-eaten robes and hairballs. Dirt devils with a knack of jumping out at her whenever she least expected. The task was a hard fought, never-ending war of attrition. Confronted with the fruits of her labour, the result was a minor consolation compared to the overwhelming background of disappointment, his promise of training so far amounting to nothing.

"Where's my lunch?" Encased in his favourite tree stump chair, the octogenarian pored over a paper-thin parchment, which was so cracked and translucent that Quill expected it to disintegrate at any minute.

"I thought we agreed no eating in this room. You're lucky we're not overrun with rats, the state of the place."

"We agreed on no such thing. Are you mad? Where else am I supposed to eat?" He glanced up before saying, "and don't say the dining hall. If you think I want to sit and listen to the scholars' inane chatter, then you're a bigger fool than I imagined."

Quill sighed, the tirade flowing over and around her like a diverted river. She had known his benevolence couldn't last, and his cantankerous mood wasn't personal. It was part of his nature, like a graft stitched to his skin, seamless with the rest of him. The words of admonishment never hurt, but the broken promise was altogether different. No matter how hard she pushed it to the back of her mind, telling herself it didn't matter, or made excuses for him, like perhaps he'd forgotten, nothing worked. She picked at the wound like a dried scab. Shifted from leaving it to heal, to prodding, gouging at the hurt with an imaginary sharp stick, until the slick, bright red blood flowed again with angry betrayal.

"This parchment written by the revolutionary astronomer, Anastarchus, is over five hundred years old. I knew I still had it somewhere. It's the last known record of a guest star. That is what we're dealing with, don't you agree?" The master formed a triangle with the fingertips of both hands, which he bounced backwards and forwards off his craggy chin, thoughts of lunch no longer a topic of conversation.

"Perhaps. It's difficult to say, as no one alive has ever seen one. But I've read about Anastarchus' sighting, so I suspected as much when I saw it from the garden. A guest star or supernova. That it's visible in daylight is unique—so powerful that it outshines the sun."

"How long will the phenomena last? That's what I want to understand." A rhetorical question she'd asked herself at least a dozen times.

Perched on top of an enormous stack of black leather-bound encyclopaedias, Quill shrugged. "Who knows? From memory, the last one appeared in the night sky for twelve days, according to Anastarchus' record. This supernova is so bright it could signify a shorter appearance in the atmosphere. A star in its last phase, burning fast and bright before it dies, returning its energy to the cosmos. Still, what do I know? I'm just a defecto with a passion for astronomy."

The old man grunted, hauling himself from the chair. "Good point, well made. I'll need to consult an expert." Then Wittgenstein paced as he ordered his thoughts aloud. "I think we should assume there's a brief window of time. Maybe a week, possibly less, to harness such an auspicious moment in history. Anastarchus' records document every detail. The Ortus, the ceremony which signifies every new scholar's birth, timed to coincide with the exact moment the guest star dies. The natural cycle of death and birth played out for the entire city to witness."

"But the ceremony isn't due to take place for six weeks. Can we be ready in a few days?"

"I'm not sure. Though sitting around here won't help. First things first, pass my coat, will you? I must speak to Dr Novack. Only the Head of the Protectorate can move the ceremony, and the sooner the better. It might mean working round the clock, but it'll be worth the effort."

Chapter Seven

The intense heat sucked the energy from their legs like a parasitic insect. Sweat dripped from them both in a stream, from their scalps to the soles of their feet. Quill and her master arrived at Dr Novack's front gate, both taking a moment to slouch against the white border fence. They panted like dogs, throats scratchy and dry from dehydration. The midday sun, amplified by the supernova's yellow-green flash, blinded them with its intensity, driving the heat haze from the pavement. While the lush trees and shrubs of the Physician's District turned brown and brittle like crisp, burnt skin.

Montague Hall nestled at the end of Willow Lane. Typical of the district, the building was clean and white and surrounded by the calming influence of nature. The house was a symmetrical vision with five bays spaced across the second storey, the same on the ground floor plus a central door. Beneath the roof line stretched a dentile cornice, like a row of gleaming white teeth, across each face of the building. Decorative quoins in contrasting red brick connected the structure—vertebrae which supported their respective corners, rigid and true. To no-one's surprise, it was the biggest and grandest residence in the district and perfect for the Head of The Protectorate.

The pair often visited in the weeks running up to the annual Ortus. A destination Quill never grew tired of visiting. Unlatching the gate, they stepped onto the gravel pathway which led to the solid black front door, grateful for a little shade beneath the marble columned porch. The master lifted the thick brass door knocker and pounded rhythmically as Quill rested her forehead on the cool marble, enjoying the sensation. They waited for what seemed like an age, exchanging quizzical glances as the door remained shut.

"That's odd," he said, "where's Yulia?"

"And I don't hear the dog barking." Quill's pulse quickened as Wittgenstein knocked again, louder.

After several further minutes of inpatient waiting, a faint sound of shuffling beyond the door elicited relaxed grins from the pair as they expected the housekeeper's arrival. But as the front entrance swung open, nothing could have prepared them for the individual who greeted them.

The gentleman resembled nobody Quill had ever seen. Short and stout, his girth was at least double his height. Much to her embarrassment, he wore an enormous fur robe and nothing else, through which protruded an expanse of naked chest and an even bigger gut. Beneath the robe, fat calves attached to his turned out feet which were encased in green leather mules. Quill imagined that if she lay this man on his side, he'd be the perfect shape for rolling down a hill. Yet those details paled into insignificance compared to the fact that someone had painted almost every inch of his bare skin in permanent ink, including his face. The designs combined intricate swirls and flourishes, symbolising who knew what. Together with images of women of every colour, shape and size, many of whom wore a smile but nothing else. Quill sensed she was gawping. Her mouth hung slack as she studied the semi-naked gentleman like an extraordinary curiosity. But she couldn't help herself. Whoever he was, he didn't belong in Scolaris. A body like a walking piece of art, taut skin a tapestry upon which he declared his passions and personality. The confusing effect reminded her of the forbidden texts locked away in the library and the book of the Meraki hidden in her Lilith bird box under her bed.

Was he dangerous?

He broke at least half a dozen laws she could think of by existing.

"What do you want?" The man's voice was deep and smoky. "Can't a man sleep?"

Quill and the master exchanged confused looks, signalling that neither had any clue who he was or what he was doing there. Before she said a word, the scholar placed a hand on her shoulder and gripped it tight, showing that he was in charge. When the old man spoke, he projected his considerable age and experience into his posture and tone. "Good afternoon. My name is Master Wittgenstein. I am the Custodian of the Library of Scolaris, and who, Sir, are you?"

"Are you indeed? Very interesting. How do I know that's true? You could be anybody." The egg-shaped man chuckled, the voluptuous women on the front of his chest jiggling alarmingly in response.

The master's bony grip clamped harder on her shoulder, forcing Quill to bite her bottom lip to stop herself from crying out in pain. "We're here to see Dr Novack. It's urgent. Please, can you find Yulia and tell her we're here?" That the ancient scholar had stayed calm was a minor miracle, in Quill's opinion, and she expected the stranger to set off in search of the housekeeper, Yulia Pomerenke.

Conversely, with a sharp shrug of his thick shoulders, the odd fellow retreated from the doorstep, pushing the door closed as he went. Suddenly, a flurry of yapping and barking followed by a blur of black-and-tan fur interrupted the awkward meeting on the doorstep.

"Luna!" Quill dropped to her haunches to greet the little spaniel, who hurtled through the legs of the surprised stranger. With a warm feeling spreading through her chest, she scooped the soft bundle into her arms, pressing her nose against Luna's wet muzzle. "Where's your daddy? Where's Dr Novack, girl?" she asked, revelling in the warm body held tight to her chest. At the sound of Novack's name, the young dog pricked up her floppy ears. Wide eyes like black pools of ink as she whimpered and whined and prodded at Quill's ribcage with her front paw. Instantly on the defensive, Quill stepped in front of her master. "I don't mean to be rude, but something's wrong with Luna. So please, can you let us in so we can help the poor little thing?" As she said her piece, she took a tiny irresistible paw in her grasp and waved it in the tattooed man's face.

Chapter Eight

If you ignored the open-mouthed ecstatic stare, the male might have been asleep, an expression Chief Red preferred never to see again. Headquarters had logged the call within five minutes of him leaving Fox, and he'd come alone as soon as he'd seen the report. As chief, it was now his responsibility to secure the scene and discover whatever he could about the latest victim before briefing the guards. The fact this one had died at home, in his own bed, was the break he'd hoped for. At least the identification process should be straightforward, unless the deceased was a stranger who'd broken in to take a long nap in the unsuspecting home owner's bedroom—an unlikely scenario, in his opinion.

Red stood at the foot of the bed. Isaac, the dead engineer's defecto, hovered in the doorway, shaking.

"What time did you arrive today?" asked Red, pulling his pocketbook and pen from the inside pocket of his blue jacket.

Isaac swallowed hard, the enormous protruding Adam's apple in his neck adding to the visible vibrations which emanated from his body. Unable to blink, a sheen of sweat glistening on his forehead, the servant stammered. "Hmm, um, er, I'm not sure. Sorry, it's all a bit of a blur. Am I in trouble?"

Red glanced up from his notebook. A witness asking if they were in trouble always raised a red flag. "That depends. Have you done something illegal?"

"No, I swear. Never, but I know how this goes."

"How what goes?" Red strode to the headboard to inspect the dead man.

"Well, I'm a defecto," said the servant, nibbling his fingernails and hiding behind the door frame to leave his face barely visible. "So this part is where you blame me for Mr Vaughn's state, report me to the authorities, I lose my job and become destitute. If it's possible to be worse off than I already am, living in the defecto quarters."

"Not while I'm in charge. Now where were we? The time, Isaac?"

"To be honest, I'm getting here later and later. That's why I'm not sure."

"How so?"

"Mr Vaughn's been acting strangely, sleeping most of the day until dinner. It's a waste of effort arriving early to make breakfast, or even lunch, because he doesn't eat it."

"What about work?" Red wondered how an engineer made a living at night. Followed by reminding himself that he didn't know any engineers, so he should keep an open mind. That was an unwritten rule of criminal investigation.

"I've been wondering the same thing and I wish I knew the answer. He always used to work the day shift, but the job's all freelance projects, so he's not tied to an office anywhere. It's possible he got moved to nights. Also, he hasn't paid me for a couple of weeks, told me it was a temporary cash flow problem. As things stand, defectos don't receive a living wage. It's barely enough to put food on the table. I'm desperate." The word *desperate* hung between them like a black cloud, and the pained expression on Isaac's face showed he regretted his choice of words. "Not desperate in that way." The defecto wrung his hands and chewed his bottom lip like a man possessed.

Red pointed at the unfortunate Mr Vaughn with the tip of his pen. "You mean not bad enough to do this?"

"You're making me nervous. I swear he was like that when I found him. I reckon I left my place after nine."

"You live in the DEQ, correct?"

Isaac scowled. "Yeah, if you can call it living. The roof on my unit leaks and now we have a rat infestation. People have been getting sick. Vaughn said he'd help with the leak and find the source of the vermin, empty promises, as usual."

With each new titbit of information, the list of motives for Isaac killing his employer grew. Red wondered if the nervous fellow could dig a deeper hole for himself. The servant couldn't have made the situation much worse if he chucked in the spade for good measure.

It would have been simple to arrest the man, and he doubted anyone would question Isaac's guilt, but that wasn't Red's style. Justice meant finding the truth, not an easy scapegoat, and the look and smell of the body told its own story. This bore the hallmarks of another drug induced death, and he needed to find whoever was supplying the toxic liquid and fast. Isaac continued, interrupting his chain of thought. "It's roughly a half-hour walk here, but it took me longer this morning. This weather is too much. If there's one thing I can't stand, it's overheating. I had to keep stopping to catch my breath. How do you manage in that uniform?"

Ignoring the attempt at small-talk, Red noticed Vaughn's hands, which lay on top of a beige blanket, clenched tight like fighting fists. He edged closer, trying to glimpse the engineer's fingernails, hoping to rule out evidence of a physical assault or altercation. "Did you find him like this as soon as you arrived?"

"No. I have my own keys, so I let myself in as usual. The house was dark, but I'm used to that, so I wasn't suspicious. I started in the kitchen and downstairs toilet, then I came upstairs to the shower." Isaac gestured towards the vacant bathroom, opposite Vaughn's bedroom, across the hallway. "At first, I thought he was just asleep with the door open, but no-one looks like that, do they?" The poor man shoved his hands into the front pocket of his tunic and studied the faded green carpet.

"Did you touch anything?" Isaac shoved his hands into his pocket, silently mouthing no. "You're sure? Everything is just as you found it?"

"I was too scared to step inside the door. I've never seen a dead body."

"Wish I could say the same thing, but unfortunately, it goes with the territory. Thanks, you've been helpful. Could you make coffee while I finish in here?" Red was eager to investigate without an audience and hoped his ploy would work.

The servant hesitated, scratching his head, still white and pasty, much like his employer. After several awkward seconds, Isaac disappeared into the hall, followed by the thud of footsteps on the stairs. Red removed the gloves he kept in his trouser pocket and prepared himself mentally for the task ahead.

The bedroom was tidy and functional. Its plain beige walls and green carpet were patchy and in need of a refresh. Heavy brown curtains hung at the window like folds of skin, blocking the daylight apart from a tiny crack of light where the cloth met. In a show of respect to the deceased, neither Isaac nor Red had opened the drapes, instead relying on the solitary bare bulb hanging from the ceiling. The iron bedstead dominated the space, merely leaving room for a narrow bedside table, on top of which stood a small glass of water. On the opposite wall, crammed together, a battered mahogany wardrobe hugged a pine chest, the uppermost drawer of which was half-open. None of the furniture matched, and no photographs of family or personal trinkets were on display. Nothing suggested there was a Mrs Vaughn, or anyone else of any importance, and from what little he'd seen, the rest of the property was no different. No-one could accuse Mr Vaughn of being house proud or extravagant with money, all of which prompted several questions.

What was he spending his earnings on? Why didn't he have enough to pay Isaac, and was it related to his death?

Eager not to compromise the crime scene, Red peered into the half-open drawer, finding forlorn folded piles of underpants and socks. A cursory glance in the drawers below revealed nothing of interest, either.

What a sad existence. A middle-aged man, all alone in this shell of a home.

A fleeting image of roles reversed taunted him. His future-self alone in the shabby surroundings, unloved and forgotten, and he banished the thought as he slammed the bottom drawer and turned to the bed.

Draped neatly over the foot of the bedstead were Vaughn's clothes: black starched trousers, a shiny satin stripe down the sides and a pristine white shirt with a boned collar.

I wonder?

As he turned to the door, Red pushed it with the tip of his pen and watched as it swung closed, creaking on its hinges. Hung on the back, where he'd expected to find it, was a matching jacket. Usually, finding a black suit shouldn't have raised an eyebrow, but in this dilapidated setting, the stiff, shiny new dress suit seemed out of place.

Where might a single, middle-aged engineer be going in such a sophisticated outfit?

As he removed the jacket from the hook, Red frisked it with his gloved palm from the collar to the waist, squeezing as he went. Despite sensing nothing obvious, he turned the inside of the garment to face him and groped in the front pockets, again finding them empty. He was about to give up when a sudden flash of green silk on the interior captured his attention, revealing an inner pocket fastened with a zip. A cursory sweep of his fingertips suggested it contained something flat and hard.

His wallet?

Red clasped the metal between his thumb and forefinger and pulled, simply to find the teeth catching on the lining, snagging and impeding access to the inner compartment. Impatiently, he fought with the fastening, tugging, pulling, and yanking increasingly forcefully, but simply seized more of the verdant cloth in the zipper. Disgusted with himself, he laid the jacket over the matching trousers.

Perhaps brute force isn't the best approach?

As he paced around the narrow strip bordering the bed, he stretched his arms above his head to relieve the tension in his fingers, taking a few deep breaths to calm his heart rate and clear his mind. "Focus. It can't be that hard. It's just a zip."

With renewed purpose, adopting a stealth approach, he teased the bunched up material millimetre by millimetre from the metal teeth. Little by little, perseverance paid off, and he freed the jam, unzipping the pocket with a satisfying buzz of metal. Gingerly, Red prised open the compartment between two fingers, surprised, and a little disappointed, not to find Vaughn's wallet. The interior contained a stiff square of cardboard. The kind you removed before wearing, a detail the engineer either didn't know or hadn't got round to completing. About to give up, he felt something else, rigid and flat against his fingertip, tucked against the tailor's card in the pocket's corner. Pulse quivering, Red reached inside to retrieve it. In one smooth motion, he dropped a white shiny square into his outstretched palm as he laid the jacket over the bedpost. Innocuous yet puzzling, it opened out from a flap on the front to reveal a double row of wooden matches, their pink tips glittering in the lamplight.

"All that effort for a match-book." Sweat trickled down his neck from his cropped black hairline as he griped to the empty room. Then Red flipped the card over and saw something altogether more intriguing.

Chapter Nine

Beyond the front door to Montague Hall, a grand hallway extended through the centre of the house, an air of peace and tranquillity enhanced by white walls. Its marble floor gleamed, a wide stone staircase swept from left to right in a pleasing ascending curve. Six alcoves decorated the vast entrance, three on both sides. Each displayed a bust of a past Head of the Protectorate. The solitary pop of colour came from a majestic silver vase which was bursting with foliage fronds in all hues of green, together with flower heads of blue delphiniums and pink hollyhocks. A riot of shades plucked fresh from the garden.

As Quill and Wit crossed the hallway, the pat of the stranger's mules echoed around the space as Luna struggled against Quill's grip, wriggling for freedom. Bent down, Quill opened her forearms. "There you go, little girl." Without wasting a second, the scrap of black-and-tan fur bounded from her arms.

Claws clacking syncopated with slippers slapping as the puppy scampered toward the back of the house, stopping to sniff at regular intervals. "There's nothing wrong with her." The rotund man grumbled, still ill-tempered.

"Maybe not," said the master, "but it's unusual to see that dog without Dr Novack, and where's the housekeeper?"

As he arrived at the opposite side of the entranceway, the strange man pushed open the door leading to the rest of the ground floor. "I wish I knew. My stomach's telling me it's time for brunch." To emphasise his point, he rested an inked hand on top of his gut like it was a shelf. "I hope she's in the kitchen."

With that desire shared, the unusual trio filed through to the living room.

The grand salon enjoyed a view of the magnificent garden at the rear of the property. Lush pea-green walls textured with symmetrical panelling melted into a rich beechwood floor. Blood red mahogany console tables framed the doorway and all three of the windows at the rear. An urn topped each surface, hand-decorated with leaf designs, echoing the colour of the paintwork. On every available section of wall hung an oil canvas of the most important figures in Scolarian history, including the most recent edition—a likeness of Dr Novack himself. Paintings were rare. Society frowned upon art as frivolous and illegal, but these recorded men of importance, which apparently excused their existence. Though the artists had taken great care to present them without embellishment.

Stood facing the full height image of their leader, Quill couldn't help grinning. The image bore an amazing resemblance to Novack. More than that, it captured the essence of the man she knew. Short and solid, with a wide stance, arms relaxed at his sides, he looked indestructible. As always, he wore an olive-green thick wool suit with a matching collared waistcoat, a pristine white shirt and a green velvet bow tie. Despite being young for a man in his position, his hair had been as white as spring snowdrops for as long as she could remember. A perfect head of hair swept across a high forehead. Novack's astute hazel eyes gazed into the room from a square angular face with a fleshy nose and a thin lipped serious mouth cut in a straight line. Somehow, although he wasn't smiling, not in the usual sense of the word, a quirk of the composition suggested he saw something she couldn't—something vaguely amusing.

After circling the area at least a dozen times, sniffing the elegant green sofa and chairs which faced the new canvas, Luna halted. Her perfect domed head tilted upward to examine the image of her owner. No sooner had she spotted the green suited replica than the whining and whimpering returned. The puppy dropped to the floor in front of the picture, body curled tight in a ball as she hid beneath her right fore-paw.

Quill and the master exchanged concerned glances, both noticing the puppy's unusual behaviour, but the orotund unknown visitor soon distracted them. "Well, this is awkward. Is this the way you usually treat important guests who visit Scolaris?" he asked, stretching out the entirety of his enormous frame along the length of the sofa.

"Aha, now I understand." The master lowered himself into a chair. Quill didn't comprehend what he was talking about, but kept quiet, anticipating further clarification. What came next was unexpected. "Why didn't you say? You're the Asterian envoy."

Quill froze, wondering if she'd misheard, her gaze flicking between the two men in rapid succession.

Was it true?

She'd met no-one from outside the city and suddenly realised she assumed she never would. Though his hailing from Asteria explained a few things; his unusual attire, or lack of it, sleeping all day, and not forgetting the strange images adorning his body.

"You're correct. Uriah Crisp, special envoy. Pleasure to meet you," said the visitor, as he struggled to lever himself out of the sofa, his palm outstretched towards Wittgenstein in greeting.

The master waved a bony hand toward Crisp's beached expanse. "Likewise, Mr Crisp. I haven't seen an Asterian in a long time, but you are welcome in our fair city. I believe you're here for the Ortus?"

"Indeed I am. Dr Novack kindly invited me and I also hope to connect with key members of the council. We wish to establish trade links between our communities and understand each other's way of life."

"The Scolarian thirst for knowledge drives us all, so I'm sure we can learn a great deal from one another. I've been looking forward to your visit. Though it's only fair to warn you that your appearance might cause, er, how can I put this, a certain amount of consternation? We are not used to seeing body art, nor indeed any art. In our search for information, we pay no attention to the aesthetic of objects or people, choosing the purity of learning over the self-indulgent nature of design and creativity. You should bear that in mind when you leave this house to enter the city proper."

"Thank you for your concern. Dr Novack has already explained, but we are all human beings, are we not? I'm sure we can find common ground. Now I'd love to chat more, but my stomach is growling like a beast. Do you people ever eat?"

"Of course, of course. I expect you've had a long journey and I honestly don't know where Yulia is. Quill, child, go to the kitchen. Hopefully, Yulia's there. If not, fix our esteemed guest some lunch."

Quill frowned. She hated to leave and miss out on the conversation. Mr Crisp, a visitor from Asteria, the country the master had sent her father to visit, the place from which he never returned. A million questions gathered in her mind.

Did Uriah know her dad? Unlikely. Though, as a prominent figure, could he find him?

What she needed was an opportunity to ask. Desperate for answers, she was about to risk the master's wrath when his husky tone interrupted her thoughts. "Quill, good grief, stop dithering and do what you're told."

With that ultimatum ringing in her ears, she knew the questions would have to wait. Resigned to her fate, she set off toward the kitchen, through the dining room to her right, followed by the forlorn trot of her little friend Luna.

Chapter Ten

With Luna tight to her heels, Quill jogged across the expanse of the formal dining room. Desperate to return to the intriguing Mr Crisp, she planned to locate the errant housekeeper, pass on the lunch order, and head back as fast as was humanly possible.

The pastel blue elegance of the banqueting area, complete with wallpaper panels covered in flocks of bluebirds with bright pink beaks, usually took her breath away. Golden chandeliers hung from thick gilded chains like shining bunches of grapes, glittering in their opulence, spraying a kaleidoscope of coloured dots across the patterned carpet. Though today there wasn't time to stop and admire the décor. Spurred on by the four-legged, black-and-tan ally who now pulled ahead, Quill sped up, the pounding of her feet mirrored by the thud of her pulse.

At the far end, she stopped, breathing laboured as she turned the round porcelain handle. To the soft sounding click of the latch, Quill pushed the door open and stepped inside the kitchen.

Expecting to find Yulia Pomerenke hard at work, it was disappointing to see the room cool and empty.

So much for getting straight back to the action.

Hands on hips, pondering what to do next, a creeping unease wormed its way into her gut, sending a shiver through her spine.

Where was the housekeeper?

Frustrated but out of options, she'd have to fix lunch by herself. The kitchen was vast, occupying the entire rear right-hand corner of Montague Hall. Quite how Yulia managed alone had always been a mystery.

How often Dr Novack entertained guests she didn't know, but as the man in charge, Quill guessed it might be a regular occurrence. The dining room seated at least two-hundred visitors, so the kitchen had to accommodate that number.

Like the rest of the property, sunlight flooded in from the window bays, which stretched from waist height almost to the ceiling, double, maybe triple, the elevation of the master's rooms. Beneath the panes, a multitude of range cookers spread along the full length of the space, each hob laid out with copper pots and pans of every imaginable size. In the centre, parallel to the ovens, solid beechwood trestles stuck end-to-end formed the grandest work surface she'd ever seen. Supported by wheels, each unit could be repositioned at a moment's notice. On top stood sturdy wooden carving boards, lethal meat knives and sharpening blocks. Jars of cooking oil in diverse shades of olive-green, gold and the palest yellow caught the light from outside, glistening like liquid metal. While copper fish kettles, flour dredgers, wooden spatulas and spoons, arranged in neat rows, slept—poised, waiting for action. Metal utensils sparkled and gleamed, none out of place, and she struggled to imagine finding the courage to use anything for fear of making a mess.

Luna trotted away, sniffing in the vain hope of finding a hidden spillage or delicious morsel, but she was out of luck as the kitchen was spotless. Quill followed the meandering path taken by the dog, tentatively brushing her fingertips along the closed oven doors to discover that they were cold to the touch. No-one had cooked in them for several hours.

In the far right corner, a set of double doors opened onto the garden. Next to those, a full height oak dresser comprised a base cupboard below row upon row of shelves. The unit housed Montague Hall's extensive collection of crockery; pristine white bowls and plates decorated with a single pink-beaked bluebird, plucked from the wallpaper in the dining area. Headed for the pastel-blue fridge to the cabinet's right, Quill expected to find a treasure of culinary delights inside. Her stomach grumbled, reminding her that neither she nor the master had eaten since breakfast. The cheese and pickle spread abandoned to Bran Harland and the rest of the new scholars.

How did I forget? We missed lunch to come here in search of Novack.

Beside the larder, she grasped the two nearest handles, pulling them together and almost falling as she did so, the weight of the doors affecting her centre of gravity. Vacant shelves and a distinct twang of disinfectant were not what she'd expected. The ticking of the black-rimmed clock on the wall above the dresser taunted her, growing louder by the second and reminding her of the inexorable march of time. Slamming the first pair closed, she moved onto the next, then the next, but the outcome was the same. They were all empty and the chemical taint of bleach grew stronger, burning her delicate nostril hairs.

Perhaps this explains the housekeeper's absence? Every cupboard is clean and empty to prepare for Crisp's visit, and the woman's out gathering supplies.

Unfortunately, that didn't solve the immediate problem of feeding Mr Crisp when the cupboards were bare. To her surprise and relief, as she opened the final set of doors, Quill spotted a pie-dish, solitary on the third shelf from the top and propped against it, written in a small neat hand, a note which read,

Dr Novack,

If I'm not back in time to serve luncheon, here's the meat pie we discussed. There is a supply of home-made cranberry relish in the dresser. I need to restock from scratch, but will return before dinner.

Your faithful servant, Yulia

So, her guess had been correct, but what it didn't explain was Novack's absence, particularly with such an important guest in the house. As she grabbed the platter, the smell of golden buttery pastry wafted up, masking the chemical twang of cleaning. Followed close behind by the earthy, full-bodied aroma of spiced meat. Quill salivated, balancing the large dish on both palms, drawing it to her chest. After closing the larder door with a flick of her hip, she headed toward the cabinet, hunting for a jar of cranberry sweetness to cut through the rich meatiness of the filling. A cursory glance at the lower shelves revealed stacks of serving dishes which matched the table crockery at the top. With the pie tucked under her chin, its size was an obstacle which jutted out beyond her line of sight. Undeterred, she turned her whole body, peering over the crust's edge, but there was no sign of the recommended accompaniment.

Let me check the base cupboard.

Crouched onto her haunches, unwilling to surrender lunch, she balanced the dish on her left fingertips, like a bartender holding a tray of drinks. It was a delicate balancing act, but she was used to manoeuvring in the confined space of the master's closet kitchen. Overconfident, Quill scrabbled through the eclectic contents with her free hand, like a thief hunting for expensive jewellery. Hand-labelled in the same neat script as the note in the fridge, jars squeezed together, packed tight, filling every centimetre. Salad dressings separated into layers of different coloured oils with ruby-red vinegar, others with thick black balsamic. Each infused with generous sprigs of rosemary, dill, sage, or thyme, which grew in the herb garden.

Items in the shadow at the cupboard's rear were impossible to identify. So, shifting her weight forward onto her right foot, she stretched further inside to lift each jar and examine the condiments. Mayonnaise and mustard pots, pickled cabbage and beetroot, slid out as she worked methodically from side-to-side. Then, out of nowhere, her calf muscle contracted, sending a spasm of pain shooting up the back of her leg and into her hip. "Argh!"

Forced to stand in one swift motion by an involuntary reflex, she pitched forward, forgetting the finely balanced meat dish which, to her horror, launched in an acute arc as if she'd hurled a spear. Desperate to rescue lunch, she opted to harness the onward momentum to her advantage. With outstretched arms, throwing her body after the pie, they sailed through the air, heading for doom and destruction on the frigid stone floor.

For a few deluded seconds, Quill thought she'd make it, until a black-and-tan ball of disaster hurtled straight at her to ruin the fantasy. "Luna, nooo!"

In reply, the little dog barked a triumphant series of short yaps, like a blast of trumpets announcing the victor of a battle. Suddenly, Quill detected the hard, crisp texture of pastry against her outstretched fingertips, which led to one final fatal mistake. Thinking she had the situation under control, Quill relaxed, losing a nanosecond of momentum. It wasn't much, but it was enough for Luna to snatch the prize, catching the meaty delicacy between her sharp teeth to steal it from Quill's desperate last-ditch lunge.

As the forward energy of the puppy collided with the opposing force from the pie, the top crust exploded, prised open like an erupting volcano. Quill crashed face-first onto the kitchen floor, unable to cushion her landing. Winded, she groaned, ribs throbbing alongside the complaints pulsating from her knees and elbows, each of her bony extremities taking the full force of the collision.

The ignominy didn't end there. As if to add insult to injury, a shower of compact meat globules and detonated pastry rained over her prone body. Bruised and battered, reluctant to move and berating herself for her mistake, Quill studied the stone flags. With her face millimetres from the floor, she turned her head left, dismayed to watch the fur ball demolishing the remains of the enormous patty, wolfing lusty gulps as if she'd not eaten in a month. "Luna, what have you done?"

The bulk of the delicacy vanished in less than ten seconds, followed by the puppy hoovering up any remnants while circling toward the exit. Still horizontal, Quill watched as any trace of lunch disappeared, along with her hopes of a miracle. At the rear doors, Luna pressed her muzzle against the glass, growling and whimpering, scratching with her front paw as she turned to Quill and back again.

"I expect you've got a tummy ache now, haven't you?" Quill pushed herself onto all-fours before standing upright. Her body ached, and she could already see a purple bruise growing on her left elbow. As she brushed her uniform, her nose wrinkled at the discovery of meat and jelly entangled among the waves of her hair. After hobbling to the doors to let the dog out, she stepped onto a crispy double sheet of newspaper, on which stood a small pair of outdoor walking shoes.

These must belong to the housekeeper.

Next to them were large twin boot prints.

Prints, but no boots?

Luna's paw-scratching increased, and Quill turned to fetch the leash from a hook on the wall, but it wasn't there. "Can't go without the lead, can we? We don't want you to get lost. I'm in enough trouble. Why am I talking to the dog?"

The animal cocked her head to one side as if she understood every word, then circled, snout sniffing the boot prints. A low growl rumbled from her chest as Luna returned to the door, butting her furry face against the glass, determined to leave.

"All right, all right, you need to go out, I get it." Opening them a fraction, Luna squeezed her wet nose into the gap. "Just don't run off, okay? Be a good dog for once."

As Quill pushed the doors wide, dutiful as ever, the puppy bolted, disappearing like a fugitive into the garden.

The change in temperature between the cool kitchen and outside was startling. Humidity gripped Quill's arms as she paused in the doorway, lamenting the wayward dog's disappearance. As she pondered the footprints on the newspaper, she noticed two salmon-pink ceramic bowls, which were usually filled with dog biscuits and water. Like the rest of the kitchen, they were spotless. Dr Novack doted on little Luna, having no human family known to her, so the vacant containers added to the growing sense of concern nibbling at her insides.

No wonder the dog gobbled the entire pie. Poor girl, they haven't fed her today.

With that realisation, the earlier frustration at the dog's demolition of their lunch vanished. Replaced by sympathy, then amusement, as Quill replayed the episode in her mind.

Still, none of it solved the immediate problem.

Should I go back to the living room minus brunch, or follow the naughty pet into the garden? Wait, if Dr Novack's boots created those prints, maybe that holds the key to explaining his absence?

With that in mind, and a deep-rooted wish to delay the inevitable telling-off, the decision appeared obvious.

It should be easy enough to locate the doctor. No doubt Luna's acute snout's sniffing him out as I stand here wasting time. At least if I find them both, I'll avoid returning empty-handed. With any luck, once they heard that no-one had fed the poor dog, they'd forgive the whole sorry incident with the pie. Nobody could be angry with that adorable ball of trouble for long.

With her sights set on locating the puppy and her owner, Quill strode out onto the gravel pathway, closing the double doors behind her. The track snaked its course through stepped flowerbeds, each full and heavy with the colour and scent of glorious blooms. With the sun at its highest point, amplified by the pulsating yellow and green of the guest star, the temperature was unbearable. Humid, sucking the moisture from every living thing.

"Luna, come here girl," she called, though the sound didn't carry far in the stilted air. Ranks of white and mustard foxgloves, interleaved with notched-petalled lilac and pink hollyhocks, towered above her. The terrace sloping upward into the distance toward the back gate, which was hidden from view. Silent floral watchers, immovable in the foetid heat, seemed to mock her, blocking her progress and line of sight through the grounds. A perfect hiding place for a mischievous dog.

Onward she pressed, sweat dripping from her forehead as she trudged along the shale track, scanning for the slightest movement that might show Luna's current position, but nothing stirred. The garden was quiet—*too* quiet—no birdsong to lift her spirits. At first, this struck her as odd. Until she realised the birds were doubtless roosting in the thick bank of beech trees behind the gate, sheltering from the oppressive warmth.

Surprised, a ripple captured her attention, to her left, among a mass of bulbous violet alliums. Energised, picking up the pace, Quill headed toward the border, forcing her way between the wide, hairy stems. As she did so, a thick smog of trouble engulfed her, biting and crawling into her eyes, ears and mouth, every crevice of her body and beneath her clothes. Quill gagged, spitting out the invaders, shaking her skull to dislodge them from her earlobes and clawing at her skin and hair to brush them aside. The swarm of flying ants charged from all directions, driven wild with desire by the aroma of spiced meat and jelly. Conjured by the hot weather, the plague of vicious insects rose like a lone behemoth from the tranquillity of the peaceful garden and attacked without mercy. Within seconds, saw-like mandibles had ravaged every inch of her skin, leaving angry red welts that itched and throbbed. Just when she couldn't bear the irritation any longer, the cloud moved on, hunting for its next meal, human or otherwise.

Palms on her knees, bent forward, still spewing out ingested bugs, Quill panted, the panic subsiding as she groaned, inspecting the damage to her wrecked skin. The low growl to her left made her smile as she pumped her fist between the nearest flower heads, trying to ignore the horrendous sight of her bloated knuckles. Silently creeping through the overgrown forest, she stalked the dog, keen not to frighten the little creature or to disturb any additional pests. As she edged onwards, the rumble grew louder, vibrating the soil under her toes until she saw a flash of black-and-tan among the green stalks. Breath held tight, Quill tiptoed the last few centimetres to the scatterbrained pup. Until finally, ahead of her moccasins, the tiny dog hunkered on her belly, grunting an intense and insistent warning in a continuous stream.

In front of her wet nose lay two objects that rarely belonged in a planted bed, a duo pricking Quill's neck hairs—a poppy-red leather lead and a solitary abandoned brown boot.

Chapter Eleven

"Where have you been?" Seated opposite the blue sofa, which overflowed with the unique figure of Uriah Crisp, Master Wittgenstein addressed Quill through gritted teeth.

"And," said the semi-naked man, bristling as he rubbed his stomach, "where is my brunch?"

"Err, would you believe me if I said the dog ate it?" Quill chewed her cheek, peeking at Luna, who slept across her moccasins like a loyal and obedient pet.

"Don't be ridiculous." The ancient scholar wrung his hands in exasperation and turned to the guest, lowering his voice. "I'm so sorry. What must you think of us?"

Crisp's inked features remained impassive as Quill waited with trepidation for his reaction to the unfortunate events. Even the mansion held its breath, embarrassed in front of the important visitor. As she was ready to fill the uncomfortable silence with inane comments concerning the unusual weather, the immense man threw back his head, erupting into uncontrollable laughter which reverberated around the elegant room—a full-bodied, exuberant mirth at odds with the formal surroundings. Awkwardly exchanging glances with her mentor, Quill wondered how to react.

Was he laughing with them, or at them? Should they join him?

It was impossible to fathom the answer. Even Luna started, head cocked to one side, unsure what to make of the commotion.

Quill nibbled her rough cuticles, keeping silent as the awkward moment stretched into eternity. With his cheeks getting redder and redder by the second, Uriah Crisp wheezed like an antique kettle, launching himself from his reclined position, clutching and clawing at his windpipe. A white-eyed stare of panic appeared across his face as he fought for breath. Roused from inaction, picturing the gossip and scandal following such an extraordinary visitor suffocating in Montague Hall, Quill leapt forward, dislodging the dozing puppy.

Caught between not wanting the fellow to expire in front of them and terrified to bash him on the back, Quill stalled short of the settee, fist inches from his spine. Paralysed by indecision, to her significant relief, Crisp raised his palm and inhaled a ragged, lusty gulp of air, as his choking subsided. "Stop. You're killing me. I'm fine. I haven't laughed this much in ages. You should be on the stage. Forgive me, that was insensitive."

Quill risked a glance across at the master, gauging his reaction to the gentleman's cultural faux pas. Then she added it to the list of questions to ask the envoy. Obviously, Asterians didn't share the concerns of Scolarians in celebrating the creative arts. A picture of settling in a city full of colour, music and theatre built in her brain. The prospect was something she'd dreamt about since Wittgenstein had given her the black book of the Meraki. The volume of mind-bending text that no-one could decipher without a magnifying glass.

"Are you hurt?" asked the ancient scholar, his weather-beaten features a picture of benevolent unease.

"Fine, honestly I'm okay. The thought of Luna demolishing the lunch was too hilarious. I got carried away. It's been an honour and a joy to meet you, Wittgenstein, and I very much look forward to conversing with you further during my stay. I hope you'll excuse me. All this excitement isn't good for my health and I'm still exhausted from the lengthy trip. I'll retire to my room for some further rest, and hopefully, once my nap is over, Yulia will have returned and I can satisfy my hunger."

Both men rose from their seats, the scholar most easily of the pair, despite his advancing years, while the now jovial Mr Crisp fought to lever his massive frame upwards. They shook hands; the master clasping his free hand over the top of their entwined palms in a surprising show of warmth and affection given they'd just met. "The pleasure was all mine. We wish you a happy and fruitful stay in Scolaris and please come and visit me. Do me the great honour of giving you the grand tour of the library."

"Thank you. Marvellous idea." Then the emissary bent over, creaking at the waist to ruffle the thatch of fur on Luna's head, as the dog nestled again on Quill's feet.

"I discovered these," said Quill as soon as they were alone. She reclaimed the poppy-red dog lead, and the abandoned brown boot from behind the master's armchair where she'd secreted them.

Wittgenstein frowned, the canyons on his forehead deepening with every passing moment. "Why are you wasting my time with these trivial objects? Do you appreciate how embarrassing that entire situation was? Thank goodness Mr Crisp is so understanding. Honestly, child, I don't understand what's got into you lately."

"Before you go any further, listen to what I'm telling you," she said, fighting the urge to list out her frustrations in words of one syllable. "It's not the items themselves, it's where I found them."

"You've lost me. What are you trying to say?"

"I went to the kitchen for food, expecting to find Yulia, but she wasn't there. The whole place is clean and emptied, I assume, before Mr Crisp's visit. She left a pork pie with instructions for Dr Novack to serve lunch. In case she hadn't returned in time from restocking the larder. I expect she's doing that now. Then we had the mishap, something I'm not proud of. But I noticed the dog's bowls were empty. They're never empty. I don't think anyone fed Luna today, which explains why she devoured the meat and pastry. He loves the dog. I can't imagine him not feeding her."

"Hmm, I see. Me neither. What about the lead and boot?"

"After eating so much, Luna needed to go out, but her leash was missing. Next to a small pair of walking boots, there's a set of larger boot prints—they must belong to the doctor."

The master nodded, staring at her, waiting for her to continue.

"When I opened the back door, Luna ran off. I wondered if the missing items meant Dr Novack was outside somewhere and that Luna would take me to him. Finding him seemed the best way to make up for ruining lunch. But I couldn't, and when I caught up with the dog, she'd brought me to the leash and this boot. Both were lying together in the flower bed. I can't imagine why they'd be there, but the doctor isn't. You've simply got to watch the puppy to see there's something wrong. Poor little thing, she's very clingy, and she was growling at thin air in the garden. I'm worried something's happened to him."

"Listen, I'm confident there's a sensible explanation. You said yourself, Yulia is out shopping and Sterling is a very busy man. There could be many reasons he's not here; official engagements, committee meetings. Not forgetting he still consults on complex medical cases. He may be the Head of the Protectorate, but he is also a doctor. I must talk to him soon, but I'm not convinced we should get carried away by a stray lead and boot. Maybe Luna grabbed them and hid them. Let's be honest, she is prone to mischief. We'll wait an extra half an hour, but then I'll have to leave. I must meet with the scholarship mentors at the appointed hour. We'll have to come back afterwards."

No sooner had those words escaped his lips than the puppy bolted upright onto her forepaws. With massive round eyes, she stared toward the entrance, ears flapping as if hearing a sound they couldn't. Seconds later, confirming their suspicions, a shuffling, rustling sound, like shoes dragging through dry, brittle leaves, came from beyond the doorway.

"Ah, there we are, you see? There's someone now. I told you there was nothing to fret about." The academic pushed up on the chair, heading toward the front entrance. "Let's get this resolved and go home."

A twinge of apprehension gripped her, the nagging cry of anxiety chattering in her brain. Quill brushed a palm across her cheeks, sensing the feather-shaped birthmark's vague edges as she urged herself to follow.

I hope the master's self-confidence rubs off on me one day.

Luna criss-crossed the room ahead, then scratched at the exit, eager to investigate the sounds coming from the entrance.

Light flooded into the lobby from the transom window above the front door, illuminating the tiny figure of Yulia Pomerenke, Dr Sterling Novack's housekeeper. The woman was shorter than Quill, her trade-mark high bun tight and perfectly formed on her crown, not a single stray wisp of hair astray, even as she leaned over the bags at her feet. That she didn't wear the defecto uniform always struck Quill, opting instead for a practical two-piece dress suit—still brown, but not the misshapen sack the rest of them had to bear.

Perhaps that was a perk of the position? Though the injustice of that insignificant detail stung more than it should have.

The middle-aged woman stopped, hands on her hips, breathing hard, surrounded by copious paper sacks bursting at the seams with groceries. The dog scurried over, sticking her snout into every carrier, sniffing for a treat. Quill found it difficult to believe there was any spare room in the pup's stomach. Yulia waved at Luna, steering the pet away from the shopping, but the gesture was futile. No sooner had the puppy removed her head from one pouch than she was dropping her nose in the next.

After a while, the housekeeper's patience grew thin. "Stop it. Silly dog, this isn't for you. There are no treats here. If you want your biscuits, they're in your bowl. Go on, off you trot."

But Luna simply sat on her haunches, peering up at the housemaid as she gathered the supplies, wedging bags under her armpits and the rest in both fists. Master Wittgenstein cleared his throat, a polite form of letting the servant realise she had an audience. "Quill, don't just stand there. Help Yulia, will you?"

The startled woman's chin shot up, a faint blush spreading across her cheeks. "Dear me, I didn't notice you there. You gave me a fright."

"Apologies. We didn't intend to alarm you. Quill will assist with those bags."

They tracked Yulia to the kitchen, walking the servant's route, accessed to the right of the hallway, opposite the sweeping staircase. The narrow passageway led straight to the rear corner of the house, accessing the kitchen without having to enter the living or dining room. The Hall was a big place, and the expedition took even longer when manhandling awkward shaped bags weighed down with groceries. Pomerenke led the way, followed by the master, and Quill brought up the tail. Luna had long since scampered ahead, the promise of biscuits impossible to resist. Though Quill expected the pup to be disappointed by the barren containers.

"Where's Dr Novack?" Yulia's stern tone echoed along the corridor, as Quill wrestled with a cabbage which attempted to escape the bag under her left armpit.

The master replied, a slight tremor in his voice. "We hoped you'd tell us that."

"Do you mean he's still not here?" Yulia halted so sharply that the old man almost collided with her. Followed by Quill, who veered right and around the pair to prevent a repeat performance of the pastry episode. A deviation which wasn't entirely successful, as the errant cabbage catapulted out of its sack, bouncing past like a severed head along the passage and into the kitchen.

Quill stifled a giggle, to which the master glared, then turned to the housekeeper, a placating smile imposed on his face. "Let's discuss this in private, once everything's stored away. I don't know about you, but I need a cup of fresh tea. Shall we?" he asked, gesticulating with his fingers toward the kitchen.

The woman nodded, pale as her lower lip trembled, and without a further word, the trio headed through the doorway.

Unloading the food, Quill listened as Yulia recounted the circumstances of her morning. The unease percolating since arriving at Montague Hall, caught in her throat like a stone. To dislodge the sensation, she gulped the boiling tea, despite burning the inside of her mouth.

"I arrived as usual at seven thirty prompt," said the housekeeper, gripping the steaming hot mug until her knuckles turned white. "Luna was on the front doorstep, howling like a baby. I assumed Dr Novack had an early meeting, that Luna had escaped again, trying to track him by squeezing under the gate between the back garden and the front. It wouldn't be the first time. I finished cleaning and left a note for the doctor regarding lunch, knowing I might not return on time from my trip to collect provisions. We have a very important visitor staying with us from Asteria, Mr Crisp."

"Yes, we've met. Singular fellow. Such a fascinating man, looking forward to exchanging ideas."

"Oh dear, I hoped he'd still be asleep. He landed a few days ago, but we haven't seen a great deal of him, to be honest. It's a protracted voyage by ship and he's done nothing but sleep since his arrival. He's been eating his meals in his room, none of which have been breakfast, as he doesn't surface until mid-afternoon. I didn't leave a tray outside his door this morning because the last few times he hasn't touched it and I do hate waste. Good grief, what will he make of us? He certainly has a healthy appetite when he's awake long enough to enjoy a meal. Perhaps I shouldn't have assumed he was a man of routine like Dr Novack."

The prim lady swept a palm from her forehead to the top of her bun, as if to catch any loose hairs, but she needn't have worried. Nothing moved. Not satisfied, she worked clockwise, retracting and reinserting each metal pin in a slick motion she'd clearly performed on countless occasions. A ritual which produced a perfect coil of hair.

"I don't think you should worry too much," said the master, in between gulps of drink and mouthfuls of oat biscuit served to him from the groceries. "I'm afraid we woke him. His state of dress, or should I say undress, suggested he'd not been up and about any earlier this morning. Unsurprising in the circumstances, it's a tiring trek, yes, but we mustn't forget that our culture isn't his. He ordered brunch, which we tried our best to provide, but without success." The ancient man gripped his hands together, shifting on the wooden bench while glancing between his plate of crumbs and Quill. She did her utmost to ignore him as she loaded the fridge. "Never mind. That's a story for a different day. Mr Crisp retired to his bedroom right before you came home. Fatigued still from his travels, he said he'd survive until later. Well, thank you for the refreshment and the delicious biscuits. I'm sure you have plenty to do, so we'll leave you to get on with it."

Quill mouthed at her mentor, hiding behind an enormous slab of ham. "Aren't you forgetting something?"

The scholar frowned, though whether that was confusion or annoyance, she couldn't tell. The multitude of lines criss-crossing his face had that effect. "Eh, what? Oh, yes, it's imperative that I speak to Dr Novack as soon as possible. Do you know where he could be?"

Yulia shook her bun, straightening a series of cooking utensils which might have been a millimetre out of line. "Sorry, no. I run the house, but Sterling, Dr Novack I mean, controls his diary and appointments himself. I keep saying he should employ a secretary, but he's a very private man and prefers to maintain a limited staff. There's only me and Bob, the gardener."

The term *gardener* jolted Quill out of the monotony of stacking row upon row of shelves. "Sorry to interrupt. I'd almost forgotten. Luna's food and water dishes are empty. I've never seen them empty before, have you?"

Three heads turned in unison, searching for the salmon-pink ceramics, which remained bare. Luna's black-and tan-body snuggled up against them, the little pet comatose, worn out from the drama.

Yulia stood, smoothing the creases from the front of her dress. "No, never. Dr Novack feeds the animal. If I had my way, it wouldn't step foot in here. Dogs and kitchens don't mix." The maid slid out a huge carving knife from the nearest sharpening block, examining the blade with alarming intensity. Until, emerging from an unnerving trance, she slammed it into the sheath. "Of course I do what I'm told. Sterling is kind enough to take responsibility for the creature. He replenishes the bowls first thing after their dawn stroll. I can't understand why they're empty."

"Perhaps he had an early appointment that prevented him from walking Luna today?" asked the master.

"It's possible, but I doubt it. As I mentioned, Sterling's a man of habit. He would've risen earlier."

The threesome fell into an awkward silence as they each contemplated the situation. Then Quill joined the conversation. "Does the doctor wear brown walking boots?"

Yulia responded, pointing toward the back door. "Yes, they're next to mine." She paused mid-flow, a pained expression across her features, as if she were struggling to complete the sentence. "Or they should be there. Where have they got to?"

The teeny woman crossed from the trestle table to the rear doors, gaping first at her trail boots, then at the space beside them on the newspaper.

With the woman's scrutiny elsewhere, Quill retrieved the two articles she'd dropped into a bag for safekeeping. A task accomplished while the housekeeper was distracting Luna from destroying the shopping. Items held aloft, she searched her mentor's face for permission to go ahead. In response to an imperceptible nod of his brow, she continued. "I found these discarded in the middle of a flower bed. Are they Dr Novack's?"

The neat woman turned and despite not making a sound, from her bulging-eyed crumpled demeanour, Quill and Master Wittgenstein instantly knew the answer.

Chapter Twelve

Despite plying the woman with copious cups of sugar laden tea, Yulia Pomerenke still embodied the distress of someone who'd received news of the unexpected demise of a close relative, which Quill found odd in the circumstances. True, the middle-aged lady had worked for Dr Novack for as long as she'd been visiting Montague Hall, but she was his housekeeper, not his wife.

Huddled by the boots, Quill and the master whispered, exchanging furtive glances as they attempted to pull a plan of action together. "We should contact the guard," said Quill. "This is the Head of the Protectorate we're talking about. The most important man in the city. We must do something."

"That's precisely why we can't call them, and what exactly do you suggest we tell them? We found a dog lead and a boot in a flower bed and from that we conclude that some terrible fate has befallen Dr Novack. Do you hear how ridiculous that sounds?"

"You have a point, but what happened the last time you kept a secret? A dead protector, six dead defectos and you almost framed for murder."

"Another factor in favour of not telling the guard if you ask me. They have no experience dealing with serious crime. Not that I'm saying anyone's committed a crime. I'm sure there'll be a reasonable explanation."

"I wish I shared your confidence. You saw the look on Yulia's face and she's still shaking like she's seen a ghost. See. There's no doubt she thinks something's happened to him."

"Dr Novack isn't home, but I know how dedicated he is to this city. He wouldn't want anything to tarnish our reputation, particularly in front of such an important visitor like Mr Crisp. We must tread carefully. Sometimes acting for the greater good takes precedence, even when that conflicts with our hopes and desires."

Was that aimed at me?

Irritated by his last remark, Quill broke eye contact, hiding the disappointment and betrayal bubbling millimetres beneath the surface. As soon as her pulse slowed, she glanced back at him. "What are we going to do, then? You said yourself that you need his approval to bring the Ortus forward. If we can't locate him, what are the options, and how long can we keep his absence a secret?"

The master scratched his scalp, snagging his fingertips in his lengthy, white mane. "He'll return soon, I'm sure of it. I have to attend my meeting or people will gossip. She must have more to tell us," he said, head flicking toward the housekeeper.

Striding to the seat opposite, leaving Quill in his wake, the old man grinned at Yulia, teeth on full display. "Are you feeling any better?"

Pomerenke pushed her cup away, then rose from the bench. "Yes, thank you. I've taken up too much of your time already. The doctor's fine, I'm sure. I expect the dog dumped those things in the garden. I don't know why I didn't consider it before."

It struck Quill that the tiny woman had slipped into a mask devoid of emotion, but a faint twitch at the corner of her lips hinted she didn't entirely believe the words that came out of her own mouth.

"Perhaps we should think back to yesterday. Do you remember what he did last evening, for example?" asked the master.

"I do. I began clearing old food stock in the afternoon and passed him on my way to the compost with some rotten fruit I discovered at the rear of a shelf. Goodness knows how it got there. I certainly didn't put it there."

"You said you crossed paths. Did he say where he was going?"

"Yes. He wished me a good evening and told me not to wait up as he was meeting Mr Paine. Said it would probably be late, and he'd lock up on his return."

"Dorian Paine?" asked the master and Yulia Pomerenke's bun bobbed forward and back in agreement.

Standing inside the enclosed porch of Mr Paine's residence, a building that screamed modernist architecture from every surface, Quill waited for the young defecto boy who'd answered the door to reappear. Yulia's telephone call had elicited no response and so, on the master's instructions, they planned to make discreet enquiries, with a firm emphasis on the discreet. The scholar had toyed with sending her alone, knowing he couldn't miss his meeting, but eventually decided that two brains were better than one, which she assumed was code for him not trusting her capabilities—an all too familiar attitude.

They'd left the housekeeper to the solitude of her kitchen, though not before she'd gained assurances she'd be the first to know when they located the doctor. The hint of desperation in the woman's voice echoed in Quill's mind in an irritating circuit. Which, coupled with dehydration from the long, hot walk, culminated in a distinct throb across her eyebrows.

If only I'd persuaded the master to let me bring Luna.

Yulia was clearly not a dog person and she couldn't help worrying about the animal's welfare. But the master had steadfastly refused. The library was off-limits to a plant, let alone a pet.

Sudden thoughts of home reminded her she still had to fix Scholar Leitch's notes, a memory that didn't benefit the headache. Waiting was tortuous, as she envisaged the many ways Aric could make her life even more difficult if he set his mind to the task, an endeavour he'd doubtless enjoy. While the master had so far reneged on his vow to teach her, leading her to conclude he'd lied, there was still a tiny part of her clinging to the possibility that he might fulfil his promise. Though none of that would matter if Leitch poisoned the master against her.

"What's taking so long?"

With the hem of her tunic, she dried the pool of sweat collecting under her chin, grimacing at the dusty, wet stain left behind. The master glared, centimetres from her nose, in the confined space of the glass porch which acted like a human greenhouse under the glare of the afternoon sun.

"Be quiet," he said through his teeth, just as the boy returned to let them inside the house.

The child slumped at the shoulders, crestfallen, visibly shaken, as if Wit meant the rebuke for him. "Sorry, master. Mr Paine is in his office. Please go through, you know the way."

"Er, right, yes, hmm, I didn't mean you. I meant to say, em, thank you." The old scholar bumbled through a meaningless exchange with the poor boy as he led them into the building.

Unsurprisingly, the residence represented a feat of architectural ingenuity. A cuboid turned on its point, it balanced on a column attached to the glass porch. Beyond the lobby, no light penetrated a short hallway leading to the stairs, which spiralled inside the windowless column and up into the cube. Left of the staircase, the architect's office swept along the tube's curve, a glorious man-cave cut-off from the world outside.

Dorian Paine rose to greet them from behind a tilted desk, awash with reams and reams of architectural designs. He tossed his pencil into the tray along the bottom edge of the stand and greeted the master with a vigorous handshake that almost lifted the old man off his feet. Quill had seen Paine once or twice in the library, no doubt researching a project. Excluding the fact that he was a key member of the architect community, a protector on his district's council, she knew nothing else about him. Tall and broad, his fingers were thick like plump sausages, fingernails bitten down to the quick. Quill wondered how such hands produced the precise, accurate drawings required to conjure a building.

Much like the master's study, floor-to-ceiling bookshelves lined the office walls. Slate-grey, masculine and filled with every conceivable book on technical drawing and construction styles through the ages. Though a random assortment of handicraft books on a shelf were odd additions to the collection.

Perhaps they belong to Mrs Paine?

"What a wonderful surprise. What brings you here?" asked Dorian, his deep tone reverberating around the cave-like space as he directed the master to a precarious looking spindle-legged stool. The old man perched on the edge, unwilling or unable to balance upon it. Quill shifted her weight from one foot to the other, questioning whether to stand behind him, in case he toppled backwards and cracked his bony skull on the floor.

"Sorry to disturb you, Dorian. I appreciate you're busy with all your marvellous projects. I hoped you might have seen Sterling today, or know of his whereabouts?"

"Unfortunately, no. He was here last evening, but he left at about 11 PM, heading home."

"Did he mention his plans?"

"Let me think. Not that I recall. Our meeting was more of a social gathering, two old friends sharing conversation and a brandy. You know what it's like for us confirmed bachelors. Human company is lacking when work is your sole focus. May I ask what this is about?" The architect's thick, bushy eyebrows pinched together to form a single black line across his umber forehead.

The master paused, leaning backward, his ancient bones searching for a backrest—dangerous when there was none. A manoeuvre which squirted the legs of the stool forward, its rubber feet screeching against the polished concrete floor. The scene played out in slow motion as the scholar's lower limbs flung upward in an arc, sending the top half of his body toppling backwards. Quill and Dorian reacted in unison, the latter hurling himself across his desk, clutching for a handful of the master's robes with his stubby fingers as Quill launched herself to the right to catch the scholar from behind. Wit yelped as Paine grabbed a clump of hair besides the white cloth, but between them they halted the inevitable. Held in suspension by the architect's grasp in front and Quill's at the rear, the old man cleared his throat. "Er, thank you. I think I can manage from here."

Then panting from exertion and fear, she stared into Paine's bloodshot eyes. "It's okay, I've got him. You're safe to let go now."

The architect hesitated, lowering his gaze to the floor as he relinquished his grip, but not before discovering a large clump of white hair in his fist, which he tried to hide behind his back, as if hoping no-one would notice. Not wishing to witness a repeat of the near miss, Paine called to the young defecto. The boy arrived soon after with a more suitable seat for the ancient fellow, who now sported a distinct bald patch on his crown.

Safely ensconced in a black wing-backed armchair, Quill perched on the deadly stool, ensuring she pushed it up against the wall next to the door. When everyone had caught their breath, the conversation continued as if nothing had happened. "We're not sure, but we cannot locate Dr Novack at the moment. He doesn't appear to be home. The housekeeper last saw him yesterday, late afternoon, early evening. He suggested he was coming here, hence our visit."

"I expect he's at a meeting. He's a very busy man. Is that all? There's something else you haven't mentioned. You know you can rely on my discretion?"

The master crossed and uncrossed his legs, making a triangle of his fingers in front of him. "Yes, yes, I do. Dr Novack is very fond of his dog."

Paine frowned. "Luna? Yes, what about it?"

"It sounds petty when I say it out loud, but Sterling did not feed the animal this morning, and Quill found the dog's lead and one of his walking boots discarded in a flower bed. Luna seems—different."

"The dog? Different, different how?"

"I knew this sounded ridiculous," muttered the scholar, glaring at Quill before returning to Paine. "She's acting strange, whining, and growling at something we can't see."

"Is that all? It doesn't seem very significant to me. What exactly are you saying?"

"To be honest, I'm not sure. It's a feeling. Lots of random details that mean little by themselves, but put together makes me question whether something's happened to him. You know the special envoy from Asteria is staying with him?"

"Uriah Crisp? Yes, Sterling mentioned him last night. He seemed quite taken with the man. Personally, I don't like the sound of him. Covered in artwork, not something we should be encouraging. Don't you think?"

"I find it difficult to believe that Doctor Novack would leave Montague Hall without mentioning it to the housekeeper, knowing that they are entertaining such an important guest. Add that to the dereliction of his duty towards his beloved pet and the unusual positioning of his walking boots. Causes for concern, which couldn't have come at a worse time."

Quill noticed the master did not answer Paine's question.

Was that a choice or an oversight?

Understanding him as she did, she settled on a deliberate evasion of the subject.

The bags under the architect's tawny eyes rippled as he raised his mono brow. "I agree that it's unlike him not to pay particular attention to guests, but he trusts the housekeeper implicitly. I'm sure she can manage."

"Forgive me. I wasn't referring to Mr Crisp's visit."

"What? I'm sorry, I don't understand. What else is there?"

"Have you noticed anything unusual in the sky today?" asked the scholar, smoothing his hair and discovering the bald patch, which he explored with his fingertips.

"To be honest, I've been here working since before dawn, so no. What am I missing?"

The master stole a glance across at Quill, who straightened her posture, expecting what came next. "We have a celestial visitor, a guest star bigger and brighter than anything recorded in history. So bright, in fact, that it's visible during the day. It flashes yellow and green, emitting immeasurable quantities of light and heat energy. If you venture outside, even if you can't see it, you feel its effects. Combined with the intensity of the sun, it's sweltering out there."

As the master regaled the architect with news of the supernova, Paine grew still, transfixed by every added detail. "Can it be true? There's been nothing similar for centuries."

"Correct, not since Anastarchus, and he doesn't mention the star being visible during the day. You know what must be done."

"Of course, now I see. We must bring the Ortus forward, watch and wait, timing the ceremony to align with the rise and fall of the star. A spectacle to renew the city's vigour, reaffirming our commitment to the pursuit of knowledge. Will we be able to accomplish this without Sterling? Doesn't he need to ratify the decision to reschedule the rite?" Then the architect paused, a puzzled expression sweeping across his countenance. "Ah, that's why you're concerned."

"I'm concerned because he's a friend and I want him to be safe. But you're correct, without his agreement, there's only one alternative course of action."

"Another way? How?"

Quill already knew the answer. She'd read it once, years ago, in an ancient text which set out obscure rules and regulations of the Protectorate, most of which were obsolete. A throwback to the early days when the council comprised only five scholars, one for each district, all a distant memory from today's complex set-up of committees and subcommittees.

"The Protectorate must vote overwhelmingly to assume control in Dr Novack's absence. Then we can reschedule. There's no alternative."

"I'd like to think that would be a straightforward process," said Paine, resting his skull in his hands which stretched behind him, fingers interleaved.

"I wouldn't be so sure. My biggest fear's that protectors will panic when we reveal he's missing, particularly as we've only recently recovered from the Hawkin episode. Certain individuals might push to hold an election for a new leader, but we cannot afford to get sidetracked. We must advance The Ortus in alignment with the star's trajectory. We could rest our hopes on him turning up for dinner, assume this is all a misunderstanding, but I'd prefer to plan for the worst and hope for the best."

"Agreed. It doesn't help that Novack has a visitor. What did you have in mind?"

"First, we wait to see if he's returned by this evening. If not, we call an emergency meeting of the Protectorate early tomorrow. We'll tell them the doctor's ill. By morning, news of the guest star will have spread throughout the city and that alone might persuade them to assume control and move up the ceremony."

"And if they won't?" asked Paine, leaning forward, elbows on the desk, chin resting on his hands.

Master Wittgenstein paused, tapping his right foot on the concrete and adjusting the front of his robe before staring down the architect. "They must."

Chapter Thirteen

Inside the evidence bag, the book of matches silently mocked Chief Red as he sat behind Jim Ross's old cherry-red desk in his new office at Guard HQ. When he described it as his new office, he meant it was new to him. He'd tried to put his stamp on it, resurfacing the desktop by filling in the dents and scratches and applying wood stain until it gleamed like the sides. Unfortunately, there was no rescuing the battered filing cabinet hunkered in the far corner, and its replacement hadn't arrived. The unusual pyramid of stone which he'd inherited from his predecessor stood on the top, waiting for an improved home.

Focused on the matchbook, willing the innocuous object to share its secrets, the plain white front disguised the back—dead centre, a familiar black swirl like a G. Today, the symbol curled around an intriguing silhouette, a woman with voluptuous curves, long limbs and calf length windswept hair. Of greater interest, a single intriguing word encircled the design—*Euphoria*.

But what did it mean?

Certainly the toxin left a lasting impression on those whose lives it took. He was unlikely to forget the frozen, ecstatic expression in a hurry. While the lab still hadn't confirmed the drug's involvement, euphoria seemed an appropriate concept in the circumstances. The question he couldn't answer was whether the match-book represented a discreet way of advertising the stimulant, or something else.

Red knew his father was partial to the odd cigar, an indulgence he enjoyed at his members-only club. An exclusive group of gentlemen who'd climbed high up the ranks of Law and Order. This clique provided patrons with match-books.

But they don't decorate them like this.

The specimen was positively artistic and broke at least half a dozen rules and regulations he could remember. If it belonged to a society or organisation, he'd never heard of it. It was possible the use of that word was a coincidence. Though his training had taught him never to discount any piece of information as a coincidence, however innocuous, and he wasn't planning to start now.

The door to his office swung open, slamming against the inside wall with a loud crash as Guard Jackson blundered in unannounced.

"Don't you ever knock?" asked Red, trying and failing to hide his irritation.

"Didn't see you there, Red, my man. I'm hunting for the latest case reports." The gangly, towering guard ignored the simple question, droning on in his familiar tone.

He'd tried to allow the rest of the guardsmen an opportunity to get used to the idea that he was now chief. Telling himself that given the chance, he'd earn their respect, but his patience was wearing thin, particularly where it concerned Jackson.

Perhaps it's time to set some boundaries?

"Jackson, I'm the Chief. You will address me with my title and knock before entering my office. Is that clear?"

"It doesn't suit you, you know? You'll never be like him."

"Like who?" As soon as Red asked, he immediately wished he hadn't got drawn into the inane discussion.

"The boss."

"I am the boss. I assume you're referring to Jim. He's gone, retired. You'd better get used to it. The case files are on your desk if you'd taken the time to look properly. I want you to divide them among the men. They can work in teams of two. Return to where they found the bodies and widen the search areas in the immediate vicinity. We need to identify these people. Somebody must know them. But be discreet. We must avoid panic spreading through the city, so I don't want any details leaked. Don't even mention that we're dealing with unexplained deaths. If anyone asks, we are following up on missing persons. Have you got that?"

Jackson slouched against the front edge of the desk, a sneering grin across his lips as he enunciated each syllable of his reply. "Yes, Chief." Then the insubordinate wretch returned to the outer office, slamming the door behind him.

Red wondered if he could to transfer Jackson to a different unit and made a mental note to find out as soon as there was a spare minute. He'd had a difficult discussion with Mr Tedesko earlier, his contact with the council for Law and Order.

A conversation which continued to play in his head, stern words which relayed the need for a result. Veiled threats about removal from his post before he'd even got going, unless this situation disappeared. He wasn't altogether sure what *disappeared* entailed, but he didn't like the sound of it and, for reasons of expediency, chose not to ask.

Tense across his tight forehead, he rotated his head anticlockwise to relieve the pressure on his neck. Startled by the shrill ring of the telephone, Red tensed, undoing his recent efforts.

Please, not Tedesko again.

Steeling himself for a further dressing-down, he reached for the receiver, taking his time, secretly hoping that the ringing might stop. Finally, he lifted the earpiece. "This is Red."

"Hey, it's Fox. I've got the tox screen on the first body. The results confirm our suspicions. Whoever he is, his blood is swimming in *M*."

The guardsman hit the tabletop with the side of his fist. The momentary celebration was short-lived, as Red reminded himself that this wasn't a game. These were real people. "Thanks, doc. Oh, the chemical might have a better name."

"Alright, what did you have in mind?"

"*Euphoria*. Seems to fit, don't you agree?"

"Now why didn't I think of that?"

"In all honesty, I can't claim the glory. In Mr Vaughn's jacket pocket, I found a matchbook. I'm looking at it right now. The word *Euphoria is* on the back. I'm wondering if it's a calling card for getting hold of the drug, or possibly it's a club. Ever heard of it?"

"Nope, that's a new one on me. Though I must confess, I'm not the club type, if you get what I mean. Smoky, sweaty places. Nothing appealing about that, and anyway, I'm far too busy. As far as I know, each district's council runs the few licensed clubs in existence. I can't imagine them using a fancy title. Jim invited me once. That environment suited him. From recollection, it didn't have a name."

"Yeah, my dad goes, and you're right, the place is toxic and, as far as I'm aware, it's simply called the club."

"Perhaps Law and Order is an outlier. It's possible one of the remaining districts is more inventive."

"Perhaps. I'm not convinced. It's not just the word, there's a design too. I'd almost suggest it's artistic."

"Are you serious?"

"Deadly. On reflection, I think we should make Mr Vaughn's body a priority. As he's the lone victim identified so far, and we found him in situ, I'm hoping you'll capture additional evidence compared to the others. Can you do that for me?"

"It's not exactly procedure, but I can see the sense. I'll start right away. Did you have any luck finding me an assistant?"

Red faltered, hopes of avoiding that question dashed. With a deep sigh, he thumbed his ear. "Sorry, no. Tedesko wasn't interested in discussing it. He suggested that if I don't get this situation wrapped up quickly, I might not be chief much longer. So, I decided it wasn't the best time to be asking a favour."

"As much as I sympathise, if I can't process these bodies, you'll be hunting in the dark without a flashlight trying to solve this case. That, my friend, is a recipe for early retirement. You should have asked."

Red closed his eyes, his eyelids scrunched tight, angry at himself as he recognised that Virgil Fox had a point. He felt inadequate, walking a tightrope with his hands tied behind his back, as he discovered that being the boss wasn't as easy as he'd imagined. At the outset, he'd vowed to forge his own path with no ambition to be another Jim Ross, commanding with brute strength and ignorance. Instead, he intended to inspire through truth, honesty, and loyalty. So far, he'd inspired a lack of respect, and colleagues trampling over him. Clearly, he needed to be more assertive.

How to achieve that without becoming a bully?

"You're right," he admitted, "I guess I'm a work in progress as chief."

"Hey, give it time. My advice, for what it's worth, is to go straight to the top. I've always found Dr Novack approachable. Tedesko might not thank you, but there won't be much he can do about it."

"Thanks for the tip. I'll call him."

"Any time. Good luck. Oh, chief?"

"Yeah," said Red, grinning at the sound of his title echoing through the line.

"Get me that matchbook."

Chapter Fourteen

5 weeks, 6 days to the Ortus

The previous afternoon and evening had passed in a blur of action. From the less than fruitful trips to Dr Novack's residence, followed by Paine's, the master had gone directly to his meeting—a gathering of the experienced scholars assigned to be the new trainees' mentors. He'd left Quill tidying the Compendium Room ready for day two of training.

She'd hoped the defectos had cleared up their master's mess, so finding the place in disarray was disheartening. The beautifully laid out lunch that once adorned the trestle tables looked as if a swarm of locusts had attacked, leaving scant breadcrumbs, flakes of cheese and globs of pickle spread like multicoloured bloodstains on the tablecloth. Tirelessly she worked, scraping the rubbish into an orange sack with the side of her forearm, her nose wrinkling at the sour odour and sharp shards of bread. The soles of her moccasins soaked up spilt pickling liquor, which she spent a significant chunk of time scrubbing out of the carpet.

At least the colour covers a multitude of stains.

With the remnants consigned to the bag, Quill gathered up the not-so-white cloth, drawing each corner into the middle to catch any missed debris. Whether she could restore the material to its pristine whiteness was doubtful. For now, it needed a new cloth.

It was already late by the time she finished cleaning the space. The master had eaten his usual light supper. A plate of bread and cheese that she'd slung together in readiness before the cleaning began. Quill's energy levels flagged. Her back twinged, complaining from the exertion of the long walk in the stifling heat, followed by hours of bending and stretching. She longed to curl up beneath the star-covered quilt and sleep till morning, maybe glimpse her father's face in a dream. But there was the small matter of fixing Aric Leitch's ink stained notes.

Sat massaging her spine against the side of the bed with her toes stretched out to greet the skirting board, she spread the mottled sheets across the rug. Aric's writing, what little of it there was, looked barely legible. Thin upright strokes scratched into the surface like the claw marks of a desperate animal. As she rotated a smudged sheet, the black blobs transformed in front of her eyes. Outstretched wings, delicate legs and proboscis primed to fly out of the paper. It could have been the butterfly she'd rescued from the clutches of the spider web those few weeks earlier. It felt like a lifetime ago, even though it wasn't.

Facing facts, the pages were beyond saving. With drooping eyelids, knowing that she might not be sleeping anytime soon, Quill sighed and started afresh. How long it had taken her, she couldn't be sure. Though the guest star's glow against the backdrop of the night sky through her window was the last thing she remembered. Followed seconds later by the mechanical voice of the 6 o'clock alarm call, "Knowledge is King". The sound rousing her from her awkward position curled up on the rug, pen and paper clutched to her chest and cramp in every muscle.

To know that the clean, detailed pages sat on Aric's desk, waiting to be claimed, settled her nerves.

Surely that should put an end to the young man's hostility?

That was the hope, anyhow.

As she bustled around the cupboard kitchen, preparing the scrambled egg breakfast, the low drone of the master's voice rumbled through the door from the study. No doubt he was on the telephone, despite hating the technology, branding it an unnecessary intrusion on the sanctity of his workspace. There'd always been a line to the library, but he'd resisted connecting it to his rooms. He insisted that if he wanted to speak to somebody, he could visit them in person. "There's nothing like face-to-face communication," he often said. "Telephones make you lazy." But considering recent events and his advancing years, Quill had finally persuaded him to have one run through to his study. Even though the cantankerous grump was unlikely to say a positive word on the subject.

As she balanced the plate of steaming yellow egg mounds on one palm, cutlery and an enormous mug in the other, Quill pushed open the study door with her hip. Her entrance coincided with the ding of the earpiece as he returned it to the receiver. A signal that the call had ended. She slid the breakfast onto the desktop, which remained surprisingly uncluttered. "Who was that?"

"Huh?"

"On the phone?" She prompted, filling the mug with that awful herbal brew he called tea. "Was it important? Any news on Dr Novack?"

"Erm, what? Oh, right, yes? That was Yulia. There's still no sign of him, and Mr Crisp has been asking awkward questions. The idea of eating dinner alone last evening perturbed him, apparently. The woman sounded jittery, distressed even. She wanted to call the City Guard. Some nonsense about not wanting to be blamed if it turns out he's been the victim of a crime or an accident and she failed to report it. It took me a long time to calm her down, but I think I've managed it now, persuaded her that Sterling would favour discretion in this situation. So it seems there's no choice but to gather the entire council."

With her bony arms clasped tight across her chest, Quill shivered, though it wasn't chilly. Light and heat flooded through the study window, promising another sweltering day. "Perhaps she's right. He's been missing for twenty-four hours now. What if he's laying injured somewhere, or worse? How will you live with yourself if you don't call the guard?"

"It's not that simple. There's still a lot you have to learn. Politics—unspoken and insidious, like the roots of a Willow, creeping into every situation. We can't afford the scrutiny, the amateur meddling of a bunch of ignorant goons. You saw what happened last time."

"Chief Ross, an ignorant goon? Yes, agreed. But you're forgetting he retired. Red's in charge now and I trust him."

With his left eyebrow arched, an unmistakable look of surprise on his crinkled forehead, he shovelled the last morsel of egg into his mouth. "Do you indeed? Interesting, but of no importance."

"So you're going to lie, then?" she asked, handing him his robe, which she gathered from the bedstead.

With a cotton striped nightshirt swapped for the white garment, the ancient scholar's bony head snared in the neck hem. Amidst a flurry of misdirected tugging, a blue scrap of paper fell out of the pocket at his right hip and fluttered onto the carpet. Quill stooped, scooping it into her palm with outstretched fingers at the precise moment as the master freed himself from the clutches of the unruly robe. Seeing the note in her hands, he snatched it, ferreting it into the compartment whence it came, a ruby flush rising from his chin to his forehead. But not before she'd glimpsed the rose-shaped postage mark of Asteria.

Who wrote to him from across the Chares sea? Perhaps it's another letter from my father?

Her heart fluttered, unable to contain her excitement. "Is that from my father?"

"Of course it isn't. You know I haven't heard from him in years. It's private, and I won't be lying, just stretching the truth a little."

"Is that what you call it? Does that include promising to train me then doing nothing?" The deep-rooted anger and disappointment which she'd tried to smother, betrayed by the quiver in her voice.

"Not this again. I've told you, we need to be patient. The city isn't ready for a female scholar, let alone a defecto."

"If not now, when? Five years? Fifty? I'm not sure they'll ever be ready. I don't think you intended to keep your promise."

Fully robed, the master stood, pressing his knuckles onto the desktop as his deep emerald eyes bored into her beneath furrowed white eyebrows. "I'm going to pretend you didn't say that. Training will begin when I say so. You have a lifetime to learn, waiting a little longer won't matter. This topic is closed. Do I make myself clear?"

Behind clamped lips, she ground her teeth, harnessing every ounce of willpower to stop herself from arguing further. Instead, she transferred her festering, impotent rage into a neat, ironic curtsy before heading to the exit.

※ ※ ※ ※ ※ ※ ※

A demon riled by bitterness, Quill stormed out of the study, straight into a tall figure with his ear pressed against the oak door. A man who, surprised by the sudden in-swinging exit, fell toward her at an alarming rate, leaving a nanosecond to take evasive action. Ducking beneath the man's right armpit and launching forward, Quill grabbed a handful of the eavesdropper's clothing on the way, saving him from the ignominy of falling face down at the master's desk. Then, the unidentified male lunged for the doorknob, grabbing it in both hands to break his fall. Simply to find himself at a forty-five degree angle, shoes grazing the floor as his body stretched at full length to the door handle. The man grunted, his frame elongating further still, as the tips of his toes barely contacted the carpet. To avert the disaster she could foresee, Quill tugged harder at the back of the man's brown uniform, yanking him upright onto the soles of his feet as the door closed with a satisfying clunk.

Still none the wiser as to his identity, Quill released her vice-grip and waited for the unfortunate fellow to regain his composure, wiping sweaty palms on the front of her tunic. Eager to interrogate him about his reasons for snooping, biding her time, eventually he turned, and she found herself face-to-face with Norris, the Leitch's defecto. "What do you think you're doing?"

With a sneer of distaste, he straightened his uniform. "None of your business. Though I have to admit, it was a fascinating conversation to tune into."

He couldn't have heard through a closed door, could he?

Flustered, finding it impossible not to stare at the man's chin, she fidgeted. "Didn't anyone ever tell you it's rude to eavesdrop?"

"Perhaps, but life's much more exciting when you know everyone's juicy secrets."

Quill swept a hand through her hair, sensing sweat collecting on her scalp. "Okay, well, you've had your fun, but there's a lot to do today to catch up on the hours missed yesterday. Between us all, we can get set up in no time."

The way Norris laughed made her skin crawl, a slow monotonous sequence of barks timed to synchronise with staccato steps as he crossed the short distance between them. The odious man towered above her, his pointed nose millimetres from hers.

"Suddenly, I don't feel so good, so maybe I should lie down? I wish someone could take my place and do the work while I recuperate."

"Well, don't look at me." Quill hugged her sides. "Anyway, you sound fine. I'm sure you'll be all right once you get started."

"No no no, I think you're mistaken. Let's say, hypothetically speaking, that the Custodian of the Library secretly intended to train a girl as a scholar. Not just any girl, though that's bad enough, in my humble opinion, a defecto girl. Imagine the scandal."

So it was true, Norris had overheard every word and planned to use the conversation to his advantage.

"You're blackmailing me?"

With his head shaking nonchalantly, Norris tutted. "Blackmail's too strong a word, don't you think? You're simply helping a fellow defecto in his hour of need. Correct?"

Backed into a corner, Quill couldn't find a solution to the Norris problem, not one with a favourable outcome. She wanted to remove the smirk from his face, but sensing that would have to wait, she sighed, resigned to her fate. "I'll take care of your duties for today. But that's it."

The odious fellow slow-clapped like a seal. "Is the correct answer. We'll talk about what happens next later. That's all for now. Off you go."

Norris peered along the length of his nose, shooing her away with his fingertips as she headed into the library on her way to the Compendium Room, sensing his gaze at her back.

Chapter Fifteen

By mid-morning, Quill's feet told her they'd had enough. They were victims of the countless trips back and forth with the water jugs to keep the trainee scholars well hydrated in the oppressive heat. As well as escorting a constant stream of senior protectors and their defectos summoned to the Judgement Chamber by the master and Dorian Paine. A call the pair had made following Yulia Pomerenke's frantic dawn appeal, which confirmed Dr Novack's continued absence. While she ran herself ragged, Wittgenstein extended his teaching, doing his best to ignore the awkward questions raised by the more forthright of the students.

As the chamber sat across the corridor from the Compendium Room, hiding the unscheduled council meeting proved impossible. With the district's subcommittees conducting the routine administration of city business, the Judgement Chamber remained inactive for most of the year. Infrequent scheduled meetings took place once a quarter and were largely ceremonial affairs. The genuine power in Scolaris lay with the Head of the Protectorate. By a ballot of the ruling committee members, whoever held the position then took unilateral decisions in their place. For this reason, Dr Novack's disappearance was more than a simple inconvenience—it left the city without its decision-maker.

With hindsight, the set-up was disastrous. In her bubble at the library, Quill's life was relatively untouched by the machinations of politics. Though now, the idea of so much power in one man's hands made her uneasy. Fortunately, the Novack she knew was straightforward, honest, and kind. Precisely the high calibre person you wanted to hold the fate of the entire city in the palm of his hand. Also, for selfish reasons, it crossed her mind he might also be open to the idea of female scholars, maybe even defectos.

By splitting her time and energy between the rooms, she was privy to the whispered conversations and suppositions of each. The students' gossip—fuelled by the Leitch brothers—was considerably less imaginative than the councillors. After the sixth or seventh protector's arrival, the pupils' curiosity waned, dismissing it as a meeting to discuss the guest star's arrival, which, as predicted, everyone had noticed because of the unseasonably hot weather.

Though no-one appreciates the situation's ramifications—the date of the Ortus will have to change, which will mean a lot of extra work. Perhaps if they did, they might stop gibbering on and focus on their studies.

The atmosphere in the chamber felt altogether different. As the numbers of protectors swelled, they congregated in distinct factions. One representing each district, sending their defectos out of earshot but primed and ready should their masters need help.

"Do you know why we're here?" said Protector Belasy to Protector Shanour.

The latter shook his head. "Not a clue. All very cryptic. I assume it's related to our cosmic visitor, but then there's no necessity for a formal meeting. Sterling is more than capable of making all the relevant decisions in that respect. I won't lie, I've got better things to do. I'm in the middle of upgrading the pumping station, which controls the clean water output in Law and Order. We reached a critical step, so I need to be on site, not cooped up here for no reason."

As Quill moved through the room, filling and re-filling glasses as she went, it was impossible not to hear snippets of conversation.

"Who called you?" asked Protector Loughran, huddled with fellow physicians.

"Mr Paine. You?"

"Yes, me too. Very irregular. I don't know why, but I've a bad feeling about this. I asked why he was calling instead of Novack, but he just said to be here and cut me off. Rude man."

"At least it's cooler in here. My clinic is like the inside of a furnace. I appreciate we're supposed to be excited about such an auspicious celestial event, but I can't wait for it to end so life can return to normal."

With the glasses filled, Quill retraced her steps, threading her way through the disparate groups despite longing to hear more. When she eventually arrived at the door, an unfamiliar face met her. If the master was old, this protector had both feet in a grave. Almost bent double at the waist, he relied on dual hand-carved sticks, supported by both, as he hobbled into the room. How the decrepit stranger could see his destination from that stooped position Quill couldn't fathom. No sooner had he passed than she recognised the figure behind him.

"Kai, I wondered if I'd see you today."

"Hey, it's great to hear your voice. It's been a while. How have you been?" His mahogany skin clung tight to his cheekbones, which were now well-established, his features better defined than the last time they'd met.

Had he lost weight?

"Busy," she said, before changing the topic. "So I take it that's Professor Moore. What's he like? How are you both settling in?"

"Er, not bad, I suppose. It's interesting."

Interesting? Was that the best he could do? He appeared to have relinquished the boyish confidence she found so endearing. *Is he hiding something?*

Before she dug deeper, Moore's staccato voice startled them both. "Boy. Here. Now."

Quill rolled her eyes as she reached out to touch her friend's forearm. "What a charmer. Is everything okay?"

Staring through her from those liquid gold orbs, Kai plastered on a smile, a rictus grin of someone in excruciating pain. "Sorry Professor, I'm right behind you." None of which answered her concerns.

🐾 🐾 🐾 🐾 🐾 🐾 🐾

By midday, the chamber was abuzz with the undulating hum of competing male voices. Opposite the doorway, against the far wall, stood a raised dais upon which sat a stout oak chair—the seat of power reserved for the Head of the Protectorate. An intricate diamond lattice punctuated its arch topped, high-back. Carved with symbols, its edges epitomised the city and each district. Books represented knowledge, scales for justice, the physicians' garlic bulb, spokes characterised the engineers and the architects' circle signified the infinite universe. Below this lofty position were two further seats, undecorated versions of the first, one occupied by the Custodian of the Library, its companion by a rotation of district leaders. On the legislature floor, rows of wooden chairs with burgundy leather backs arranged in a horseshoe formation faced the elevated platform, strips fanning out like a ripple of waves towards the entrance.

With an early lunch called for the student scholars, another chore for Quill and the defectos, the master arrived. The respected, confident fellow strode through the crowd to his seat. The move silenced the room, like switching off a light and plunging them into darkness. Obediently, the council members took their seats, which cued the servants that it was time to leave.

Once the scrape of chair legs and the rustle of clothes ceased, the venerable scholar cleared his throat and addressed the audience. "Gentlemen, I thank you for your patience. We are all busy men, so I propose to get straight to the point. I'm sure it won't have escaped your attention that we are witnessing a moment in history, a cosmic event beyond compare. Our traditions are clear, we must bring forward the Ortus to coincide with the rise and fall of the star. Our fledgling scholars will complete the ceremony, relinquishing their old lives, reborn into the new. Exciting times indeed, but I digress. Unfortunately, it is my sad duty to inform you that Dr Novack is ill."

With that revelation, the polite silence descended into chaos as everyone spoke at once. Councillors expressed a myriad of questions and concerns to their neighbours before the master's husky voice took control. "Quiet gentlemen, please. I appreciate this is difficult, but reserve your discussions for after I've outlined what we should do. We must bring the ceremony forward. Such a decision would usually be straightforward, but we find ourselves in uncharted territory. I have discussed matters at length with Mr Paine." With an open palm, he gesticulated toward the architect, who sat in the front row. Dorian nodded, exuding authority as he met the collective gaze of a hundred plus pairs of eyes. "We propose this council assumes temporary rule of the city in Dr Novack's absence. Then members may set the schedule for the rite."

With that astonishing declaration out in the open, the cacophony returned. Voices echoed, crescendoing in a wave which swept from the back row.

"You haven't told us what's wrong with him," said Protector Xavier, a man with such a bald pate that it shone like a ripe peach.

"Didn't I?" The library custodian plastered a strained, false smile on his lips that didn't fool Quill at all. She'd adopted her usual position, hiding in the gloom cast by one of the marble columns which marked the room's corners. She was acutely aware she shouldn't be there, but persisted in perfecting the art of disappearing into the shadows, though she suspected the master knew her secret. With the delicate nature of the meeting, there was no guaranteeing a favourable outcome if they caught her, something she didn't intend to discover.

"I'm not at liberty to discuss Dr Novack's private medical affairs and am surprised that you have the temerity to ask. He needs time to recover, rest and recuperate without the burden of duty and responsibility. We owe him that much."

Suitably admonished, the quarrelsome rabble examined their shoes or chewed their fingernails. Their muttered conversation decreased a notch as they faced the enormity of the situation.

A tall dark man rose to his feet from among the architects and silenced the room. It was like looking at Bran Harland twenty years into the future. "If he's truly incapable of fulfilling his duties, then perhaps what we in fact need is a new Head of the Protectorate. We have always governed the city in this manner. I see no reason to divert from a centuries old reliable system. If we assume control while he recovers, if he recovers, I fear the city's business will grind to a halt under the weight of bureaucracy. We all know the disastrous effect this has on progress from the endless tiresome sub-committee meetings. This is precisely why we invest in a single leader, someone with the presence and foresight to make unilateral decisions that benefit us all. So as much as I respect your proposition, master," he said, bowing in feigned deference, "I propose a fresh election."

To which the argumentative din returned with renewed vigour, as every councillor resumed a heated debate with his nearest neighbours. From the concerned expression on her mentor's face and Paine's lurid flush, Quill knew the prospect of a ballot wasn't something either of them had seriously considered. What she couldn't decide was whether their anger stemmed from the warring protectors, or themselves.

Chapter Sixteen

The stifling heat brought with it swarms of marauding insects. Thousands hatched at once, gathering in thick, black, cloying clouds and attacked any living thing with a pulse. The ravenous creatures crept into every orifice, stinging and sucking blood from any patch of bare flesh.

Red fought his way through the relentless seething hordes, flailing his arms, swatting and slapping himself to avoid being eaten alive. He cursed the bright blue uniform which he usually wore as a badge of honour, sure that its vibrancy turned him into a walking target. It was an additional frustration to add to a long list.

If Novack's housekeeper had answered the telephone, she'd have spared me the wasted journey to Montague Hall and these bites.

His conversation with Ms Pomerenke on the doorstep replayed on repeat, the lady insisting that Dr Novack was too unwell for visitors. He'd asked to speak to a member of the family, a question met with a peculiarly enraged response that her employer had no living relatives. Yet, the woman kept peering over her shoulder as if she were worried about being overheard.

And unless he'd been mistaken, her pale complexion and the deep purple circles below her eyes suggested she hadn't slept.

None of that means a thing. After all, if she's nursing the poor doctor, stress and lack of sleep's understandable.

But there was something else. A gut feeling nagged him that there was more to this than Yulia had let on. In fact, his instincts said it went further than that. He couldn't shake the uncomfortable conclusion that she'd lied to him.

As he made his way through the library's central corridor, the countless rows of dusty books towered over him, piling in like phantoms from a childhood nightmare. The faint tang of bile registered at the back of his throat, a sheen of sweat forming across his forehead as the all-too-familiar and unwelcome claw of claustrophobia plucked at his sanity. The terror could strike at any moment, even in a vast open space. He tried to make sense of it, rationalising, hunting for clues to when and where it might hit, but fear was intangible, irrational and beyond understanding.

"Can I help you, Deputy?"

The sudden unexpected interruption from behind made Red flinch. With an influx of adrenaline coursing through his veins, he spun one hundred and eighty degrees, fists raised in a defensive position. The owner of the adenoidal voice shrank against the nearest bookshelf, arms outstretched in surrender, abject horror across his slack-jawed face. "You shouldn't sneak up on people like that. Not unless you're intending to induce a heart attack." Red lowered his fists and straightened his uniform. "And for the record, it's chief now."

Master Godwin conformed to the academic stereotype with his intense, inquisitive eyes behind thick, wire-rimmed glasses. At a guess, Red reckoned the man was in his seventies, not as old nor as wise as Wittgenstein, but not far off it. He reminded him of a fox. A long projecting nose, which could have been mistaken for a snout, overpowered his face. Whilst there was no official hierarchy among the scholars, Godwin acted as second-in-command, a potential custodian-in-waiting.

"My apologies. I saw the uniform and assumed. I hope you're not here to find more bodies. We're still trying to recover from the last time."

"Not if I can help it. Unless there's something you need to tell me?"

Godwin's right eyebrow detached itself from the left, arching upward at an astonishingly acute angle, merging into the liver spots crowding his forehead, before Red put the officious man out of his misery. "Don't look so worried. It was a joke."

"A joke in very poor taste."

"I'm hoping to speak to Wittgenstein. Can you take me to him, please?"

"He is engaged at present. May I help you at all? Perhaps a tour or a closer inspection of our most precious artefacts?"

"Err, interesting, I'm sure," said Red, trying not to hurt the eager fellow's feelings. "Maybe another day, when I'm not on duty. It's important that I speak to him today."

"I see. Well, I suppose you'd better follow me."

Led in the opposite direction to Wittgenstein's private rooms, the chief endured the less than friendly glances of the library patrons, who squinted up from their books. Made to suffer like an unwelcome intruder, he was relieved to enter the empty corridor leading to the Judgement Chamber. Unfortunately, the silence was fleeting as the passageway filled with chattering protectors, joined by their attending defectos, a brown retinue from across the way. Hemmed in, swimming against the human tide, the chief could no longer see the back of Godwin's head. With his torso ricocheting between one suited man and the next, like wading through treacle, the relief of finally exiting the throng was palpable but short-lived as he realised that Master Godwin had vanished from view.

Tentatively, he crossed the threshold and entered the chamber where a few stragglers remained, speaking in hushed tones in groups dotted about the place. The tall, long-haired, white-robed figure was recognisable, even from the rear. "Master, you're a hard man to track down."

As Red crossed the space between them, Wittgenstein spun round, head drawn back as he rubbed his breastbone. Followed by something else, twitches at the side of his mouth and over-blinking. "Chief, what a pleasant surprise. I haven't congratulated you on your new position. Nor indeed thanked you for your help in the, err, other unfortunate business. You've met Mr Paine, I presume?" The scholar turned sideways, a move which exposed an impeccably dressed gentleman hidden from view.

"I don't believe I have, though my father speaks highly of your work. Pleasure to meet you," said the guardsman, extending a hand towards the architect who grasped it in a firm handshake.

"Your father is too kind. A great legal mind, I might add. It's a wonder you didn't follow in his footsteps."

Although he'd heard the same thoughtless remark at least a hundred times, it smarted more than it should. Still, he clamped down hard on the urge to defend his life choices, preferring instead to redirect attention to the matter at hand. "A council meeting in May, master? That's unusual, isn't it?" He could have sworn that the pair exchanged nervous glances, but it was over in a flash.

"It's an unusual time. There were decisions that couldn't wait."

That made sense. The entire city was talking about the supernova, expecting an announcement that the Ortus would take place earlier. It was the one day in the calendar that everyone looked forward to, the only time when work stopped and people gathered to celebrate the continuing success of their way of life. But he still had a job to do and pressed on, regardless. "I don't see Dr Novack. Where is he?"

An uncomfortable interlude followed, during which both Dorian and Wittgenstein fidgeted, their awkward body language speaking volumes, before the architect broke the silence. "This is a top secret matter. I need your word that the information will not leave this chamber."

"I'm Chief of the Guard. Unless what you're about to tell me threatens law and order, there's no-one you could trust more."

"Very well," said Paine, straightening his tie as if it were strangling him. "Dr Novack is ill. We don't know the nature of his illness, but he's incapacitated to the point he's unable to fulfil his duties. After notifying the council of the situation, they retired to their districts to debate the next steps. We're reconvening in a couple of hours."

"Hmm, that's exactly what the housekeeper told me." With Red's admission, the atmosphere shifted. Tight-lipped scowls on both of the important men's jaw lines reflected their mood had soured.

"Why are you asking a question to which you already know the answer?" asked Paine. Barrel chest puffed out in a demonstration of unbridled masculinity.

"Because I didn't believe it then, and I don't believe it now. My job is to ask tough questions."

"Are you questioning my integrity, young man?"

"No, I don't doubt there's a reasonable explanation behind this—this story." Red avoided the expression he wanted to use, the word *lie*. "But despite my inexperience, to date my instincts have proved right. Let me get straight to the point. I don't know what, or who, you think you're protecting, but I swore to serve the city, and I can't do that if you don't tell me what's going on."

Paine's chest shrank, deflated like a punctured balloon as again the architect exchanged cryptic looks with Wittgenstein, who smoothed his straggly grey hair. Finally, the master said, "Let's talk somewhere more private."

Chapter Seventeen

Returned to the Compendium Room, sneaking out of the chamber before anyone noticed, Quill discovered that lunch had finished. The defectos, whose numbers had swelled with those serving the protectors, made light work of tidying what little remained of the buffet. A significant number stared longingly at the remains.

I must parcel up anything salvageable and gift it to the thinnest.

Though, in truth, it was difficult to separate them. She paused for a moment, having not stopped since dawn, and smiled as she watched Kai on duty. His hands were nimble and decisive as they moved over the trestle tables, collecting and gathering plates and cups as he travelled from end-to-end. Movements carried out with ease, fluid and yet precise, he was the equal of the rest.

"I love your boyfriend." A clipped voice over her shoulder startled her, the sound jolting her back to reality. Quill didn't need to look to know the statement belonged to Aric Leitch. Self-conscious but ignoring the jibe, she strode away, hoping to convince him she hadn't heard.

"You make a splendid couple." The nit-picking tone continued, the volume telling her Leitch had followed. "I suppose he's the only boy who'd have you, seeing as he can't see that thing on your face."

Aric had stepped across an invisible line, aggravating the raw nerve that refused to heal. Further fuelled by the trials and tribulations of the past few days, her self-control fled the scene. Quill spun, pulse pounding in her ears as she fought the urge to cry. Hot angry tears welling at the corners of her eyelids as her mind raced, searching for the perfect retort. But logic and reason vanished as she stuttered and stammered before blurting out the feeblest of replies. "Shut up Aric." As she spat the words at full blast, she groaned inwardly, cursing herself for reacting, while the triumphant expression on Leitch's twisted lips confirmed she'd made a huge mistake. Quill held her breath, dreading what might come next, sensing that the entire room was staring at her. The servants assessed the carpet, as horrified at her outburst as the scholars.

In the blink of an eye, Kai appeared, occupying the space between her and Leitch with his youthful body. "Where shall I put these dirty dishes?"

At first, the mundane question sounded ridiculous against the backdrop of her outright insolence, but something about the way Kai shielded her from Aric's reach told her this was no accident. A clever ploy, designed to dupe the malevolent student into thinking that nobody had heard her harsh remark. Silently, Quill begged the universe to let the ruse succeed, but either Aric was too dense, or he simply didn't care about saving his reputation. "How dare you speak to me like that? I'll have your job for this. You jumped up ingrate."

"She didn't mean it. It's the heat, it's getting to all of us. Please, she begs your forgiveness. Don't you?" Kai grabbed a handful of her tunic and tugged.

Impotent rage boiled through her veins.

Apologise on her behalf? Who did he think he was? If she needed rescuing, she would ask.

The boy, tugging again at her clothes, flung his head toward Aric to emphasise the point. "Quill. Your apology"

As she was about to give up her righteous indignation in favour of self-preservation, help arrived in the most unlikely of guises.

Chapter Eighteen

"Why didn't you call me the second you suspected he was missing?" Red scratched his head in disbelief, shocked. The gentlemen should have known better. Although his hunch had proved correct, it was impossible to derive any satisfaction from knowing that the most important man in the entire city had vanished. "The first twenty-four hours are critical in any investigation, particularly with a missing person. Forensic material contaminated or lost altogether might wreck the chances of finding him. I need to report this immediately. We can dispatch a team to Montague Hall within the hour. I should charge you both."

"What exactly would you charge us with?" asked the Master, closeted in his favourite tree stump chair. "We don't actually know that a crime's been committed."

"Correct. The task is now a hundred times harder thanks to the pair of you. What possessed you?"

"I understand you're new to the job, and I don't doubt you're a fine officer, but you've got a lot to learn." Dorian Paine chimed in, his thumbs hooked into his waistcoat.

"Be my guest, Mr Paine. Perhaps you can explain it to me?"

"That Sterling is the most prominent fellow in the city is precisely the reason we had to keep the current situation between ourselves. Scolaris woke to the news that we're about to witness a supernova event. Influential visitors are gathering from across the continent of Neorah, and more will follow to observe the greatest spectacle for centuries. If the man to lead us is gone, can you imagine the fall-out? I can't even bring myself to think of the consequences. Yes, we told a white lie, but I won't apologise for it."

Ugh, politics.

A dirty word he couldn't seem to avoid, no matter how hard he tried to stick to the solid ground of truth versus lies. "Gentlemen, I see your point, though I don't have to like it. So what you're saying is that I'm to investigate with one hand tied behind my back. True?"

The venerable scholar raised an eyebrow as he picked at his teeth with the pointed tip of a fingernail. "This requires the utmost discretion, the personal touch, all details kept away from prying eyes. I'm sure you could re-allocate any remaining duties to your men, throw them off the scent, so to speak."

The sensational suggestion reminded him why he'd visited Novack at the outset.

Fox needs a pathology assistant. How could I forget?

"Hmm, I can't promise anything, but maybe we can help each other."

In a move which elicited a low growl from the ancient man's throat, Paine leaned toward Red, his fists on the scholar's desktop. "What do you suggest?"

"We need to recruit an assistant for Dr Fox."

"The forensic pathologist?"

"Yes, that's him."

"Whatever for? We're hardly swimming in suspicious deaths, are we? I appreciate there was that unfortunate business before, but that's history now."

Red wiped his sweaty palms on his trousers and practised what to say at double speed in his mind. "Don't take this the wrong way, but I can't divulge the details of an ongoing case, so you'll just have to trust me. You do me this favour and I'll find Novack."

While cringing at his own manoeuvring, Red's skin crawled like he needed to take a shower, a sensation that escalated as Wittgenstein winked and tapped his vein-ridden nose. "We'll see what we can do."

Chapter Nineteen

"Aric, let it go." The smoky voice ripped through the apprehension pervading the room like an electric current. Every gaze directed toward the unexpected sound and the sight of Bran Harland stood behind her right shoulder was unsettling. Though no-one could miss Aric, who glared at Harland, a defiant stare mirrored by his puffed-up body language. The crowd held their collective breaths, glancing from one young scholar to the next, eager to discover who, if anyone, might capitulate.

Kai took the stand-off in the conflict as an opportunity, grasping Quill's forearm to remove her from danger. Still in a rebellious mood, she resisted, jerking from his grasp as she peered into Bran's dark eyes, attempting to read his mind, to figure out why he'd help her. The energy in the atmosphere collected around him like a lightning rod, and Quill sensed the prickle of downy hairs standing on her forearms. Close to him, she noticed he had a scar, roughly two centimetres long, parallel to the left half of his lower lip. As soon as she saw it, Bran responded, parting his lips as he traced its line with a fingertip. No-one would dare deny a single simple fact: Harland was enjoying every second of the attention.

To the collective relief of the audience, Bran stepped toward Leitch, using his height in a show of force as he lowered his voice. "You've made your point. Now let's set a good example. Agreed?"

"I suppose, though, this is not over." Leitch glared, his vitriolic veiled threat hurled in Quill's direction before Harland strong-armed him away.

Seconds later, the realisation of how near she'd been to disaster struck as bile rose in her throat, shivers wracking her entire body. Beside her ear, Kai asked, "Are you okay? That was close. What were you thinking?"

With hindsight, recognising she'd jeopardised her future for the sake of her pride was difficult to acknowledge. Still, she wasn't altogether ready to admit it to the outside world. "I don't need you stepping in to fight my battles. Thanks." The harsh sound of her voice made her wince the second the words left her lips.

Kai took a step backward, followed by a slow disbelieving shake of his forehead. "When *he* did the same, you didn't mind. Maybe they're right after all. You think you're better than the rest of us?"

Quill scowled, acknowledging that she remained the focus of defecto chatter. The hurt of that realisation manifested itself in her response. "And I thought *you* were above listening to idle gossip, but I see I was wrong."

"Kai. Home. Now." The forceful single word commands of Professor Moore brought the spat to an early conclusion and sent the throng scurrying back to their respective places. Then the protectors' defectos took their cue to leave, joining their masters in the corridor as they left.

Kai tutted, shaking his head at her. "Coming Professor." With his wooden stick extended, he tapped in an arc around his feet, scoping out a path toward the door. As he passed Quill, he spoke from the corner of his mouth. "Speaking as your one and *only* friend. My advice is to stay out of trouble. And as for Bran Harland, from what I hear, he's precisely the trouble I'm talking about." With that cryptic announcement, Kai followed Moore.

What's he talking about?

Quill rubbed at her arms, trying to erase the goosebumps from her flesh. As she expected her master to appear at any moment to recommence the day's teaching, her thoughts shifted to the debate across the hallway.

Headed toward the exit, she flinched, surprised to find Bran behind her once more. "I see you noticed my scar," he said, grinning while running his fingers along the pink line. "Childhood accident, or so I'm told. How did you get yours?"

The direct question startled her. No-one ever asked her to explain the feather-mark. People stared or muttered under their breath or crossed the street to avoid her, but this was a novel experience. She tucked a stray curl of cinnamon brown hair behind her ear. "It's not a scar, it's a birthmark."

Before she could react, he'd reached out, touching the blemish on her face, stroking its raised brown edge. "It's one added thing we have in common."

Confused, struggling with the overwhelming sensation, she felt a rush of blood to her chest. A flush grew from her core, enveloping her torso before invading her cheeks. "Erm, I'm not sure I understand what you mean." While wishing he'd remove his hand from her skin, she found herself rooted to the spot.

"Well, we're both intelligent and capable young people with a bright future. If our nearest and dearest supported us, it would make life less, err, what's the word I'm thinking of? Frustrating."

"You must mean someone else. After all, I'm just a defecto."

"You don't need to pretend with me. I know there's a lot more to you than serving. My father told me all about your recent exploits. He's quite the fan. The defecto girl who can read and solve murders. To be honest, he's never spoken about me in such glowing terms."

While stuffing her fidgeting hands into her tunic pockets, Quill had no clue how to respond. Embarrassment mixed with a dash of arrogance as she considered the possibility that some gossip was positive. "Surely your father's proud of you? You're about to become a scholar."

"That's the problem right there—a scholar, not an architect. I'm not following him into the family business, and that's the issue. What about you? Why is Wittgenstein on your case?"

"Who said he was?"

"No-one, but you'd have to be dense to ignore the tension between you. Perhaps he didn't like you having to rescue him from a murder charge. A man of his age, you know, behind the times, saved by a woman?"

Interesting theory. Why didn't I think of that? He could be right. Though which is worse, the master's blatant lie about his plan to teach her, or rampant sexism?

Bran closed the gap between them to a few centimetres until she could feel his breath on her face. "We can help each other, you and I."

Quill gulped, her mouth dry, lips glued to her teeth. "I don't see how."

"For a start, I'm the only one who can keep Aric under control, and believe me, he's desperate to find any excuse to humiliate you, or worse. Plus, I can sing your praises to Wittgenstein, tell him how useful you've been to me, helping me to learn the material."

"So you just want me to help you study?"

"We can start there and see what happens."

With such a reasonable proposition, Quill examined Kai's earlier warning and dismissed it as petty jealousy.

Why shouldn't Harland be interested in what I could teach him about scholarship? After all, I know more than most and it would be worth the effort to keep Leitch at bay. What could go wrong?

She smiled and dipped her chin in agreement.

"What's with the meeting? It's a bit early for the council session, isn't it?"

Quill studied his face, unsure how to proceed. "Er, I don't know."

"Oh, come on, we're friends now. I know you were in there. I watched you sneak out."

"Nothing major. They're meeting to discuss moving the Ortus to coincide with the star imploding."

"But shouldn't Dr Novack make that decision? He has the power."

Quill stopped, shifting her weight from side-to-side, weighing viable options as she scrutinised Bran's eyes, searching again for signs of danger. But seeing none, and before talking herself out of it, she took a leap of faith. "This isn't common knowledge, so I'm trusting you to keep this to yourself. Dr Novack is missing, so the council has to decide whether to assume collective control in his absence."

Bran gaped and, for a second, seemed lost for words. "Whoa, err, sorry, that's devastating news, but don't worry, you can trust me to keep the secret."

Chapter Twenty

Red opened the master's study door on his way out, to find the short, intense figure of Yulia Pomerenke centimetres from rapping on the wood with her knuckles. A motion which almost led to him being punched in the naval. "Hey, that was close. What are you doing here?"

A high-pitched whining noise at floor level drew his attention from the housekeeper. Then to the black-and-tan body of a spaniel puppy huddled on top of the woman's utilitarian brown shoes. "I could ask you the same thing." The neat woman adjusted her dress suit as if it were chafing. "Are you going to let me in?"

"Of course, sorry." He stepped aside, allowing the woman to enter with her canine companion. Wittgenstein and Paine shifted their gaze from a vast array of texts and manuscripts—statutes built up during centuries of Protectorate rule.

"Yulia, what's wrong," the hunched old man asked, "and why is Luna in the library? She can't be here—the books—what were you thinking?"

The housekeeper's head jerked in all directions as her mouth opened and closed like a starved fledgling, but nothing came out of it. Red grabbed an armchair, sensing the housekeeper was struggling with the enormity of the situation. Deftly, he slid it to her rear, then pushed it forward, forcing her legs to bend at the knee which deposited her in the seat. Brought to her senses, she said, "Sorry, I forgot. She's pining, making that terrible griping sound morning, noon and night. It's driving us wild. Mr Crisp has threatened to go home, so I couldn't leave her behind."

"We cannot afford to upset Crisp. You shouldn't have come. Your job is to make sure our guest is comfortable." Wittgenstein finger-tapped the open books, his sour mood clear to see.

"There's something I should explain, but I didn't want to risk anyone overhearing. It's delicate." Pomerenke's gaze flicked toward Red and then at the floor.

Observing the woman's obvious discomfort, the guardsman intervened. "If you have information about Dr Novack's disappearance, I need to know."

Yulia's Adam's apple darted up and down as her gaze latched onto the scholar's for approval. "You can speak freely. The Chief has agreed to help us navigate this difficult situation—*discreetly*." Wit emphasised the last word for everyone's benefit.

"It maybe nothing. I feel silly now I'm here, interrupting your important work."

Red drew closer, crouched on his haunches, eager to learn what the lady had to say. "Please, Ms Pomerenke, let me decide what's important. Often, the most inconsequential detail can unlock a case."

"Sterling had a visitor, last Friday, as I recall. I'd never seen her before. She said her name was Blackwood. He called her

Olga. She'd dressed all in black, like she was in mourning. The doctor welcomed her into the house, but she didn't seem happy to be there. She made me feel uncomfortable, so I—I'm not proud of it—I stayed in the hallway. I was about to withdraw when I heard raised voices, hers first, then Novack. Seconds later, she flew out of the living room and almost sent me flying. Her eyelids were red around the rims. As she left in a hurry, this piece of paper fell out of her skirt pocket." Yulia produced a folded item from her suit. "I went after her, but it was too late. I couldn't find her."

"Luna! Hey there, girl, what are you doing here?" Everybody stared as Quill arrived, fussing over the little dog, squatted on her knees on the rug.

"Don't you ever knock, child," asked the master, his forehead furrowed, frustrated by the interruption.

As Quill rose to her feet, she clasped Luna to her chest. The dog's lead dangled in front, swinging like a pendulum. Then she spoke to the puppy as if addressing a toddler, nuzzling her nose into its soft body. "Why is he so grumpy? I know, he's an old grouch, but don't you listen to him, his bark is worse than his bite." Followed by chuckling to herself at the pun.

Silence reigned supreme as those assembled failed to share the joke. At once reading the room, Quill stopped her cooing and took in the serious expressions surrounding her. "What did I miss? Did somebody die?"

The master rose from the hand carved chair as if he'd sat on a sword, launched into action. "Hold your tongue. What an insensitive thing to suggest. To be frank, I don't know what's got into you recently. Either be quiet or disappear."

Chastised and cursing herself for making such a social faux pas, Quill shrank into the corner of the study. Still clinging to the spaniel for comfort, she waited for someone to speak.

Chief Red reached his hand toward the housekeeper. "What's on the sheet?"

Intrigued, wondering what she'd walked in on, Quill observed the woman relinquishing a folded cream square, edged in black, unable to make eye contact. "I don't know. I didn't look."

Hmm, I don't believe that for a second.

Quill couldn't explain her disbelief, or the potential significance of the document.

They watched as the muscular, stocky guard unfolded the piece of stationery, his dark, brooding eyes scanning the contents as he did so. "It's a death certificate dated more than a decade ago."

"That explains the black, then." Paine's whispered declaration delivered deadpan as he stared into space.

"Over ten years in mourning? That's rather extreme, wouldn't you say?" The master's rhetorical question didn't call for an answer, but Paine obliged, sounding like an expert on the topic.

"It depends. Grief is such a personal thing."

Red cleared his throat, signalling his intention to continue, and the two men returned to their seats to hear the rest. "The deceased is Otto Blackwood. He was only four years old by my calculation. Dr Novack certified the death. Though this is odd." He pulled the sheet closer to his face. "The box for recording the cause is empty."

"Tragic loss. No wonder the woman was distraught, but how does it help to locate the doctor?" asked the scholar.

"No idea, yet, but with no other potential leads, it can't hurt to investigate further."

"Hmm, I suppose, if you think so. Yulia, you must return to Montague Hall and entertain Mr Crisp. Dorian and I have a monumental task before us to convince the council to assume control. Harland senior, the bright spark, suggested an election—give me strength! That's the last thing we need. We're trying to keep the situation out of the public eye."

Red raised his palm at the housekeeper. "Before you go, have there been any other unusual visitors you've forgotten to mention?"

Yulia bristled, sucking in her cheeks as she rose to leave. "Um, like who, er I mean no, not that I'm aware of."

Suddenly in a hurry to leave, the woman slipped away while the Master spoke over her awkward reply. "Quill, I want you to get that dog out of the library before it contaminates the precious artefacts. You seem to have a knack for unearthing secrets, so go with the chief."

"Now, hold on," said Red, pulling on the cuffs of his jacket.

Before he could proceed, the gruff scholar interrupted, arching one grey eyebrow. "I'll see what we can do about your staffing issue. Unless there's a problem with anything I've suggested?"

Red paused, fuming behind gritted teeth. Not that he disliked Quill, but as Chief of the Guard he didn't need an ad hoc assistant.

Still, Fox does, so I might have to play the politics game, however much I hate the idea.

With that in mind, he plastered on a tight-lipped smile. "No, master, and thank you for offering your support."

Chapter Twenty-One

At almost one hundred metres tall, Equity Towers was a prime example of Law and Order's less ostentatious residential blocks. The building could not compare to those in the district's heart with their slick glass frontages and vertiginous proportions. For that reason alone, it stood relegated to the outskirts, bordering the Defecto Legal Quarters (the DLQ). Utilitarian in design, its concrete façade encased a long, thin profile. Next to which rose a separate elevator and service tower, linked by access corridors to the primary structure on alternate floors. A handful of residents enjoyed the luxury of accommodation split over two floors, but most of the two hundred and nine dwellings were single storey apartments.

Of course, the lift wasn't working. The six hundred and fifty-three steps, coupled with the ongoing heat problem, sapped their energy by the time Quill and Red arrived at Flat 98 on level thirty-three. Over-breathing, Quill leant her forearm against the cool concrete wall and rested her forehead on top, closing her eyes for a second as she waited for her body to recover. In the remaining arm, tucked under her armpit, nestled Luna. Fast asleep, the puppy had missed all the excitement, though the extra exertion of the climb meant the bundle of fur felt like a dead weight. Red winced, palms on knees, torn between relief at having avoided a claustrophobia inducing ride and annoyance at the inconvenient exercise.

"I thought—guards—were fit," she said, wheezing between words.

"We are. But that climb is something else. Blasted lift. How do people manage?"

While arching his spine to ease away the tension, Red rapped on the solid grey entrance and stepped backwards to wait for a reply. Quill's nose wrinkled at the unmistakable odour of over-ripe fruit and rancid meat. Stacks of orange refuse bags lined the gantry in front of the apartment, spewing out their contents. "This place needs condemning." Red muttered under his breath, cutting himself off as the door opened a sliver, revealing a lone dark brown almond-shaped eye.

"Yes?" a thick, dusky voice answered, muffled from behind the door. "Who are you, and what do you want?"

"Mrs Blackwood?"

"The name's *Ms* Blackwood; if you don't mind. Who wants to know?"

"I'm Chief Red from the City Guard, and this is, um, this is—" But he tailed off, unsure how to introduce Quill into the proceedings without it sounding odd.

"He's trying to say that I'm Quill, a defecto, and this is Luna."

As she produced the puppy from under her arm, like performing a magic trick, the flat door swung wide, exposing a tall, willowy figure dressed top-to-toe in black, tight, springy cork-screws of jet-black hair held in check by a voluminous matching scarf. The woman grabbed the dog, cradling it in her arms like a newborn baby as she headed inside, leaving the door open behind her. Quill took that as an invitation to enter and Red followed.

From the condition of the communal areas, she had expected a dingy interior, but the opposite was true. The place opened into a single space, glazed in a wide stripe, letting in as much light as possible. Beyond the glass, a narrow balcony provided an outside area with an exciting view of the community's elite residential quarters. Although perhaps that was a bad thing for residents keen to avoid comparisons.

On every available surface, wall, or table, pictures of an infant gleamed in the bright room, from sleeping newborn to tiring toddler. The life of a small boy documented and displayed by proud parents. Blackwood sat, rocking Luna, attention rapt, apparently oblivious to the pair of them as they marvelled at the apartment-come-shrine. Red leaned out to pick up a framed image, but the curious woman intervened. "Don't touch him." The command delivered in a strangulated, high-pitched cry at odds with the tone from a few moments earlier, though she didn't look up from coddling the dog.

"Forgive me, I meant no harm."

Olga tore her gaze from Luna, staring at them both through cold, dead eyes. "The harm's already done. My poor boy, Otto. What did he do to you?"

Quill and Red swapped awkward glances, stood in the middle of the residence, not knowing how to continue. "I'll make tea, shall I? Tea always makes everything seem better somehow," said Quill and Olga nodded, pointing to her right.

Accessed via a sliding door, a clever space-saving feature, the kitchen was the colour of sunflowers. Through various cupboards, Quill rummaged for supplies and headed back to the living area within minutes, sunflower tray in hand, complete with lemon tea and ginger biscuits, which she'd found on top of an old newspaper cutting lining a shelf. With refreshments set on a photograph free spot—a yellow foot-stool—she passed Olga a cup. "There you go. Shall I take Luna while you drink it?"

"No, I can manage. Why are you here?" asked the woman, turning to the chief, drink in one hand, dog nestled in her lap, snoring.

"I need to understand why you visited Dr Novack recently?"

The woman tensed, eyes flicking between them and her cup, before blurting out a terse response. "Who?"

"We know you paid him a visit. His housekeeper let you in and saw you leave."

"Maybe she's mistaken. Have you considered that?"

Red pulled the death certificate from his uniform pocket. "You dropped this, Ms Blackwood. So perhaps you might tell the truth?"

Blackwood shot forward from the pastel blue sofa, dislodging the sleeping Luna and sloshing most of the tea over the cup's rim and onto the floor. Not an animal to miss an opportunity, the pup lapped up the spillage in seconds. Then, trotted over to Quill, who'd perched on the edge of the pouffe with the tray. Olga snatched the certificate from the chief's grasp and clutched it to her chest. "This is a private matter. It's none of your business."

Red changed tack, seeing that he was getting nowhere fast but unable to disclose Novack's disappearance. Moving positions to sit alongside the lady as she retired to the sofa, her outburst over, he said, "Otto, your son?"

The olive-skinned lady clenched her eyelids and nodded, resting her skull on the top of the settee as they descended into a deep, painful silence.

"I'm sorry for your loss. I can't imagine your suffering. Dr Novack signed the death certificate. Is that why you were visiting him?"

Olga remained silent and immovable. If it weren't for the shallow rise and fall of her rib cage, she might have been mistaken for a corpse.

Quill's heart ached for the miserable soul. Although she'd never known her mum, she still felt her painful absence.

Imagine losing a child.

With great care, she lifted Luna, returning her to Olga's lap, offering consolation in the single way she could. The grieving mother responded to the warm bundle, opening her eyes, which sparkled with silent tears. Quill whispered, laying a palm on Blackwood's knee. "Can we get somebody for you? Your husband?"

"He's gone, gone."

Whilst sympathetic to the wretched woman's plight, his job was to find their leader, so Red pressed on with gentle questioning. "It must be a tremendous comfort to you, talking to Dr Novack, a chance to reminisce about your child with his physician."

Olga's brows pinched, as if processing what he'd said, palm stroking the dog from tip to tail in a slow steady rhythm which increased to an erratic pace. "Yes. Yes, that's right."

Quill and Red exchanged side-glances, doubt mirrored in their expressions. The lady's answer was devoid of feeling or detail.

With suspicions aroused, he leaned in closer. "What was the row about?"

"What row?" she shot back, the sudden forceful retort strange.

"You met Dr Novack. He entertained you in the living room. The maid heard raised voices, an argument. Then you left in a hurry, dropping the death certificate. If the doctor consoled you over your son's passing, what were you arguing about?"

"I don't like your manner, young man. And you still haven't explained what you're doing here."

Frustrated by the woman's continual deflection and now by her belittling use of the term *young man*, Red stood, his stocky frame casting her slim silhouette into shadow. "Why won't you answer the question? I'm Chief of the Guard, so I don't need to explain. I'd prefer to discuss this here, where you're comfortable. But if necessary, I'll have to ask you to accompany me to Guard HQ, where we can conduct this conversation more formally." The ploy was a risk. He had no intention of conducting a formal interview. After all, he'd never keep that a secret. Then the woman's shoulders sagged, signalling the gamble was about to pay off.

"We disagreed. I don't even remember what about being honest. Do you have children?"

Red shook his head and returned to the seat adjacent, softening at the needy woman's obvious distress. "No. I'm sorry to ask this, but what did your son die of? The death certificate doesn't say."

"Ha, well, it wouldn't, would it?"

"Excuse me, I don't follow."

Olga Blackwood sighed. An immense release of air escaped her lips, shrinking her frame before she fixed him with her gaze. Her reply came in a tone which cracked under the burden of emotion. "Inadequate care. He died because of medical negligence."

Chapter Twenty-Two

"I agree with Harland. We should hold an election." Mordecai Templar's orotund proclamation injected a fresh dose of chaos into the proceedings as Master Wittgenstein and Dorian Paine grappled with maintaining order.

"Here, here." A supporter from the architects shouted, standing and raising a plump fist, which garnered the rest into stamping their feet in agreement.

"Be quiet," thundered a voice within the physicians, followed by unruly laughter across the chamber.

The master stood, palms raised, signalling his intention to address the protectors and without a word, he restored order as silence descended. "Gentleman, how many times must we debate this? An election is a distraction we don't need. Dr Novack is our elected leader. True, he's currently incapacitated, but this is a temporary issue that cannot interfere with the most important issue of the day. We must begin the Ortus while the supernova rises. Who knows how long we have left before it's too late?"

The harsh sound of competing voices rose afresh, like fingernails scraping across a chalkboard as individual comments for and against developed into group conversations, then into full-blown arguments. A state of affairs akin to children fighting in a school playground, thought the despairing scholar, before once again using his authority to bring the councillors to heel. "Consider this: if we schedule an election, what will we say to the wider community about Dr Novack's condition?"

"We'll speak the truth," said Belasy, to the assembled masses, "what else is there?"

Paine stood, joining the academic at the lectern, slotting his stubby thumbs inside the collar of his waistcoat. "Are you mad?" he asked, first to Belasy, then fired a withering glare at Templar. "Such an announcement would hurt civic confidence when the eyes of Neorah are upon us. Are you prepared for the turmoil that would follow? Scolaris might suffer economic and cultural damage for years to come. How should we explain electing a new leader while the incumbent remains in office?"

The murmuring returned, though unobtrusive, as the mass of men contemplated their options. The ancient man drummed his fingertips on the leading edge of the lectern, waiting for a hush as he winked his appreciation at Paine's intervention.

Shanour, the engineer, rose. A bow of his rock-shaped head and a click of his heels showing his deference to the venerable teacher. "Mr Paine makes a strong case. I, for one, have no appetite for a ballot. Sterling was this council's choice a decade ago, and it pains me to see those who would cast him aside at the earliest opportunity. No doubt those in favour of a vote do so for self-serving reasons. You should be ashamed." He stood a little taller, appreciating the vigorous round of back-patting received from the engineering faction.

Templar scowled, disapproval etched on his cheeks, though the remaining architects did not rally around to support him.

"Well said, Shanour. We've been talking in circles for the last two hours. Let's vote and then we'll consider where we are. Agreed?" Taking a lack of objections as the signal to go ahead, the master tapped a jolly rhythm with his fingers. "Excellent. So the motion entails that we assume collective control of the Protectorate in Dr Novack's absence. Because of the ramifications of such an agreement, the regulations stipulate—err, let me see now," he said, squinting along the length of his elongated nose at an ancient text. The enormous book strained at its bindings, revealing the inner stitching, its blue cover faded almost to grey. "Ah, yes, I thought as much. The decision requires a seventy-five per cent majority, votes to be cast by private ballot in the usual way. We begin in half an hour."

The choice to assemble the council at Guidance Grove, instead of continuing at the library, had already proved sensible. The official home of the Protectorate, nestled in the pleasant surroundings of the Physician's District, offered the utmost seclusion, hopefully ensuring that no awkward details leaked out into the public domain. There'd been extensive grumbling from the architects who preferred the library's central location to the longer journey across the city. Still, they'd soon agreed, rather than infuriate Wittgenstein any further.

Three white clad interconnected buildings and a round bell tower came together to complete the seat of power. A rectangular residential block formed the top of a T-shaped construction while the twins of the Judgement Chamber and the ballot room made up the rest. The circular spire nestled under the left crook, commanding a view of the leafy sanctuary hidden by laurels on three sides and locked wrought-iron gates on the other.

The lone complication had been the sudden arrival of Mr Crisp. A fact-finding mission, he'd called it, to understand the inner workings of the city. Despite conveying that Protectorate business was strictly a behind-closed-door affair, the special envoy insisted that did not matter. He could learn much from the ambiance, and hoped to bump into Dr Novack, who was never at home. Unable to think of a reasonable excuse to refuse, optimistic that Crisp, true to form, might spend his days in bed, Wit allocated a room in the living quarters as far from the action as possible.

As a single sonorous chime rang throughout the grove, signalling it was time to vote, Wittgenstein hurried through the stone-clad walkway which ran the entire span of the building. An intricate, arched roof protected his head from the sweltering heat. Its curves criss-crossed from one surface to the other, stretching away in an endless array of interconnected curved triangles.

Moments later, he climbed the five wide steps at the entrance, crossed the reception lobby into the hall and joined the queue, ready to register his preference. As the bell chimed three distinct notes, utter silence reigned supreme as each protector bowed his head in contemplation, proceeding in single file. Then, in perfect unison, they each took a pace forward. Right foot first followed by left, choreographed like an enormous worm. As the column moved inexorably onward, the master soon departed the Judgement Chamber and entered the ballot room. A smaller space, cocooned in wood panelling, in its centre stood a wooden cubicle, accessed through an aquamarine velour drape. As the man ahead entered, pulling the curtain behind him, Wittgenstein paused, preparing to instigate the next step. A moment which arrived seconds later as he stepped through himself, drawing the drapery for privacy.

The battered ballot box's slit mouth waited to be fed. Without hesitation, Witt selected a white stone disc from the bowl on his left and dropped it into the container. Those on his right, the red ones, represented a *no*, and he tried to estimate their number, wondering if he could glean the likelihood of a favourable outcome. But there were too many to count. He quickly gave up, making space for the man beyond the curtain, as he returned to the chamber to await the result.

Stalemate. Not the outcome he and Paine had hoped for as they huddled together behind the stand.

"What do we do now?" asked the architect, scratching his scalp.

"The only thing we can. We apply pressure to the ignorant bunch."

"How do we do that?"

The master tapped the side of his nose with a skeletal finger. "Watch and learn, my friend. Watch and learn."

Turning to the throng of fellows all engaged in heated debate, Master Wittgenstein cleared his throat, a signal which sent the unruly group scurrying for their seats. Delineated by their factions, the old scholar took his time, dissecting each individual as he scanned their faces. At one end, the lawyers in their staid pin-stripes and black robes gathered next to the doctors in brightly coloured scrubs. At the other, suited architects contrasted with the utilitarian garbed engineers, a sea of brown and green, not forgetting the scientists in the centre, a stripe of white lab coats.

"You have failed to achieve the three-quarters majority required to carry the proposal. It's a wonder that anything gets done in this city if this ridiculous situation is the norm. Each second that passes is a second wasted. Scolaris is relying on us to do what is necessary to secure its future. You must assume control and bring the Ortus forward without further delay. I should not be here. I have would-be scholars to train and you are keeping me from my duty." The canny teacher paused, repeating his deliberate pass of all the eyes trained on him before delivering his killer blow. "Very well. Under regulation 423, paragraph b, sub-section 3: in the event of an emergency which threatens the safety and security of Scolaris, a member of the upper tier of the Protectorate—that would be me—can, and I quote." Peering down at the pages of the rule book, following the text with his finger, he read. "Sequester the council until such time as is reasonably practicable to enable decisions of state to be made in response to the threat or threats as aforementioned in regulation 423, paragraph a, sub-sections 1 to 5."

The second he paused for breath, the masses erupted for the hundredth time into a melee of sound and wild gesticulation. Snippets of speech bounced around the room. "What's he talking about?"

"Anyone understand what that means?"

"Can he do that?"

"What about my work?"

"My wife's expecting me home for dinner."

Eventually the din subsided and the perplexed gentlemen retook their seats, all save for Mordecai Templar. "On behalf of the architects, please explain, in plainer language, what the statute means in practice."

The old man gripped the top edge of the rostrum, his protruding knuckles white as he smiled, a thin-lipped horizontal slash across his face. "It's simple, really. Nobody leaves until we've voted to take control, supported by a resolution to move the Ortus. We vote again in fifteen minutes."

After that pronouncement, Wittgenstein swept away, ignoring the haranguing shouts and protestations, in search of a secluded tree under which to hide.

Chapter Twenty-Three

Pressed against the front of the narrow tallboy, back against the bed, the firm contact between her right arm and Bran's left distracted her as Quill taught him the nuances of the forthcoming Ortus. All while trying her best to ignore the knowledge that she might never get the chance to take part.

A cloak of darkness signalled the late hour, punctuated by the eerie yellow and green flashes of the supernova which cast psychedelic shadows. Colours refracted through the windowpane, scattering to the compact room's four corners as Luna, the four-footed fugitive, snored on top of the star covered blanket adorning her bed.

I wish the dog was bigger, then her sleeping frame would cover most of the childish stars. At least the master shouldn't discover my rule-breaking while he's holed up at Guidance Grove.

Olga Blackwood's unbelievable accusations continued to swirl in the back of her mind, but Quill still couldn't decide whether they were simply the ravings of a grief-stricken woman.

"Where do we begin?" asked Bran, his voice deep and hypnotic, caressing her eardrums.

While tucking a stray curl behind her ear, a creeping awkwardness stole her voice as she scrambled around her brain for the right words—any words. "Ortus means rising, specifically in relation to the sun and, of course, the sun is a star, our closest star. That's why the supernova's rise in the heavens is such a monumental event."

"Because the star will rise, then die?" Bran asked, the shape of his scar manipulated by the words as they left his ripe mouth.

"Correct. That's the reason the master's pushing to advance the ceremony, though it's difficult to be precise about when the star might implode."

"Best guess? How long do we have?"

"Well, as far as I know, there's never been a supernova like this, where it's so bright that we can see it in daylight, so nothing else quite compares. There is an account recorded by Anastarchus, from over three hundred years ago, which gave the duration of rise and fall as approximately ten days, so no longer than that, I'd guess. Although, if the heat is proportional to the rate it's using energy, it may be much less."

"You're quite something, aren't you? How do you know all this stuff?"

Quill shrugged, sensing the flush rising from her navel despite her finest efforts to grapple with the overwhelming embarrassment activated by the compliment. "Erm, I live in a library surrounded by every text known to man, and I have a particular interest in cosmology. My father shared his love of the universe and passed it on to me."

"And now I feel even more pathetic." His fingers interleaved behind his head as he stretched out on the rug, a manoeuvre fraught with difficulty for tall people. "Your father sounds interesting. The only thing my father is passionate about is power and money and how to make more. I don't remember him talking about anything else, if I'm honest. What does yours do?"

Quill turned, searching Bran's face for a sign that he was mocking her, but his eyes were closed.

If he's playing games, he doesn't seem invested in witnessing the fun.

"He's a defecto, I'm a defecto. You're born into it, then you die," she said, grimacing at her own fatalistic assessment of life. "Shall we continue?"

In response, he opened his dark brown eyes and smiled. Taken as a cue to continue, Quill explained the significance and meaning of further facets of the Ortus. Enraptured, Bran listened. "The definitive guide to the ritual is this book, *Ortus: Born In Light*. It contains detailed instructions for every aspect from dress to deportment, the use of symbolic objects and their meanings, and even questions of morality."

"Where to start?"

"Let's look at the process in chronological order. The first step is *Emergence*. This marks the seven days prior to the ritual. We seclude new scholars from society, an act of purification from worldly concerns. Meals should exclude meat and fish, and fasting during daylight hours prepares the body for a life of intellectual stimulation. From this point on, wearing the brown robe is mandatory," she said, glancing across at Bran's tailored black trousers and shirt, his robe nowhere to be seen.

"Hmm, not sure I approve of that one. I don't think brown's my colour," he said, eyes crinkling at the corners.

Distracted by his casual manner, Quill lost her place in the text and spent too many awkward seconds trying to find the last sentence she'd read. "Non-negotiable, I'm afraid, as is shaving off all your hair."

"What?" Bran launched forward, his relaxed posture vanishing. "My hair? No-one touches my hair."

Quill chuckled. Whether this was vanity or his attempt at humour, she couldn't judge. "Your personal appearance doesn't matter. *Knowledge is King*, remember? And it doesn't last. The shaving signifies your re-birth as a scholar, then you should never cut it again. It'll soon grow back."

Harland stroked the black waves from his prominent forehead, silent and pensive, before staring straight into her eyes. "What about women?"

Focused on avoiding his intense stare, shifting from one side to the other, Quill struggled to form a reply. "Erm, well, scholars may marry, but most don't. A lifetime's study is not conducive to a family life."

"I didn't mean that. Do female scholars have to shave their hair?" He feathered the ends of her curls with the faintest touch of his fingertips.

The sensation overwhelmed her intellect, freezing her to the spot as her autonomous nervous system failed and forgot to breathe. As her lungs screamed for oxygen, Quill came to her senses in a rush of air. "There are no women scholars. Never have been, never will be."

"How last century. Rules change. Don't be so pessimistic. Your time will come."

With his hands removed, relieved, Quill studied the text in her lap, chewing her bottom lip, wondering how her dreams were so obvious. "I don't know what you mean. Anyway, this isn't about me. Let's move on."

"If you say so."

The rest of the night into the early hours passed in a blur of ritualistic delights and Quill revelled in teaching the finer details. Whilst she had the book to guide her, mostly she spoke from memory. The years of serving Master Wittgenstein had taught her well.

Bran was an attentive student, though he wrote nothing, something she urged him to do frequently. His response, a casual wave and a gut-clenching comment about the impossibility of ever forgetting anything that came out of her mouth.

※ ※ ※ ※ ※ ※ ※

As the sun crept over the horizon, she crawled beneath the covers, but the sleeping spaniel didn't stir, bobbing like a boat on the ocean. If she could catch a couple of hours' sleep before the city-wide alarm, maybe the day could be bearable, but try as she might, sleep eluded her. Each time she closed her eyelids, her brain filled with the photographic images of Otto Blackwood.

A boy with feminine shoulder-length corkscrew curls like his mother, deathly white skin untainted by the Sun. His cheeks were plump as apricots, a vision of purity and innocence shining through electric-blue eyes. Followed by a larger-than-life Dr Novack, irises black as coal, brandishing surgical tools like instruments of torture, opening his mouth to speak and purging a torrent of thick sludge.

Knowledge is King. The mechanical voice boomed, catapulting Quill upright, sweating and hyperventilating as she searched for the devilish doctor. But found instead the bemused stare of Luna, who licked her face with a raspy tongue and shattered her stupor. Olga Blackwood's allegation that Dr Novack's treatment of Otto caused the innocent boy's death clearly tormented her imagination.

But the man wasn't a monster. Was he? No, it was a dream, a terrible dream.

Chapter Twenty-Four

5 weeks, 5 days to the Ortus

Thunder growled, prowling low in the atmosphere, stalking pedestrians as the humid heat spiralled upwards from the tarmacked streets of Law and Order. Battered by a bruising gust of wind, Red hunkered into the crimson doorway, prevaricating as he weighed the pros and cons of his current plan.

The two-storey dwelling sandwiched between a pair of towering office complexes harked back to a different era. It declared its stubborn defiance of progress simply by existing and must have caused the developers no end of sleepless nights. Constructed with stone blocks, barely wide enough for a single casement window above and below, the house was small but well proportioned. As he banged on the front entrance with his fist, red paint chips shot toward him like blood pumping from a vein. While brushing the debris from his uniform, the door whipped open, revealing a bleary-eyed figure clad in striped pyjamas. "What do you want, sunshine?"

The unmistakable gruff, gravelly sound of retired Chief of the Guard, Jim Ross, historically inspired a sense of anxious trepidation, but spoken from the lips of the virtual stranger before him, Red felt nothing but sadness and a considerable dose of pity. Without saying another word, his former boss loped inside, leaving the vacant doorway as an invitation to follow.

An opening left of the hallway revealed a view into a tiny sitting room, yet Ross continued into the property's rear, to the kitchen, which overlooked a concrete yard cast in the neighbouring offices' shadows. Well-thumbed newspapers, piles of grimy washing and part-eaten tins of food thrown into a corner, Ross cleared a couple of wonky chairs of detritus and beckoned him to sit. "Coffee?"

Red nodded, checking the seat before deeming it safe and making a mental note to dry-clean his suit. Neither spoke as Jim filled a dented copper kettle and hunted through the teetering mountain of mugs in the sink before settling on one emblazoned with the term *BOSS*, then another which read, *I'm allergic to mornings*. Ross gave them a cursory rub and rinse under the tap before filling them with thick black goodness. His nightclothes fitted loosely and though it was difficult to be positive, Red suspected Jim had lost weight—a significant amount of weight in the brief spell since he'd seen the man.

An earthy, bitter aroma saturated the air, fighting to suppress the odour of mould and rotting fish remnants. "Suppose you should have this one, now," said Ross, sliding the *BOSS* cup over the sticky crumb covered surface.

"Thanks." Red cradled the drink in both palms, inhaling the vapours, while he contemplated his next move.

The pair sat that way for several minutes, staring into space, supping coffee while the young chief became convinced that the stack of dirty washing moved of its own accord, infested with something hideous.

"I assume this isn't a social call?"

"Er, well, I was wondering how you're enjoying your retirement?"

The ex-guardsman cocked his skull to the side, eyebrow raised. "Never kid a kidder, sunshine. Now spit it out."

While chugging the caffeine, burning the innards of his cheeks, Red pushed back on the chair and rose to leave. "Honestly, I was passing and thought it would be rude not to stop by. I must run, lots to do."

"It's not all it's cracked up to be, being chief, is it? What's the problem? Lack of a social life? Insubordination? Politics?"

Red sighed and re-took his seat, rubbing the tension from his neck muscles. "Is it that obvious?"

"'fraid so. Okay, I'm glad you came. Now don't give me that look. I know we didn't always see eye to eye, but you're what the guard needs. The right candidate at the right time, hence my recommendation. Dr Novack wants to modernise Scolaris, relegate us primitive dinosaurs to history, where we belong."

"It's nice to hear that someone has faith in me, and I'll be honest, I'm surprised it's you, but thanks. There are countless obstacles I didn't envisage, so many, I don't know where to start."

"Take your time. I'm not going anywhere."

"The men don't respect me, because they're older and have way more experience, or they're jealous that I'm the chief, not them. Then there's the mounting body count, drug deaths which I'm sure relate to Professor Hawkin's toxin, if I could prove it."

"How many deaths are we talking about?"

"We're into double figures, and rising. There are so many questions I can't answer. Where's the drug coming from? Who's distributing it? And most puzzling, who are the victims? We've only been able to identify one so far, because he died in his own bed. Each found in isolated spots, no identification documents and no-one's reported them missing. The victim profile seems to be a middle-aged man with no family. Don't get me started on politics. I didn't know that I'd have the Protectorate in the shape of Omari Tedesko watching every move I make. I wouldn't mind if their concern was for the fatalities, but it's all about keeping up appearances, preserving the city's reputation. Also, Dr Fox desperately needs someone to help him deal with all the bodies, but Tedesko is about as approachable as a cactus."

"Have you tried Novack?"

Red paused, twirling a loose thread of cotton from the neat hem at the bottom of his jacket around the tip of his index finger. He pondered the risks of continuing, shocked by the ease with which he'd unburdened himself to the last person he'd imagined ever doing so. Based on the mess, he figured Ross didn't possess an enormous supply of friends to shout his mouth off to, so ploughed on regardless. "Yeah, well, that's the icing on the cake. Dr Novack's missing."

"Missing?" Jim choked on a swig of coffee, which dribbled down his chin, leaving a murky brown splodge on his pyjama top collar. "Now that is serious. How many guards have you deployed? You'll need Hodges and Carrick and Kazinski. They're your best bet. Oh, and don't use Jackson, he's a liability."

Red laughed, a fleeting outburst of mirth amongst an astronomical jumble of headaches, before returning to the issue at hand. "I wish that were possible. I discovered he was gone purely by accident. Master Wittgenstein and Mr Paine insist that any investigation should take place in secret. They're worried about the ramifications if news gets out, particularly as the city fills with dignitaries from across the globe, so as things stand, I'm on my own."

The old chief rose from the table, his mottled fingers splayed across the surface, butting up against sugar crystals and breadcrumbs as he leaned in close with stale coffee breath. "Not anymore, you're not, sunshine."

With fresh drinks brewed, the duo got to work. The new chief ran through what limited information there was available. Confirmation from Fox that the dead engineer, Mr Vaughn, had ingested Hawkin's toxin, leading to heart failure. Followed by the reasonable assumption that the rest of the victims had suffered the same fate, and the guards' mission to ID the other remains. Novack's last known movements, an evening with Dorian Paine and the theory he'd returned home that night and that some untoward mishap had occurred whilst he walked the dog early the following morning. His hunch that the housekeeper,

Pomerenke, was hiding something. Not forgetting the strange Olga Blackwood, who alleged that, as a junior physician, Dr Novack had caused her son Otto's death. Ross listened, asking the odd question here and there, but mostly he let his successor talk through every angle, until Red had nothing else to say.

"So now you've got that load off your chest. You know what to do next, right?"

Jim grabbed the mugs and returned them to the stack. Although it was surprising, Red realised he was correct. Offloading aloud had given him the chance to grapple with the scant evidence and discover the holes that needed plugging. "Yeah, funnily enough I do."

"So, who's first on your list?"

Red considered the options, weighing each as he followed Jim's stripy rear along the corridor to the front door. As he prepared to respond and offer his thanks, Jim waved, large hollow circles striking beneath his eyes. "Never mind, you don't have to tell me. Hurry along now, I haven't got all day. I'm busy."

Chapter Twenty-Five

"Eight, eight, nine, ten, nine, ten." The steward called the score while jettisoning the red and white discs from the ballot box. His solemn, booming count rang throughout the legislature as the assembled protectors craned their necks, witnessing what appeared to be a further fruitless round of voting.

The tenth vote hurtled towards the inevitable stalemate, as yet again the council failed to take decisive action. The master faced the possibility that his decision to sequester the councillors hadn't worked, depriving them of their liberty to impose his agenda. His frustration threatened to boil over into anger, simmering like volcanic lava capped in an active crater.

"Motion denied." The steward threw the last red disc onto the pile. A declaration met by a collective groan from the audience.

With a face like he'd swallowed a wasp, Wittgenstein resumed his position at the lectern, awaiting the silence which never came as he observed the gaggle of chattering men. Steadfast in their obstinacy, they stuck with their cliques, incapable of taking tough decisions when it mattered most. Unable to bear it any longer, the venerable man hammered a fist into the spine of the open regulation book, shouting above the racket. "Sit down and be quiet."

Shocked by the outburst, everyone's eyeballs faced the front. A mixture of defiance and embarrassment plastered on the expressions of the chastised men. Finally, the councilmen took their seats, waiting for Wittgenstein to continue.

While taking a deep breath, the harangued scholar gripped the edges of the podium until his fingers hurt. "Gentlemen, my patience wears thin. You seem not to realise the gravity of this situation. In case it has escaped your attention, the supernova is rising. We can all feel it. This unusual weather is not a coincidence. The heat, the high winds, phenomenon linked to the energy released as the star ascends, and we all know what must come next. It's time for action, not infighting and one-upmanship. The choice is simple. Take the reins or sit back and do nothing while Neorah watches and laughs."

The deliberate stab at their collective hubris hit the mark as the grumbling and muttering resumed, each block throwing accusatory looks at their neighbours.

Quill, already suffered from a lack of sleep and running backwards and forwards between the library and the grove, added to her troubles. Now, Master Godwin had the honour of teaching the students, a task he relished if that morning's session was anything to go by. Quill stifled a giggle as she pictured the intense, diminutive man trotting around the Compendium Room. His rubbery ears protruding, hands clasped behind his back as he delivered the opening lessons on the meaning and significance of the Ortus. Nor could she forget Bran's wry smile and conspiratorial winks.

The master's imprisonment of the council at Guidance Grove was sensible in the circumstances, but it made her life much harder. To the point, she joined the groans, envisaging days of traipsing back and forth with dirty washing and provisions in the heat. That morning, the humidity took her breath away. Though that was the least of her problems, as a stiff wind delayed her arrival, ripping clean clothes from her grasp on half a dozen occasions, sending her scurrying in multiple directions to rescue them from the dusty pavements.

While watching Scolaris' finest citizens, those in charge, it was impossible to understand how any business got done. The men rejoiced in talking, appreciating their own voices, arguing from one point of view, three hundred and sixty degrees, back to where they started.

Politics is a game. A ridiculous game played by an elite few with self-interest at heart. No wonder the master is losing his composure. How's he lasted this long without exploding?

The bell tower tolled eleven echoing chimes, which signalled morning refreshments. Quill straightened her tunic and readied herself for Witt to adjourn the meeting to prepare for the next vote. Instead, Protector Reiner stood from the back row of the lawyers, his hands clenched together at chest height. "It's no good. I can't keep it to myself a second longer. Is it true? Is Dr Novack dead?"

Quill froze, gaze darting first to the dais, then around the chamber as she watched proceedings descend into chaos. The lawyer visibly trembled, sweat glistening on his forehead as he jerked at the top button of his shirt, straining his neck until it looked broken in two.

"Of course not. Where did you hear such a puerile, distasteful, fantastically preposterous suggestion?" The master swiped aside his scruffy hair, removing it from his eyes and out of his mouth as he spluttered out a desperate response to the shocking question. At that moment, Quill saw the custodian's authority slip. His angry, muddled rebuttal was too indignant to sound true as the magnitude of plans thwarted rode roughshod over good judgement. Then a pained expression across his deeply lined face, slumped shoulders and a bowed back showed he recognised the deception had run its course.

"With all due respect, we don't believe you. Rumours circulate throughout the chamber and in the hallways. There is talk of death by accident or misadventure. Whether they are legitimate, I cannot tell, but I'm sure there's something you're not telling us. Information we have a right to know and I won't vote again until I am satisfied that I understand the facts." The once timid lawyer's wordy declaration won favour with his colleagues as they mumbled in a monotone. "Here, here." Which sent, "Here, heres," rippling from one faction to the others.

The master emerged from behind the protective lectern, scratching his scalp as he examined the stone flagons on the floor. While they waited to learn how he'd respond, the throng scrutinised him. The ancient fellow paced along the front line, men shuffling their feet aside, shifting positions as he took his time before finally facing the architects at the far side. While straightening his posture, he lifted his chin, his expression calm and emotionless as he opened his mouth to speak.

To the amazement of those gathered, an endless peal of ear-splitting chimes drowned out his voice, brought to a crushing stop by the tower bell. The rabble sent their hands to their ears in a bold, fruitless effort to dampen the sound, then the chamber door flew open. The thud of heavy boots syncopated with the jarring bell strikes as a red-faced, brown-clad young man tore inside as if he were being chased by a wild dog. To the horror of those gathered, the defecto shouted, the cords on his skinny neck taut like elastic as he battled with the racket. "Help! Come quick. It's Templar. Mordecai is dead!"

※ ※ ※ ※ ※ ※ ※

The master led the way, a snaking series of protectors followed hard on his heels like an enormous brood of ducklings waddling after their mother. With Quill at his shoulder, the scholar knocked on Mordecai's bedroom door as the line of council members stretched into the distance, through the block's main exit into the grove outside. Quite what they expected to see was a mystery, yet their curiosity overrode any common sense. The master knocked again. "Mordecai? It's me, Witt, can I come in?"

No answer.

The youthful defecto who'd announced the man's demise moments earlier whispered into the scholar's earlobe, loud enough for anybody to hear. "He can't hear you 'cause he's dead."

As confusion and fear crept through the group like a disease, Quill rolled her eyes. Tutting, she forced her way to the front, grasped the handle and pressed down, opening the door with an excruciating squeak.

A gasp of horror started in the doorway, swept along like a wave to the crowd's edge—a ludicrous state of affairs, considering most couldn't see anything. Mordecai Templar lay face down on the ground, parallel to the neatly made bed, fully suited, the soles of his shoes white and worn, ready for a day he'd never experience.

Chapter Twenty-Six

"Who found him?" asked Red, whispering to the master who sat drowning his sorrows in a vat of herbal tea.

"His defecto. Young lad, he's here somewhere."

Quill refilled the scholar's enormous mug, eyeing the room. "What are you going to do now? The crowd's getting restless."

Wittgenstein tutted, rubbing his temples and muttering under his breath. Inside the Judgement Chamber was a sight to behold. Awash with fear, grown men jumped at any sound, others staring into space like automatons. The protectors battled the enormity of the situation and the gnashing of teeth was hard to ignore.

"Most likely a heart attack, wouldn't you say, chief?" Dorian Paine laid a comforting palm on the master's shoulder, despite an unmistakable hint of desperation in his voice.

Red scowled. "I'm not speculating until Dr Fox examines the body." *Ugh, another corpse to process, and I've still not found a forensic pathology assistant.* "Still, between us, I suspect it was foul play."

"What?" The master poured tea down the front of his white robe as he catapulted upright. "How could you possibly know that already?"

"Under the bed, there's a brass architect's triangular scale, a heavy-duty item and deadly sharp. My guess is the killer hit him with his own tool."

"But that means," said Quill, rubbing at the stain spreading across the master's chest.

"The murderer is probably inside the grove, particularly when most folks cannot leave. Though we can't discount the prospect a defecto's responsible. After all, they're free to come and go if their master requires it."

Quill scowled. The new chief sounds exactly like his dinosaur of a predecessor. His title provoked old prejudices. With her bottom lip protruding like a spoilt child, she muttered. "What's your name, Chief Ross?"

"Hey, that was uncalled for and Jim's not all bad. I only meant that we should keep an open mind at this stage." Red paced, circling Wittgenstein as he kneaded the tension brewing across his forehead. "This murder is a complication we don't need. I'm fighting fires on too many fronts. Novack's disappearance and a murder mean I desperately need additional personnel."

"No!" said the master, his insistent tone leaving no-one in any doubt about his feelings on the matter. "We can't risk any of this becoming public knowledge. The city's reputation may never recover. And frankly, Mordecai's death, er murder, is even more reason to have the council here, where we can keep a close eye on them. I've wasted enough energy. It's time I spoke to my colleagues." The custodian thrust the tea at Quill's chest, throwing her temporarily off balance and once again took to the podium to speak. "This has been a tough morning, gentleman. I'm sure, like me, you wish to return home, leaving behind the heavy loss we all feel. So, at the risk of repeating myself, I urge you, take control so we might move forward."

The dazed collective sat in frozen silence, like wind-up toys in need of winding, until at last Protector Belasy bumbled a response. "Here, here. Let's do it for Templar." A half-hearted show of solidarity, which garnered the merest ripple of agreement from the masses as they rose from their seats, forming the snaking line which plodded once more toward the worn out ballot box.

"Motion carried." The steward threw down the last white token onto the enormous pile next to three stray red discs. The landslide decision met with a collective sigh of relief, borne out of a deep desire to leave, to put as much distance as possible between themselves and a murderer.

Dorian Paine approached the podium, thanking the steward for his patience on his way. "I commend you, gentleman, for your fortitude in such difficult circumstances. Now that we have control, I propose we bring the Ortus forward with all haste, say, in the next three days, dependent on the progress of the supernova. All arrangements directed by Master Wittgen—"

Shanour jumped from his seat like a jack-in-the-box, interjecting before Paine finished his sentence. "I second the proposal."

"Wait," said the timid lawyer from earlier, a word met with the hostile glares of anyone within a one hundred metre radius. "You still haven't told the truth about Novack, and who will conduct the ceremony since that duty falls to the Head of the Protectorate?"

"Sit down, Reiner, no-one cares at this point. Let Wittgenstein worry about that," said Shanour, still on his feet.

"I agree. Proposal carried," said Loughran, a smug grin lighting up his chubby cheeks.

Quill absorbed it all like a sponge, astonished at the speed at which their consciences flip-flopped between opposing positions. Then the master resumed control, directing Paine back to his seat with a cursory stab of his finger.

Something about him has shifted. I recognise that glint in his eye. What is he up to?

"Gentleman, you do me great honour by bestowing the responsibility for this most illustrious Ortus on my shoulders. I will not let you down. For that privilege, I owe you honesty. While it's true that Dr Novack's indisposed, the nature of his absence isn't health related. Sterling is missing, whereabouts unknown. I am sorry for the minor embellishment, but it was necessary to secure the safety of the city."

"This is outrageous," said a pot-bellied scientist, his handle-bar moustache quivering like an enormous bow.

"Scandalous."

"The nerve."

"I just want to go home."

The master raised his crevice lined palms as he signalled for silence. "We all do, Xavier, but for security reasons, that's out of the question. I summon all protectors and students. No-one leaves until after the Ortus."

With that bomb-shell dropped, the room ignited with indignant fury at the scholar's cunning manipulation.

※ ※ ※ ※ ※ ※ ※

"Which one of you was it?" Wittgenstein tapped a foot, complaining despite his triumph over the inferior intellects of the complex.

"What?" asked Paine, as he joined Red and Quill, who stood around the cunning fellow, the chamber now empty of disgruntled councillors.

"Someone must have been talking about Novack vanishing. How else could they have been suspicious?"

"Well, it wasn't me," said Red, hands in the pockets of his trousers. "I've just arrived, remember?"

Paine took a step back, a hurt expression on his face. "And don't look at me. I've supported you all the way."

As the last viable option, they zeroed in on Quill, unspoken accusations firing from all sides like sharp knives hurled at a defenceless target. "Oh, I see how it is. I'm the defecto, so it must be me. Perhaps they figured it out. Have you considered that?" she asked, hands on hips.

Wittgenstein shook his head, pointing a sharp fingernail in her direction. "Don't be ridiculous, child. You've seen them. They're like a bunch of unruly children. It must've been you. It's the one thing that makes sense. Think, child, think, it just takes one careless word."

Quill gulped hard, fighting the angry tears which threatened to appear, protestations of innocence caught in her throat.

I shouldn't have to say it wasn't me, not if he trusted me, believed in me, cared even.

Yet the evidence to the contrary left a bitter, acrid taste in her mouth, driving a dagger into an already fragile self-esteem.

Could anything be worse than the master's distrust?

Perhaps that she couldn't protest her innocence without deceiving herself. Perturbed, she picked through the less than discreet conversations with Bran, his openness and effortless charm. He'd sought her out, become her friend, and friends didn't betray each other's trust.

Did they?

Finding solace in her answer, hiding behind it, Quill made a choice. "I haven't said a word. Not to anyone."

Chapter Twenty-Seven

3 days to the Ortus

"I thought nobody could leave?" Red posed the question as he left Guidance Grove with Quill, the servant's gate locking behind them. Passing along the side perimeter, a vast bank of laurels hid the interior from public view. At the main entrance, they passed a steady trickle of protectors from the lower echelons of the council, together with their defectos. Including Aric and Arthur Leitch and a sneering Norris, laden with notebooks and writing paraphernalia. Collectively, they greeted her with a scowl, to which she responded with the broadest, toothiest grin and a sarcastic dip at the waist.

"What's up with those two?"

"Nothing I can't handle," she said, for her own benefit. "Anyway, there's no way out, apart from the main or side gates, and you've seen the security. Why do you ask?"

"It's probably not important, but did you notice the soles of Templar's shoes?"

"Not especially. I mean, they were rather shabby, but otherwise, I can't say I did. Why?"

"They were coated in a white substance, something crystalline. I'll need Dr Fox to tell me more."

"Maybe it was already on them when he arrived?"

"Could be, though they looked wet in places, like he'd been out in the rain, but we both know it hasn't rained for days, not with this infernal heat."

It took them roughly fifty minutes to walk to the Architect's District. Mordecai's house paled into insignificance compared to Dorian Paine's residence. A modest two-up-two-down, it was an advert for architectural mediocrity. Relieved to let themselves in with the keys helpfully discarded by the dead man, the home was spartan. Neat, clean and organised, the place was a testament to the defecto employed there. The downstairs declared nothing of any importance. A front living room dominated by a rich, dark mahogany bookcase arrayed with every imaginable reference text on architecture, all painstakingly alphabetised, each spine aligned with pinpoint accuracy to its neighbour. At the rear, a small kitchen faced onto a paved courtyard, devoid of plants or colour of any kind. It reminded Red of Jim's place, minus the debris.

Upstairs was much the same. A bathroom just big enough to squeeze a person into, and two bedrooms, one at either end of the landing. Both contained single beds, and no family pictures were on display.

Another bachelor, married to his work.

With the cursory search of each room complete, Red scratched his neck, pacing the hallway while Quill restored the bedroom to its original condition. Clothes folded in drawers, bedding made with crisp corners and wardrobe doors clamped shut to keep out the damp.

With the chief beckoning her to follow, she took a final, superficial peek around the bedroom. Pleased with her efforts, she smiled and retraced her steps. Suddenly, she saw him frozen like a statue, left foot on the first step below the right. Red's head rotated, slow and steady, his index finger to his lips, signalling to be quiet.

Ears tuning into the tranquil house, Quill heard nothing except the blustering gusts of wind rattling loose windows.

As she decided the guardsman was hearing things, she set off toward him. The visit had proved a total waste of time and the list of chores that needed doing at the grove grew each minute she wasted. Red glared at her as she approached, but Quill ignored him, sidling crab-like past his athletic frame, unable to avoid brushing against him despite her best endeavours. When her frame was parallel to his, the point of greatest contact—a moment that should have lasted less than a second—she heard it too.

Rooted to the spot, staring straight into his deep, inquisitive pupils, a heavy thudding from below intermingled with the purr of his breath as it caressed her nose. Quill mouthed, "Now what?" in the hope he could lip read while cursing her impatience. Red signalled with hand gestures. He'd go first and she should follow. Nodding, the young guardsman squeezed past, tiptoeing down the stairs like a thief. As the pair reached the lowest step, they picked up the banging again, much louder, coming from inside the living area, beyond the closed doorway.

I'm sure that door was open.

Quill hesitated, watching Red take up position outside the sitting room.

"This is Chief Red of the City Guard. We know you're in there. We have the place surrounded. Come out slowly with your hands up, and no-one needs to get hurt."

Admiring the obvious bluff, Quill expected the door to open and find herself face-to-face with Templar's defecto, but the thudding resumed, rhythmical though disordered and getting louder.

"This is an order. Show yourself now, or we'll have to come in." The guardsman infused his command with a distinct hint of menace.

But the entrance remained shut while the banging continued unabated. With a firm-set jaw expressing a steely eyed determination, Red grasped the handle, turning it clockwise as he rushed into the room. "I warned you. Don't move. We're coming in."

As Red ground to a halt in the room's centre, Quill collided with his back. The momentum of rushing in to accost an unknown entity propelled her forward, powerless to stop. "Ouch," he yelled, as she trod on his heel, leaving a dusty footprint on the rear lower half of his right trouser leg.

"Sorry." Her eyes darted everywhere, searching for the intruder, but the room was empty. Confused and embarrassed, the insistent thudding returned, drawing their gaze to the front of the house. *Thud, bang, bang, bang,* followed by the whistle of the whirling wind. Dust and leaves picked up in eddies which swirled like mini tornadoes outside the windows.

The window. That was the answer.

Somebody had neglected to latch it, and the strong breeze did the rest. Quill strode toward the panes, her pent up adrenaline subsiding, and grabbing a metal shaft, she pulled it closed.

As she faced Red, embracing the relief, a shiver shattered the moment. A creeping sense of dread swallowed her whole as she spotted the bookcase. No longer a scholar's dream, its contents were in disarray. Books in haphazard piles teetered off the edge of each shelf, many discarded on the carpet, spines cracked, loose leaf covers separated and torn.

Eager to identify a reasonable explanation, to rid herself of the fear scraping her insides, Quill embraced a theory that the wind had caused the mess. But the notion didn't last long, as the guardsman said, "Someone's been in here. They must have been inside the whole time. I wonder what they were searching for?" Quill gulped. The ridiculous mind trick she'd tried to play on herself fell in tatters. Red was correct, of course, then he said, "And I wonder if they found it?"

※ ※ ※ ※ ※ ※ ※

Red searched, working from the window to the doorway on his gloved fists and knees. Relegated to the entrance, Quill watched, entranced by the rhythmical way he swept the space. Focused on the task, the examination was problematic and time-consuming. To preserve the scene, the chief examined and replaced every book dumped on the floor in the exact location he found it. Each time he turned one over, Quill held her breath, craning her neck to see what was underneath it, but aside from the faded brown carpet, each moment of anticipation led to the same disappointment. With the entire room covered, he rose, arching his spine and flexing his muscular legs to shake off the build-up of lactic acid from spending so long in a cramped position. He wiped the glistening sheen of sweat from his hair with his forearm. "So that's an hour of my life I'll never get back. I suppose it's possible there's something hidden in the books, but I don't want to disturb the site too much. Though I suspect that either the thief discovered what they were searching for and took it, or there was nothing to find."

"Do you think it's connected to Dr Novack's disappearance?" Quill at last voiced a question percolating in her brain since the discovery of Templar's body.

"I'm not sure. There's no evidence to suggest that so far, so I'm treating them as separate investigations."

"What now?" she asked, making one final long sweep of the chaotic living room.

"Well, there's no more we can do here. I'll secure the premises until Fox conducts a forensic inspection. Though he's working twenty-four hours a day beneath a sea of bodies, so who knows when that will be?"

"I'd hardly call Mordecai Templar a sea of bodies. What did I miss?"

Red blew out a sequence of brisk breaths as he fussed with his uniform, actions which suggested he'd said more than he intended. "It's confidential. Ignore me."

"Have you forgotten the help I gave you last time? How I kept my mouth shut about what Professor Hawkin did to those poor defectos. Bill and Finn and Val, she was a child."

Red turned aside, unwilling to make eye contact as he shook his head. "Of course I haven't forgotten. But things are different now."

"Perhaps they are for you, Mr Chief of the Guard, but for me, nothing's changed. I'm still the lowest of the low, a defecto with no hope of a better lifestyle. It's easy when your father is a big hotshot lawyer and your mother is a society Queen."

"You know nothing about my life, or my family, so don't tell me my life's simple, because you've no idea what you're talking about." Red stiffened, his generous chest expanding with the force of his speech, signalling she'd hit a raw nerve.

"You're right. I don't, not really, but the experience we endured together is not something I'm likely to forget in a hurry. I trusted you, and I still do. Shame the feeling isn't mutual."

Red sighed, shifting his weight from side-to-side as he examined his reflection in the shine of his shoes. "No, that's not completely true. I did trust you, but I'm not so sure now."

Quill's pulse pounded in her ears as she felt a twinge of anxiety stirring in the pit of her stomach. "Why? What's changed?"

"You told Wittgenstein you haven't discussed Novack vanishing with anyone. Why did you lie?"

Indignation simmered beneath the surface as she opened her mouth to speak. Before she'd uttered a sound, Red interrupted, eyebrows arched. "Don't even try to claim you didn't. I've had extensive training in interview technique, body language and psychology. To be honest, it was obvious."

Quill slouched against the door frame, nibbling her fingernails as her gaze darted around the living room, anywhere than straight at him. While her mind was engaged in calculating what to say next, a set of books on the top shelf attracted her attention—a series by Koepker, on Scolarian architecture through the ages. Arranged in chronological order, they charted architectural styles from the early days of Scolaris through to modern times. Each book was bound in grey leather, its title embossed in gold on the forward facing spine, every volume in the same trim size, only the width differed. At first, she couldn't decide what drew her to them. They were innocuous enough. All at once, her brain caught up as she spotted that number three of five jutted out from the rest. A minute detail that shouldn't have meant anything, but in this perfectly ordered environment, it was an obvious anomaly.

Distracted from their disagreement, Quill pushed past Red, re-entering the room, positioned facing the title. She pointed to it. "Have you noticed this book doesn't line up like the others?"

Red shrugged. "Stop avoiding my question."

"I'm not. Just look at it. You're the one with the gloves."

Red crossed to her side, and frustrated he'd not seen it himself, said, "So it's bigger than those, so what?"

"They're part of a series, so I'd expect them to be the same size. I know about books, in case you'd forgotten."

"There's been a burglary. The place is a mess, that's all."

"But this row's untouched."

Red paused, scanning the top ledge from left to right. "Okay, you have a point. It won't hurt to take a closer look."

As he slid the volume out, the pair exchanged curious glances as they peered into a hollow void to discover it wasn't empty. With gloved hands, Red pulled out a peculiar object from its hiding spot and inspected both sides. "Why would anyone keep this here?"

"I don't know, but I guess we're about to find out."

Chapter Twenty-Eight

As Quill entered the residential block through a side entrance, her brain bounced and hummed with thoughts of Mordecai's ransacked living room. The potential implications of what they'd discovered were far-reaching, though there were still unanswered questions. She was glad to escape the horrendous heat and the resultant swarms of biting insects which descended like vampiric clouds from the humid atmosphere. Inside, the corridor stretched into the distance, its temperature kept cool in the shadow of an immense oak tree, which dominated the overgrown quad in the block's centre. Doors to the captive scholars' rooms punctuated the hallway at regular intervals while the chemical taint of disinfectant mingled with the full-bodied waft of bacon and eggs. In response to the tantalising, lingering aroma of breakfast long since consumed, Quill's stomach clenched and growled, a reminder she'd grabbed nothing but a dry crust on her way out earlier that morning.

With her mind elsewhere, she ploughed straight into two figures emerging from the nearest room to her right. An unfortunate collision which resulted in books, paper, quills and piles of laundry launching upward in a graceful arc, before falling, clattering to earth and bouncing in all directions across the white-tiled floor.

The tallest of the men threw his palms in the air as he faced the source of his frustration. Quill groused, unable to contain her emotions, coming face-to-face with the man with the mountainous black mole in the middle of his chin.

Of all the people to bump into today.

Norris stood with his master, Aric Leitch, the shorter of the pair, as both bullies turned an unflattering shade of purple, stepping across the hallway, blocking her path. In his imperious tone, Norris said, "You again. I might've known. Don't just stand there, we don't have all day. Pick up this clutter."

Aric snickered, behaving like a spoilt child as he giggled behind a cupped palm. Certain the accident was not entirely her fault, Quill railed against the order. "Don't blame me. You should pay attention to where you're going." As soon as the words came out of her mouth, she regretted them. Both men stepped forward, their superior height intimidating as they glared at her like predators.

"It's time someone taught you a lesson," said Aric, moving in even closer.

She clasped her arms around her rib cage in a self-soothing bear hug. "I didn't mean any offence. What I meant to say was if we all work together, it won't take long to clear up this mess. It was an accident."

"Funny how you always seem to be at the centre of accidents," Aric said, his hooked nose centimetres from hers. "It's not my job to clean up, that's what defectos are for."

Norris clutched at his stomach. "And don't look at me either. Suddenly I'm feeling nauseous again. I guess it might be a repeat of yesterday's sickness."

"Poor dear Norris, you seem tired and under the weather." Aric smirked.

Surprised to discover the loathsome young man supporting the lies of a defecto, the injustice of the situation made her seethe with resentment. But realising she was fighting a lost cause, Quill dropped to her knees, scooping the scattered accoutrements onto her lap as she muttered under her breath.

"Is everything okay?" Quill recognised Kai's voice, together with the tapping of his cane as the young defecto approached. Forward movement which ended as his stick inadvertently hooked one of the discarded robes, sending it flying once more. The timing was perfect as Norris and Leitch turned to the sound precisely as the robe launched into orbit. A fluid motion which ended with the long brown garment wrapped around the duo's faces as both clawed at the cloth, trying to free themselves from its suffocating embrace.

While laughter threatened to escape and dig her into an even bigger hole than the one she was already in, Quill bit hard on her tongue. With her lips clamped shut, burying her chin in her chest, she performed a desperate charade of total ignorance.

"Get out of my way," roared Aric, freeing himself from the clutches of his own robe. "You think you're really clever, that you're protected somehow—some protection, a blind low-life. You want to watch yourself."

What a prejudiced jerk.

Quill stood, the pile of books and scholarly manuscripts balanced with pens on top, then thrust them toward the furious Leitch in an aggressive show of defiance. "I thought Bran told you to leave me alone. Perhaps *you* should be careful."

A trickle of sweat dripped from her hairline between her shoulder blades as she waited to see whether mentioning Harland's name might diffuse the situation, or if she'd added fuel to an already brightly burning pyre. Aric's eyes contracted to the size of pinpricks as he pursed his lips, drawing a sharp intake of breath, before erupting into unbridled laughter. Once the student could speak, he gasped, his breathing heavy. "What a fool you are. She thinks Harland likes her," he said, turning to Norris as the manservant snatched the handful of robes from beneath Quill's armpit. Both enjoyed further hilarity. Laughing and pointing, they exchanged knowing glances, wheezing and spluttering with the exertion, before Aric spoke. "You might be his little pet for now, but you're not the first and you won't be the last. He'll soon grow tired, he always does. Why he's slumming it with you is anyone's guess. Still, they say change is as good as a rest. I can be patient, so I'd watch your back if I were you, particularly as there's a killer on the loose. Who knows who's next?"

The undisguised threat fired a shiver through Quill's spine as Aric turned on his heels, barging past Kai, as Norris followed like a lapdog. Unbalanced, the sudden bodily contact sent Kai lurching to his right, flailing his arms in front of him, struggling to save himself with his stick. Quill shot forward, grasping his left arm, acting as a counterbalance until she stopped him from falling.

"Sorry about that," she said, still gripping him tight as she felt him relax, returning to an upright position.

"Why do you keep getting yourself into these scrapes?" Kai stared straight at her with his hypnotising liquid gold eyes.

"It's not intentional. Anyway, they don't scare me."

"Maybe they should. You heard what he said, and he's right, you're a defecto, no-one is going to care if you get hurt."

"No-one?" she asked, nibbling her bottom lip, feeling the throb of his pulse through her palm as she gripped his biceps.

Kai snatched his arm from her grasp. "You can let go now."

The coldness of the last remark stung like a slapped cheek.

I miss his boyish charm and relaxed company.

Somewhere along the line, the dynamic between them had shifted, but she was too afraid to ask why, preferring instead to change the conversation. "How are you finding living in the grove?"

"It's okay. I can't say I enjoy sharing the dormitory with all the other defectos, but I'm thankful for the fact I have a job. And when all this is over, I'll be lucky enough to escape to a bedroom by myself. There's plenty who'd give anything for my life, so I try to be grateful for what I have, rather than focusing on things that I don't. Anyway, the professor wanted coffee and I've been here too long already. I'll speak to you later." With that lesson in humility delivered, Kai walked away, leaving her dejected and alone.

"I reckon it was Wendell. Do you remember there was that awkward business over Mordecai's refusal to pay his fees?"

"Really? I realise he has a temper, but murder? All assuming it *was* murder."

"It's difficult to see how Templar could have hit himself over the head with his own ruler, so what else could it be?"

Similar conversations occurred in every secluded corner and alcove as Quill hurtled through with the drinks trolley, hurling mugs of hot liquid at people as she passed. Far from a respectable gathering of intelligent gentlemen, they called to mind a bunch of backstabbing gossips. The protectors of each district sounded keen to lay the blame for Mordecai's death on their nearest rivals. So much for the Scolarian way of life, an ethos of the city united in the pursuit of knowledge crept further out of reach with each overheard snippet of ludicrous conjecture.

"I heard Mordecai ripped off Jones when he designed his new clinic, charged him double the going rate. Jones has been telling all the physicians about it, urging them to move their projects elsewhere."

"Yes, I know that's true because Hubert told Nadolny, who told Ziegler they'd overheard the pair of them arguing about it in the grove on the morning we arrived."

Certain exchanges were of greater interest than others, causing her to linger a few seconds longer, using the excuse of asking whether they took sugar or cream. As usual, none of them paid her any attention, nor tempered their conversation, and quick-witted as she was, Quill made a mental note of any details worthy of closer inspection.

With the tea service almost at an end, trotting behind the rattling trolley, she caught the faint hum of more muffled voices in a recess up ahead. Intrigued, slowing to eavesdrop, she strained to hear over the squeaking wheels; with each cautious step, the words grew distinct.

"It's outrageous that they're keeping us here. Master Wittgenstein is a liar. He's proved that to be the case by deceiving us all about Novack. Why should we trust anything he says at this point? One minute the doctor is seriously ill, now we're expected to believe that he's missing. Likewise, there's Templar's death, I mean murder, to consider. You've heard what people are saying?"

"Don't remind me. It sends shivers down my spine whenever I think about it. I'm not sure we should repeat idle gossip."

"What should we be doing, then? Taking this all on the chin? Funnily enough, I'd rather not stick around to be murdered in my bed, thank you very much. I'm regretting voting to take control of the council. If the rumours are true and Novack is dead, there needs to be an election. We should have done that from the start, and if there's going to be a new leader, we should appoint someone who will protect our interests."

"Hmm, I don't disagree with you there. It's about time there was an engineer in charge. No-one should underestimate our practical prowess. We'd make considerable progress on the backlog of projects if we were in control."

Stunned, that last conversation was the most outrageous of an eye-watering collection. So much that Quill decided she'd learned enough and that whoever the conniving pair were, they didn't deserve their morning tea. So, she executed a full one-hundred-and-eighty degree turn and sped off in the opposite direction to return the trolley to the kitchen, desperate to report back to the master.

Chapter Twenty-Nine

"What is this about?" Dorian Paine asked, flustered as Quill entered the master's office. That her master had an office at Guidance Grove set him above the rest, a perk of his lofty position as Custodian of the Library. Though he never looked at home in the stark white surroundings, his robes blended into the environment, making his body disappear, leaving a skeletal disembodied head.

"Don't ask me," the ancient teacher said. His reply was gruff as they both turned to study Red, who sat at the front of Wittgenstein's desk, clutching a small brown pouch.

The chief beckoned to the white leather chair opposite him. "Mr Paine, please have a seat. This shouldn't take long."

"Tea, anyone?" asked Quill, finding an easy excuse to stay. As she laid out the cups on top of saucers on the trolley, she crafted the perfect brew as if it were a military exercise. First, she warmed the pot with scalding hot water from the urn before steeping the leaves for precisely two minutes. While she worked, Chief Red interviewed Paine.

"Why was Mordecai Templar blackmailing you?"

Dorian turned pale, a distinctive hue of green kissed his cheeks as a rivulet of sweat trickled down the middle of his forehead, then dripped from the tip of his nose like a leaking tap. "What a preposterous suggestion. How dare you speak to me like that? Wit, are you prepared to let this, this jumped up nobody, ask me ridiculous questions? I don't have the patience for such nonsense. I'm heading to my room. There's work to be done." With that overblown series of protestations ended, the architect leapt up and hurried toward the exit. Red had expected the move, so before Paine had managed two paces, the young chief blocked his escape. "Sit down, now. No-one is going anywhere until you've answered my questions."

Dorian slumped, shrinking in height. His chin dropped to his chest as he loped back to the chair.

"Let's start again, shall we? But this time I demand the truth, Mr Paine, or I'm in danger of jumping to unsavoury conclusions where you're concerned."

The designer deflated, powerless to hide the shame of the affair as he examined the blue rug under his feet, anything to avoid making eye contact. "How did you find out?"

"That's not important. What did Templar have on you?"

"Nothing, not really. I want to hear who's been feeding you idle gossip? Was it Ziegler? He's had it in for me forever."

Red swiped a hand across his face, clearing his throat. "No-one had to tell me anything. The information came from the source."

"What? How? Mordecai's dead."

"Not from him, from *you*," said the chief, producing the brown pouch found at Templar's home from the inside of his uniform jacket.

Paine's Adam's apple bounced within his neck like a cork swept along by the tide as he stammered. "What is that?"

"I believe you know exactly what it is. I'll read it, shall I?" Opening the pouch, Red removed a lone sheet of paper and read aloud, while Dorian shifted in his seat, scanning to the ceiling as if searching for rescue from on high.

> *Templar,*
>
> *I don't know who you think you're dealing with, but you are playing a dangerous game. I paid you as agreed and will not pay extra. Don't come to my house again or I won't be accountable for the consequences, which believe me will be severe. Don't forget, I hold enormous sway when the committee allocates architectural projects and can make your professional life very difficult.*
>
> *I trust we'll never need to speak of this again.*

"And it's signed D.P."

The architect paused, apparently weighing the best way to respond. "Anyone with the same initials could have written it."

Red sighed, shaking his head in disbelief. "Are you saying that you didn't write it, that this isn't your handwriting? Think carefully before you answer."

Dorian chomped on his bottom lip. First staring at Wittgenstein, then at Quill and finally at the chief before closing his eyelids and holding up his palms in a signal of surrender. "No, you're right, it was me, but it sounds worse than it is."

"Go on."

"Mordecai consulted on a project commissioned by the Protectorate. He was an expert in geotechnical engineering. I've used him before and had no issues, but this time was different. We settled on a price, then suddenly he wanted double the amount. He said I was stealing from him, that his expertise was worth a lot more. I offered to increase his fee by fifty per cent as a gesture of goodwill, even though the amount we'd agreed was fair. But dissatisfied, he turned up at the house a few times, shouting and making threats and behaving erratically. Several colleagues complained to me recently about him overcharging."

Quill interrupted. "I heard a protector talking about that this morning. So that's true."

Paine dipped his head too, grim faced despite offering her a weak smile of thanks for the vindication.

"Why didn't you offer this information straight away?" Red asked, not willing to disentangle the designer yet.

The architect rubbed his palms along the thighs of his trouser legs. "To be honest, it never occurred to me it was relevant. It was a professional disagreement, that's all."

"A professional spat that had both sides threatening the other, if you're telling the truth."

"Of course I'm speaking the truth. Why wouldn't I?"

"You tell me?"

With the frantic tug-of-war of questions and answers reaching a pause, the master's room fell silent, except for the plaintive calls of the Lilith birds perched outside on the window ledge which stabbed the hush like hot skewers.

"I've told you all that I know. But you're right, I should have explained straight away."

"For today, I'm reserving judgment while I verify your story. If I discover you've been lying, we won't be continuing our chats in private."

Paine glanced repeatedly at the door. "May I leave now?"

"No, there's one last thing." Reaching inside the packet again, Red pulled out his gloved hand, his fingers clenched around an object hidden from view. After working it from his palm until it dropped between his index and forefinger, he held out an innocuous folded piece of card. Then, manipulating the square, he flipped it over to display an image dead centre, a familiar black swirl, like a G. The symbol intertwined with the silhouette of a woman—a woman with voluptuous curves, long limbs and calf length windswept hair—identical to that found in Isaac's suit. The design encircled by a single word: *Euphoria*. Reverently,

Red laid the match-book onto the desk in front of Wittgenstein. To Paine, he said, "I need to identify this item."

The architect and the scholar craned their necks, eyeballs on stalks, as they probed the provocative scrap of card. Quill studied their reactions, which she imagined were like her own the first time she saw it. The master lifted his gaze, eyes colliding with hers as a moment's recognition passed between them, an uncomfortable but necessary pact of silence. She hated the deceit but accepted that, for now, The Meraki's secrets must stay hidden in the pages of the little black book, a treasure which nestled in the Lilith bird box beneath her bed.

Paine reached instinctively to handle the magnetic object as he responded. "I have absolutely no idea."

The chief intervened, swiping the architect's hairy mitts away from the match-book. "Don't touch. No-one's forensically examined it yet."

"Sorry. It's an intriguing little thing. *Euphoria*, what's that?"

"No clue. I was hoping you could tell me."

"Why would I know?"

"Well, the letter and the matches were together in the same envelope, so I assume they're connected."

"If they are, I've no clue why. We have similar match-books at the architect's club, but ours is blue and there's certainly nothing like *that* on it." Paine jabbed a finger, a sneer on his top lip in response to the card's image, while also transfixed, unable to tear his attention from the seductive silhouette. The artwork radiated a power she'd never witnessed. The capacity to entrance men, turning them into gibbering wrecks, and maybe that explained why it was dangerous.

Red turned to Wittgenstein. "And what about you?"

The venerable scholar had a faraway look in his eye as he rested his chin in one cupped hand. "Eh? Sorry, I was thinking about the tasks I need to complete before the Ortus. The list grows longer and longer with no end in sight. What did you say?"

"Have you ever seen anything like this?"

"Of course I haven't. Scholars do not frequent gentleman's clubs. We are far too busy for socialising. Talking of which, if you'll excuse me, I've neglected my students for too long." With that announcement, the teacher swept out of the office.

As Quill recognised that this was at a push a half truth, her skin crawled, but on this occasion she was a willing participant in the deception. Though it was another prime example of how adeptly lies rolled off the master's tongue and added further evidence to her case against him. The charge sheet grew longer by the second, but his crimes amounted to one central transgression—he was a liar who betrayed her faith and trust. A man who'd made a promise he'd never intended to keep. For that reason alone, Quill doubted she could ever forgive him.

Chapter Thirty

"Do you ever see the old chief?" asked Red, watching Dr Virgil Fox clean his instruments.

"You mean Ross? No. Why do you ask?"

Shoving his fingers deep into his trouser pockets, the guard stalled, wondering if he was breaking a confidence. "Nothing, it doesn't matter."

Fox flicked his fingers, the largest droplets of water falling from his perfectly trimmed fingernails, then he dried them on a paper towel and deposited it in the sealed waste disposal unit beneath the sink. "If there's something on your mind, you'd best share it. It's never a good idea to stew. That path leads to stress and sleepless nights, none of which is desirable for your health in the long-term. What's the problem?"

"Not sure. This case has me second-guessing myself. I feel like a rookie recruit not a competent leader. Don't ask why, I don't even like him much, but there I was on Jim's doorstep, talking through the evidence. Honestly, it makes no sense."

"Did it help?"

"Weird, but yes, it did."

"What's the problem, then?" The fellow in the lab coat turned from the basin, leaning against the edge with his spine.

"His house was a mess. Not just untidy, filthy, as if the refuse collectors had broken in and dumped the city's rubbish."

"Well, I'm not surprised. He never struck me as the domesticated type and he didn't marry, so it's not like he has anyone to keep house for him. Though I suspect there's more to it than that."

Red paced, circling the mortuary slabs as he searched for the words to describe what bothered him about his unexpected visit to Jim's home. "Hmm, well, I'd obviously caught him still in bed. He was wearing his pyjamas mid-morning."

"Ha, if I had my way, I'd crawl under the duvet and stay there for a month. Jim's retired now, so it's no surprise he's taking it easy. I'm quite envious, to be honest."

Red nodded, seeing the sense in Fox's observations, but couldn't shift the twinge of concern in the pit of his stomach. "Yeah, I know what you mean. I've recently moved into my apartment, but haven't had time to feel at home because I'm never there. Still, it wasn't the state of the place or his personal appearance alone. He looked thinner, but the heaps of food cartons suggest he's not eating well. I can't understand how anyone would lose weight based on that junk diet. And thinking back, he had dreadful dark circles under his eyes which, for someone who's in bed after ten, seem odd, don't you agree?"

"Maybe that's the reason he slept late. He had a terrible night, so with nobody to get up for, he laid in longer, makes perfect sense from where I'm standing."

Red swept a hand over his tightly clipped black hair, weighing up the doctor's dispassionate assessment of the facts. Finding them sensible and plausible, he resigned himself to accepting that he was tired, stressed and overreacting to nothing of any importance. "I expect you're right. It's been an endless day already, and it's barely lunchtime. Anyway, you called. What do you have for me?"

"One step forward, and two steps backward unfortunately, but here's the detail, for what it's worth. Vaughn's prints are all over the match-book discovered in his jacket, but nothing else. It's clean and doesn't help us."

Red stabbed the toe-end of his right boot into the concrete floor, kneading his temples with his knuckles, massaging the tight band forming around his skull. "I hope that's not your forward step, Doc, because if so, I don't want to hear the rest."

"Okay, it isn't much, but I have processed three further bodies. Unsurprisingly, they all died of heart failure caused by ingesting a quantity of *Euphoria*. If I had support, I'd get through the others faster. Any luck with Novack?"

With nowhere left to hide, Red faced the facts. Either he was about to lie to Fox about their leader vanishing, or break confidence with Master Wittgenstein. It should have been a straightforward decision. He'd given his word to the Custodian of the Great Library, the de facto head of the Protectorate, the body to which he'd sworn allegiance. Made an oath to serve and protect on the day he'd transitioned from a recruit to fully fledged guardsmen. The entire case was becoming impossible to manage. A drug epidemic, their leader's disappearance and now the murder of a protector. There was nothing to suggest there was a link between those three issues, but fighting fires on multiple fronts alone was proving insurmountable. So he repeated the one nugget he'd vowed never to tell. "This is top secret. I'm breaching pretty much every rule in the code of conduct, but I'm out of options."

The doctor stepped away from the sink, pressing his fists on the middle slab. The sterile surface gleamed under the harsh light of an overhanging bulb as the pair's eyes met across the gurney. "You can trust me. We both want the same outcome—the truth. Unfortunately, I've discovered that the path to finding it rarely runs straight. There are tough choices to be made and often you make compromises, but I think you have excellent instincts and you'll need them. So, what's so secret?"

"Dr Novack is missing. No-one's seen or heard from him in over forty-eight hours. The last known sighting is him heading to Dorian Paine's residence, the architect who swears Novack was fine when he left. His boot and a dog lead ended up in the hall shrubbery, but no sign of him, and he's hosting an important house guest from Asteria, to add an extra dash of jeopardy to the mix."

"Goodness. No wonder you're stressed. How are you supposed to find him by yourself?"

"My thoughts exactly, but politically, the whole situation is super sensitive, especially now with the supernova event. Wittgenstein and Paine insist if word gets out, it could destroy Scolaris' reputation forever."

"Whoa, yes, they have a point. Do you think there's a connection between these events?"

"Do *you*?"

"In relation to Novack, I can't assist without access to his home and that's not likely to happen, is it?"

Red shook his head, clasping his arms around his chest, resisting the urge to bite his fingernails. "How did you guess?"

"I almost forgot. I didn't tell you about the steps forward."

"Huh?" said the guard, confused by the pathologist's sudden change of tack.

"One step forward, two etcetera. I mentioned the back, not the forward. Never mind, the main reason I called you is that I've established a connection between Vaughn and Mordecai Templar."

"Did they work together on a project? It would be logical, an engineer and an architect."

"Not a personal relationship, a forensic link. You remember the mystery residue stuck to the soles of Templar's shoes? You pointed it out to me."

"A white crystalline material, wet in places, which is strange because it hasn't rained for days."

"Yes, correct. I've had the analysis of the substance."

"And?"

"Funny really. Not at all what I expected."

Red drummed his fingertips on the edge of the shiny table as the scientist basked in the thrill of his own discovery, while forgetting to explain it. "Doc?"

"Oh, goodness, sorry, got quite taken away there. It's salt."

"Salt? Like you put on your food? How does that help? Doesn't that simply suggest an overzealous application of the stuff at breakfast?"

"No, it's not the table variety. It's rock salt, hence the large crystals."

"I still don't see how that helps us."

"Remember, I warned you, it's not all positive news. I can't explain its presence, or where it came from, but there's a vital detail to add."

"Which is?"

"I also detected minute traces on Vaughn's shoes."

Chapter Thirty-One

2 days to the Ortus

Dong, Dong, Dong. The weighty clamour of the bell tower echoed throughout Guidance Grove in an unending cascade of bass notes. Sombre, they reverberated around the Judgement Chamber filled to the brim with protectors, scholars and their defectos. The room hastily rearranged to accommodate the first ceremonial act of the Ortus. No longer arranged in a horseshoe formation surrounding the dais, the steward and staff had moved the seats that morning. Two banks, one on either side of a central aisle, led from the rear entrance to the stepped podium at the top. At the sound of hammering on the door, the throng spun, eager to witness the next batch of academics arriving. Master Wittgenstein rose from his lofty seat, positioned behind an enormous gold ewer which rested in the lectern's place. Sunlight poured through the arched stained glass above his head, colours refracted through its magnificence, sending beams of light to each corner: crimson, cerulean, amethyst, gold and jade. A panoply of every imaginable hue and shade amplified by the immense power of the supernova.

"Bring forth those who seek to be purified." The master's husky voice was loud and authoritative, full and ripe, exuding the confidence befitting a man who had performed this ritual many times.

At his command, the entrance swung open, revealing the steward. He grasped a stout wooden staff carved from an oak tree with knobbly, weathered fingers which looked more like the stick than flesh and bone. As the bell continued to peal, Quill stood in the back row next to Kai, forced to watch the slow procession of young men who walked toward a future she'd never share.

Cecil Shepherd followed Prosper Foley with Aric and Arthur Leitch in the middle. Jacob Dowling and Bran Harland held up the rear of a line of roughly thirty student scholars, as one by one, they stepped up to the dais to be offered a copper plate filled from the shining vat. Icy water, which they splashed exuberantly over their faces. Once finished, each recruit turned to the audience, dripping from their noses and chins, before stepping to each side of Wittgenstein, facing the crowd with their hands clasped together. As the last recipient of the public bathing, Bran remained in position at the super-sized jug.

For the first stage, the master ducked behind the golden tub. Then, reappeared holding aloft a double-headed dagger reminiscent of a lightning bolt, with its jagged asymmetrical shape and serrated edges. While holding the blade in one hand, Wittgenstein grasped Harland's right shoulder, which he took as a signal to tip his skull until he peered up at the ceiling. As Bran did so, his thick black waves tumbled beneath his shoulder blades, lustrous in the sunlight. Then, sinking the copperplate into the water once more, raising it high above the young fellow's face, the ancient scholar flipped it over, liquid gushing onto Bran's forehead and returning to the precious vessel. When Harland's curls wept, the master raised the knife and hacked at the mane of hair.

In no time at all, Wit tapped the recruit's other shoulder, signalling that he had finished, and Bran returned to his upright position, resembling a shorn sheep. Quill stared, unable to tear her gaze away as she studied this new stripped-down version of him, and he returned her gaze, unflinching, boring into her soul.

"What's going on?" Kai's whisper right into her ear made her jump. His question interrupted the circuit of electricity flowing between herself and Harland, who stopped at the front grinning irreverently, the solemnity of the occasion apparently lost on him.

"Be quiet. You'll get us into trouble."

"Sorry. I know today's difficult, but you don't have to take it out on me. I'm only asking you to help me understand what's happening. In case you've forgotten, I can't see."

With the realisation she'd been unkind and unsure why, she said, "You're right. I'm the one who should be sorry. The bathing is complete and now it's the shaving. It shouldn't be too much longer."

By the time she turned back, Bran Harland had gone. She couldn't spot him as Jacob Dowling settled in his place and the master repeated the choreographed steps, ending with the removal of an entire head of hair.

To be frank, the ceremony was difficult to watch, even though she'd witnessed it many times. Quill seethed. The frustration and bitterness she felt at the injustice of being forced to observe the one thing she longed for was almost unbearable. The toll of the bell reverberated inside her skull, jarring and stabbing at her psyche as the intermittent tinkling of water mocked her wish to be included. But there she remained, a defecto, a woman barred from pursuing her vocation. The lone ambition left that was truly hers—a thirst for knowledge and a dream to immerse herself in a scholarly life, foregoing anything else. It took all her strength not to launch herself running into the aisle, declaring to the packed audience that there'd been a mistake. He'd promised her. No, greater than that, she'd earned a chance and the rules against women and defecto's joining were illogical and outdated. That Master Wittgenstein, the Custodian of the Great Library of the City of Scolaris, despite his power and wisdom, was guilty of lies and betrayal of the highest order.

"Hey, can you see Professor Moore?" Kai asked, disturbing her brooding thoughts for a second time.

Quill craned her neck, hunting a line of sight through the sea of bodies. "Just about. He's on the opposite side of the aisle. At least I think it's him. Yes, about midway, towards the end of a row. Why?"

"Can you describe what he's like?"

Confused by the question, still fearful of talking through the ceremony, she endured the disparaging frowns of her neighbours as she tried to conjure an exact description of the professor. It was a hard exercise, as she'd not paid close attention to him during their brief encounters. "I'll do my best. He's short. Ancient, older than the master, I'd say. His hunched spine is pronounced, as if someone's folded him in half. I expect he has arthritis, poor man. That's why he needs those sticks. How does he manage in this heat, under that enormous wool coat and all that facial hair?"

"Is that the best you can do?"

"What else is there?"

"Not what he looks like. What's he *like*? What do you think of him?"

"I don't have an opinion. I've met him twice, each time for less than a minute. There's nothing I can add, sorry. Why do you ask?"

"Err, I'm not sure. There's nothing specific, but he's so secretive. Maybe I should be grateful. Apart from preparing and serving meals and gardening, he doesn't want me to do anything else. Most of Courtyard Place is out of bounds to me. He's fitted locks everywhere. I miss Serenity Gardens. Old Jed, she was like a mother to me."

"It's bound to take time to adjust to unfamiliar surroundings and a different set-up. I miss my father too," she said, reaching out her fingertips to grasp his hand. A movement he reciprocated, squeezing her palm with his as they stood shoulder to shoulder. Giving and receiving what little comfort they could, as they watched the last sweep of the ceremonial dagger removing the remaining clump of Prosper Foley's mane.

"Let the celebration of F*east and Famine* begin," said the master, his arms spread wide, a contented beaming smile upon his craggy face. To which the steward responded in the time-honoured way, beating the hard stone floor with his oak staff in a fast rhythmical drum roll which crescendoed in volume and speed. Signalling to the gathering that the preliminary rite of the Ortus was complete.

The chamber rang out with the cheers and clapping of those assembled. Rowdy as they competed with the tower bell, which continued clanging, albeit faster now, word miraculously having found its way to whoever pulled the bell rope that the show had ended. To rapturous applause, the newly bald recruits bowed their shiny heads, retracing their steps as the steward strutted like a peacock, leading them to the exit. Headed to their rooms on the residential block, they were ready to embark upon the next leg of their philosophical journey—the step called *famine*. Confined to their cells, this was an opportunity for further study and deep reflection where the students fasted during daylight hours, sustenance limited to a few hours after sunset. A meagre offering of fruit and vegetables and last season's walnuts gathered from the grove.

The Protectorate prepared to celebrate the antithesis of *famine*; the stage known as *feast*. Indeed, the entire city would rejoice with family and colleagues. Meals, which ordinarily amounted to fuel for a day's work, transformed into opportunities to reflect on the past year's successes and to count the days to the new discoveries awaiting them. Even the defectos benefited from the overindulgence of their employers, allowed to enjoy any leftovers. No morsel should go to waste. Caught up in the contagious excitement, Quill relegated her heartache, slinging it to the back of her mind, Kai's hand squeezed in her sudden vice-grip and giggling as he did the same. Turning to face him, his golden eyes enveloped her, sucking her into his gaze like the black holes that inhabited her dreams. His nose was centimetres from her as he cracked out his boyish tooth filled grin. "I see you."

"You too." A warm fuzzy feeling surrounded the two of them in an invisible protective bubble, as those nearby continued their loud carousing, oblivious.

Suddenly, an orotund voice penetrated their intimate sanctuary, popping it in one mighty explosion. "Hooray! About time. I'm starving."

Shocked by the forceful vulgarity of the pronouncement, the duo whipped their heads around, searching for the speaker. Stood next to the glorious ewer, a position reserved for the most senior members of the Protectorate, his prodigious belly protruding from the black fur, Uriah Crisp stunned the entire chamber into silence. Laughing at his own comment, animating the inking on his skin, his enormous frame undulated like a snake traversing a dune. As the master ushered the extraordinary man away, Quill spied the line of cleansed recruits who'd halted in the aisle, accosted by Crisp's outburst. Confused, she glanced up to discover a different pair of eyes. Except these were inscrutable, beaver-brown and glaring at her waist. The scene played out in slow motion as her mind connected the dots until she jerked her hand from Kai's gentle grasp, rubbing her palm awkwardly on the front of her tunic. Seconds later, the human train set off again and Bran walked away without another glance.

The hammering in her chest gripped her as she swallowed hard, her thoughts muddled and unsure. As the cacophony of clapping subsided, Quill turned to say goodbye to Kai to discover an empty seat next to her.

Chapter Thirty-Two

Sat at the cherry-red desk in his new post, Chief Red pondered the fresh information provided by Dr Fox. Beyond his room, in the jaded outer office, guardsmen toiled over the scant details of bodies 1-10, the practical labelling impersonal and unpleasant. They were no further forward, a fact which gnawed at him like a wolf chewing a juicy bone.

How could ten grown men die unnoticed in Scolaris where most residents were born, lived and died without ever setting foot outside their own district, let alone the city itself?

No official nor exact population figure existed, not least because of the absence of any rule to register defectos. A detail that shocked him at the outset of Professor Hawkin's case, and remained a source of consternation. An educated estimate based on the municipality's size suggested the number might be somewhere near a hundred thousand. How was it possible that among those people, nobody had come forward to report a friend or loved one missing? Chilled to the core at the prospect of ending his days without family or friends to commemorate him, Red conjured up the face of his old boss and daydreamed.

An unwelcome image of his onetime nemesis laid out on a slab next to the other unloved souls filled his head.

"We've still got nothing."

Red flinched, startled by the booming voice.

Oh no, not now.

The tall, gangly figure of Jackson blocked the doorway, leaning both arms against either side of the frame.

"I can't quite decide if you're deliberately ill-mannered or you're just dense."

"Huh?" the pock-faced guard said. A question which apparently confirmed his ignorance.

"Never mind. Try to remember to knock in the future, and its chief, again. There must be something. Talk me through all the steps you've taken." Red beckoned the irritating guardsman inside, pointing to a spindly legged chair. Jackson complied, perching on the seat, all arms and legs, like a scrawny spider.

"We've done as you asked. Checked the sites where we found the bodies. Reviewed the call logs for missing persons' reports. There are none. Discreet house-to-house enquiries revealed nothing, though maybe we'd have better results if we explained our interest in recent strange comings and goings."

Red squirmed, leaning into his new, sleek, black leather chair, which smoothly and silently reclined. He'd slung out Ross's old recliner with the rubbish, squeaking and protesting every step of the way. Its skin had cracked and faded, imbued with the stink of meat grease and body odour. "You have your orders, Jackson, and I expect you to follow them."

"Like *you* did?"

"Excuse me?" Red jolted upright in the seat, the backrest of which followed the upward arc with a languid hydraulic puff of air.

"You can't lecture anyone about following orders. 'Practice what you preach,' my daddy always taught me. You didn't toe the line with Ross in charge, so why should we listen to you now?"

A vein in Red's temple pulsed, the insistent swoosh of blood rushing through his ears difficult to ignore, as he contemplated the fact that the guardsman had a point. Once more, faced with a tough choice between dictatorship or a collaborative style of leadership, he took a chance. "You're right, that's an excellent question."

Jackson's bug-eyed, comical double-take confirmed that the frank response had the desired effect, and he grinned inanely like it was his birthday. "Err, really? Thanks, chief. What do you want us to investigate next?"

Red curbed an overwhelming desire to laugh. The serotonin hit delivered to Jackson by simply telling him he'd got something right had thrown the less than astute young man off track, turning him from an angst ridden troublemaker into a pussy-cat. "I need you to widen the search zones further. Return to the streets and canvass again. I know the discretion part is hampering the investigation, but my orders come from The Protectorate. Indirectly, so do yours. Do you have any further questions?"

Jackson's cross-eyed expression always meant he was thinking, a process which looked painful. The mere mention of the council had turned the guard a violent shade of fuchsia pink, his acne pulsating alarmingly as sweat formed on his upper lip. "Ugh, The Protectorate breathing down your neck. I don't envy you."

"Good of you to say. Is there anything else?"

"No, sorry, we'll get on to it straight away."

With the latest Jackson encounter chalked up as a win, Chief Red wondered if he'd won the war, or merely a small preparatory skirmish. Suspecting it was the latter, he wrote a mental note to invoke the Protectorate whenever required. As he watched through the door, Jackson gesticulated wildly with his long bony limbs, animated like a twitching scarecrow as he took charge of the men. Ross was correct. The young man wasn't the brightest and frequently proved himself a liability, but for unfathomable reasons, the rest of the guards looked up to him. He was a joker, and that made him popular.

Unlike me, I'm neither funny nor well-liked.

With the exterior office now empty, the chief removed a file from his desk drawer where he'd stashed it the second Jackson had uttered his first comment. A brown folio wallet with a white adhesive label stuck on its top third bore the name Otto Blackwood typed in neat text. Doctor Fox had provided the papers as requested, though he'd emphasised that this was an autopsy he didn't perform. When asked if that was unusual, Fox gave a damning single word reply. "Very."

Examination of the interior took less than a minute. There were two documents. First, a copy of the death certificate reporting what he already knew, the child's name and those of his parents, Victor and Olga, and the date of death. The second wasn't much help, either: an individual summary sheet recording the autopsy findings, or rather recording *no* findings. The same phrase appeared in every box from stomach contents to cause of death; *nothing of note*. It made no sense. The name at the bottom of the page made matters worse. No matter how long he stared, wishing it might vanish, he couldn't avoid what he had to do next.

Chapter Thirty-Three

Quill busied herself with cleaning. Tidying the master's office to forget the awkward moment with Bran and Kai.

It's amazing how much work you can create out of not much if you set your mind to it.

With the teacups and saucers, she loaded up the trolley, sweeping biscuit crumbs from the chairs and desk to the floor. Next, she lifted the array of papers and books scattered across the tabletop, piling them on a chair now that it was free of debris. As she opened the wax polish tub, the smell of lavender wafted up her nostrils, the comforting aroma transporting her to the library. A twinge of homesickness threatened to disturb the illusion of safety and security she'd created. Heat from the afternoon sun poured in through the window and she wiped sweat from her brow with her forearm in between polishing. Once she'd returned several notes and rulebooks to the desktop in neat piles, she lowered onto her haunches. With a dustpan and brush, she swept from the opposite corner to the door, wiping the skirting boards with a cloth as she progressed. Aside from crumbs, the place was spotless. The steward and his team were obviously experts.

Too soon, she had nothing left to clean. Quill stopped, admiring the sparkling surfaces, reluctant to leave in case she got dragged into serving lunch. A task which might involve contact with the hideous Norris, a prospect which sent a shiver up her body. The wall clock read a quarter-to-two. *Service should soon be over and if I follow a circuitous route, hunting for stray cups along the way, hopefully I'll avoid any unpleasantness.* Set on the plan, she passed the trolley, stepping behind the desk to push the seat into place. At first it slid easily but soon halted, caught on an obstacle she hadn't noticed when sweeping. Confused, Quill returned to her hands and knees, crawling into the dark void toward the desk's backboard. Plunged into blackness, she combed the carpet with tentative fingertips, unable to see while her pupils fought to let in enough light. She promptly discovered a wad of something thick and pliable snagged around the front chair legs, preventing them from sliding any further. Frustrated at her inability to see, she grunted, tugging at the culprit as she backed out on all fours. Impatient to stretch her spine, Quill stood in a fluid motion. Her upward trajectory met with the solid wood counter-top, which cut her down like an axe felling a tree. Howling, she clutched her skull in both palms, eyes and nose streaming as the pain engulfed her. Once the worst of the agony had passed, Quill rubbed the resultant lump growing beneath her hairline as she contemplated whether it was safe to move. While wiping off tears, she spotted a heap of white cloth next to her and assumed it had caused the obstruction. Tutting, she grasped the bundle in one fist, pressing onto the chair seat, driving upwards while her limbs wobbled. As she stood, the bunched up material unfolded from her fingertips, dropping toward the carpet. Fluttering from it like a butterfly was a folded square of blue paper. Distracted by the floating scrap, it took a minute longer to detect an anomaly out of the corner of her eye. The oddity prodded her subconscious, a sharp stick, jabbing until she had no choice but to face it. Turned from the flying sheet nestling on the carpet, Quill stared at the white item still hanging from her outstretched hand. It was one of the master's robes, yet now she had recovered her senses she could see it wasn't white any longer. Stretched from the neckline to the waist, a dirty reddish-brown splat screamed foul play. With a mouthful of bile, she arched her body, desperate to escape the offending article, which appeared to be glued to her fingers. "Oh no, not again."

Crossed legged on the ground, Quill sat with her head in her hands, transfixed by the master's stained robe, which she had finally ejected from her grasp. Experience had taught her that hiding items with potential links to a crime ended in disaster, so she ruled out stashing it in her bedroom. As her brain worked on the problem, her fingers fiddled, repeatedly looping a curl behind her left ear as she hunted for a solution. The endless rumination unearthed a surprising absence of sensible options.

Perhaps I could burn it?

Flustered, she dismissed that idea as soon as she remembered she was stuck at the grove where people might notice a bonfire.

Or wash it?

But inspecting the mark, she doubted a hundred washes could remove it and her toes curled at the prospect of being discovered scrubbing a blood-stained garment. Privacy under the current arrangements was impossible to achieve, and she could imagine Norris and the defectos catching her then delighting in her misfortune.

While considering the practicalities of sneaking into the laundry room at night, Quill absent-mindedly twirled the paper rectangle around her fingers as she reached a decision concerning the robe.

It's not my problem. I don't owe Wittgenstein any loyalty at this point. After all, he's betrayed me in the most hurtful way.

That she might contribute to a killer getting away with murder by omission crossed her mind. But the scholar hadn't been responsible for Hawkin's death, and she didn't believe he was now. So, having gone round in a circle, she shoved the garment in the space where she'd found it, sliding the chair into place. With one hand on the desktop, she levered herself from the floor and brushed her clothes, checking that the bloodstain hadn't transferred to her tunic. Aware that the folded square remained in her grip, she tossed it onto the table, discarding the scrap without a second thought. As it hit the hard surface, the folds sprang open, exposing an envelope, postmarked Asteria. With her curiosity piqued, powerless to resist the temptation, Quill retrieved it and slid out the contents. Immediately recognising the handwriting, she read the message with a mixture of excitement and trepidation.

Master,

I have tried many times to get word to you, and suspect this letter is my last chance. For countless years, the authorities have held me captive in the Blackwater Maximum Security Facility. Accused of a series of terrible crimes, I await trial and fear that, as an outsider, they will find me guilty despite my innocence.

Please, if you receive this, send help before I'm executed.

Your servant,

Matthew

Chapter Thirty-Four

Time dragged as Red watched the orange lights flash through each of the seventy-six floors, gripping the lift's handrail until his knuckles bleached white. A huge iron fist breached his ribcage, squashing his windpipe, making breathing problematic. He leaned against the cool metallic interior of the box as the walls closed in around him. Just when he felt suffocation was imminent, a tuneful ironic *ping* announced his arrival at the top floor. Frantic, he lurched out of the doors, grasping his knees, sucking in giant ragged lungfuls of air while holding in the vomit.

The view from above was breathtaking, a three hundred and sixty degree panoramic study of Law and Order, dwarfed by this brand new shiny addition to the already sleek neighbourhood. Fortunately, he wasn't afraid of heights.

Claustrophobia's enough for one person to manage.

The thought made him scowl as he pushed his palms against the glass, peering at the myriad of rooftops and at the tiny moving shapes on the street below him.

It's lunchtime. I hope my timing isn't a mistake. They need me at Guidance Grove, and I could do without having to return later.

While following the view around to his left, he came reached a gilt-clad reception, relieved to discover it was empty.

Perhaps lunchtime is perfect timing?

Opposite the sinuous curved desk, four offices bore the names of those powerful enough to call the top level their domain. Two he didn't recognise, the rest he knew too well. With his ear squeezed against the penultimate door, nothing reached him, which meant one of two things, no-one was in, or perhaps most likely, the solid oak created a sound-proofed seal. Out of the corner of his eye, the name *Quentin Redmond*, embossed in silver against a black background, was still enough to provoke a cold sweat. Red toyed with going inside to play the dutiful son, enjoying a few moments of quality time with his father. The notion didn't last long, since it was pointless pretending their relationship was like that.

As he moved swiftly to the next plaque, it confirmed he'd come to the right place. Red knocked a trio of rhythmical taps before pressing the handle and entering the room. The space was magnificent. Following the curve of the circular rooftop, an elegant arc of uninterrupted glass stretched from floor to ceiling. "Who are you? How did you get in?" A trim, bewildered man glowered behind a gargantuan black desk, which turned the papers on top into postage stamps.

Surprised by the question bearing in mind the distinctive blue and red-striped uniform which he wore with pride, he said, "Um, I'm Red, sir. Chief of the City Guard."

"Hmm, yes, of course. A pleasure to meet you finally, but as you can see, I'm swamped." The man swept his arm from his body across the counter, an unfortunate motion which caused the handful of papers to fly off onto the floor. "Come back when you have an appointment."

Like a good citizen, Red scooped the debris from the thick piled bottle green carpet, returning it to the desktop in an untidy heap. "I think you might prefer to keep this conversation between us."

The man lifted his chin, holding up his hands in a defensive stance as he reclined in the chair until he was practically horizontal. "I can't imagine what you mean, but suggest you get to the point, assuming there is one."

From inside his jacket, Red produced a beige folio, Otto Blackwood, typed on a white label, stuck on the front. "Fine, tell me about this."

The recliner creaked as the man peered along his triangular bronze nose at the innocuous file. Close-set eyes narrowing as a faint twitch at the intersection of his mouth threatened to expose his calm exterior. "Never seen it before in my life. Next question."

Typical lawyer. Stick to the facts, and if you have to speak, keep your answers to a minimum.

Red wouldn't give up that easily. He opened the file, removing the death certificate and the forensics summary, laying them side-by-side, face up on the desk. "What about these?"

Wheels squeaking like a mouse as he whizzed across the carpet, the protector barely had time to study anything before scooting back to the window. "Not that I remember."

"Okay, how about this, then? Have you ever carried out an autopsy?"

The response to this question was noticeably different. The farcical chair-powered propulsion across to the desk ceased while the man weighed his options. Red imagined he could hear the whirring of the man's brain. Finally, he rolled out his favourite stock phrase. "Not that I recall."

"Are you qualified to perform one?"

"Err, possibly, maybe. No."

"Which is it?"

"No, I'm not qualified, but I command the guard, and you shouldn't forget that."

"Noted, sir," said Red through gritted teeth as he leaned across the table, turning the summary sheet to the back, pointing at the bottom of the page. "Perhaps you could explain this from the perspective of someone who's not trained to carry out a post-mortem."

The gentleman closed his eyes, laying his interleaved fingers over his rib cage. "I can't."

"Or you won't. What does this say, sir?" Red asked, jabbing his finger at the paper's edge.

"A name."

"I know it's a name. Which name?"

Then the fellow cracked, buckling under the weight of the unrelenting inquisition. "Omari Tedesko. It's *my* name."

Tedesko's forced admission that his details on an autopsy report stank like rancid blue cheese on a hot summer's day was one thing, but the man swore he didn't know why. It took little imagination to hazard a guess. The scant facts pointed to a conspiracy to cover up the circumstances of Otto Blackwood's death, but there were still many unanswered questions. What had happened to Olga's son, and was the missing Head of the Protectorate somehow responsible? That he'd vanished so couldn't clarify any details was especially inconvenient.

After taking his frustration out on the entrance of Flat 98, Equity Tower with his fists, but getting no answer, Red crouched, lifting the letter box and peering through the horizontal slit. "Mrs Blackwood, it's Chief Red. Can you let me in, please?"

Standing, he pressed an ear to the door and listened for the sounds of movement headed his way. Nothing stirred. While bobbing once more to peer through the gap, he glimpsed something black and frizzy, wafting like it was waving. Suddenly, realising what he could see, the guardsman called again. "Olga. Olga, are you okay? Open up or I'll break down the door."

Subconsciously aware that a response would never materialise, Red launched at the entrance, leading with his shoulder, using his entire stocky body as a battering ram. Pain shot through his arm and across his broad chest as he pounded on the door. Until, with a satisfying crack, the wooden frame splintered and the door swung open. Propelled by forward momentum, the robust guard fired into the hallway, grappling for purchase on the interior walls to avoid falling face first. Instead of which, he ricocheted out of breath and out of control. Finally, the corridor ejected him into the living room, where he ground to a halt scarcely centimetres from the sofa.

Wincing at the stabs of pain throbbing in his limbs, he wiped the sweat from his brow with the sleeve of his coat. He stretched, puffing, trying to dispel the sting of lactic acid from his side. "Olga, wake up. Can you hear me?" he asked, coughing between each word as he surveyed the mother. Her head lay against the settee's arm, frizzy hair waving in the breeze from an open window and covering her face.

Tentatively, he reached out his fingertips, braced for her to jump up at his touch, but she didn't stir, her skeletal frame protruding through a thin black cotton dress. As he swept aside the tight springy cork-screw shroud, Red swallowed hard, averting his gaze to the mustard tiled floor.

Olga Blackwood wasn't sleeping. She was dead.

Chapter Thirty-Five

To discover Quill wasn't where he expected was one concern. The dog curled up asleep in a wash basket was another. Master Wittgenstein strode through the corridor with Luna following, garnering curious stares from colleagues as he passed. This time, the girl had overestimated his forgiving nature. Guidance Grove was a place for contemplation, where protectors took serious decisions, a sanctuary from the stresses and strains of everyday existence, not a home for delinquent pets. Agitated, rounding a corner, he picked up the hushed murmuring of two distinct voices. The sound made him pause, knowing this section of the residential block housed the newly shaved scholars-in-waiting. Concerned that the troublesome canine might betray his presence, the octogenarian grinned as Luna rolled onto her belly, nestled against the side of his foot. Powerless to resist, he crouched to stroke the soft black fur on top of her skull between her floppy ears.

"I don't understand your interest in the girl," said an imperious male voice.

"I couldn't care less about her. The defecto is irrelevant, but she's the sole individual with direct access to the custodian, which could prove handy when they dish out assignments after the ceremony. She's fallen for me in a big way, they always do. It's a shame. For a second I thought she might be different, but apparently I'm irresistible."

With that observation, the master stepped forward, revealing his presence in the passage. Norris and Bran Harland grinned sheepishly as the servant conducted a ridiculous charade, straightening the student's pristine robe. Wittgenstein cleared his throat. "Mr Harland, are you lost? You are supposed to be studying in silent contemplation in your room. Alone." The teacher added the last word as he glared at Norris. "You should not take the period of famine lightly. Explore within yourself, examine your motives for choosing a scholar's path. It can be a difficult, lonely existence which is not for the faint-hearted. Most likely, you will never marry or have a family of your own, as you dedicate every waking hour to furthering the city's unceasing pursuit of knowledge. Spend this time wisely, search your soul, discover whether you are indeed worthy. There's no shame in admitting this life isn't for you. But mark my words, I won't allow you, or anyone else, to sully the good repute of our vocation. Now go, before I change my mind."

※ ※ ※ ※ ※ ※ ※

"There you are," said Wit, entering the office to find Quill stood behind the desk staring into space. "I looked for you in the laundry, where you're supposed to be, but found Luna instead. Fancy bringing the dog here. What were you thinking? Actually, don't answer. Clearly you *weren't* thinking." He waved a hand in her direction to usher her out of the way.

The little pet yapped, lifting her forepaws to stand on her hind legs in a show of excitement at being reunited with Quill. But the young woman paid no regard, rooted to the spot as if she'd seen a ghost. Exasperated, the aged scholar took his seat at the table. "Whatever is the matter? Are you well, child?"

Luna's insistent shrill barks captured her attention and Quill flinched, adopting a wide-legged stance as if she were expecting to be attacked. Head twisting in all directions, nostrils flaring, her jaw ached from teeth clenching. With the letter gripped in her outstretched hand, waving it in his face, she growled from the rear of her throat. "You want to know what's wrong with me? My father is languishing in a prison thousands of miles from home for the sake of a book, and you haven't even mentioned it. When were you going to tell me? Or maybe you weren't? He's supposed to be your friend. If this is how you treat a friend, I'd hate to be your enemy."

"The timing wasn't right, but of course I planned to tell you the truth. Who knows how long ago Matthew wrote it? I'm afraid it might already be too late, and I don't think there's much we can do to help, anyway."

"So you did nothing? There must be something to try. What about Mr Crisp? Surely you can use your influence there? What's the point of having connections if you can't manage them to your advantage?"

"It doesn't work like that. I can't ask a special envoy from a neighbouring country to intervene in the administration of justice at home. What message could that send to our neighbours about Scolarians?"

"I don't care. This isn't about Scolaris. My father's life is more important, though he is a defecto, so perhaps that explains why he's no one's priority."

"What a terrible thing to say. You know that's not true."

"Do I? I'm not convinced I know you at all," she said, darting beneath the desktop, pulling out the incriminating garment from around his legs. "And speaking of truth, what's this? I'm sure the chief would love to hear your explanation."

"Silly child, what do you think it is? It's a robe."

"Not the robe, all the blood on it, Templar's blood."

The scholar's emerald eyes twinkled as he threw back his tangled mane of hair as he laughed like a braying donkey until tears ran into the crevices of his skin, collecting into rock pools. "Soup. Soup," he said, struggling to form a sentence through the laughter.

"What? Stop laughing. You're not making any sense."

The ancient fellow rasped, shaking his head as he pointed at the stained cloth. Then, as he wiped his cheeks on a sleeve, chuckles subsiding, he exhaled loudly. "Sorry, too funny. You really have an over-active imagination, child. It's yesterday's lunch, tomato soup, remember? Smell it if you don't believe me. Why do you suppose I was searching for you in the laundry?"

As she sniffed the garment, Quill's heart sank as she recognised the fresh acidic tang of fruit and the unmistakable aniseed top note of basil. Feeling like a total dipstick added fuel to the anger inside of her. "I knew that. Stop deflecting from the real problem. What will you do about my father?"

"Defecto or not, I cannot interfere in the domestic affairs of another foreign state, personal feelings aside."

Sweat oozing from crown to toe, Quill's mind leapt into overdrive, reliving the hurt, shattered dreams and broken promises of the last few weeks. Unable to contain herself, she purged a torrent of bilious hatred. "Liar! You're so full of lies you couldn't recognise the truth if I recorded it in thick black ink on the front cover of one of your prized books. I'm sick and tired of being treated like a child, a second-class version at that. You don't care about my dad, nor me. We're simply the help. Here to serve. Why won't you just admit it? You had no intention of training me, what with all your precious conventions, and today I see exactly what you are, a self-serving, narrow-minded coward."

With that savage slander delivered, the pair fell silent, only the clock ticking and Luna's faint snoring interrupting the enmity pervading the space until Quill continued. "Apparently, I must do this myself. I'll board the next ship to Asteria and find my father."

The master slumped against his chair, forming a pyramid of fingers against his nose. He appeared tired, downtrodden, and Quill felt a twinge of guilt.

Did I go too far?

"I grounded all shipping until after the Ortus. The supernova affects the weather and the tides. Travel's not safe," he said, avoiding her gaze.

"Then I will leave straight after."

"What about becoming a scholar? You cannot do that in Asteria."

"You said yourself I have an over-active imagination. It was a dream, a fanciful dream, but my father's real, and he needs me. I just hope it's not too late."

Unannounced, the office door flew open and in walked the steward, red-faced and blowing the air out of his inflated cheeks. "Master, excuse my interruption. There's something you need to see."

"What is it? We're in the middle of a private discussion."

"Please, follow me. It's important."

Wittgenstein levered himself from the seat with his bony arms. "Okay, I'm coming. This had better be good."

Still dealing with the aftershocks from their bruising disagreement, Quill considered using the interruption as an excuse to make a hasty retreat. Instead she followed, overtaken by curiosity, with Luna trotting at her heels, the puppy awoken by the steward's unexpected vocal arrival. This odd procession snaked a route from the office through the Judgement chamber, outside into the grove, into the residential block, arriving at the warden's quarters. The door to his room stood ajar, and as they approached Quill glimpsed the tips of brown boots. Luna halted, alternating between whimpering and growling, baring her sharp white puppy teeth. Squatting, she scooped up the tiny animal, nuzzling her forehead into her chest as she cooed. "Hey, girl, what's wrong? It's okay. Shush, hush now."

By the time Quill lifted her head, the entrance was wide open. Stunned expressions on the master's and steward's faces should have prepared her for the approaching shock. Two men, a defecto and a dog, appraised a figure in a ripped and filthy olive-green suit. A gentleman who smiled despite the livid purple cheeks and scabby, swollen lips. Dr Sterling Novack, the City of Scolaris' Head Protector, had returned.

Chapter Thirty-Six

Their leader's reappearance met with a collective sigh of relief, conveniently coinciding with *Feast and Famine*. Novack appeared reserved. A white carnation hastily added to his lapel, detracted from his dishevelled appearance. Content, Sterling watched the festivities from the dais, while protector after protector toasted his return with flagons of frothy beer. Quill longed to know where he'd been, and the cause of those bruises, but the consensus had been to leave him in peace. He might talk about the experience when he was ready.

The mood in the grove transformed, as if someone had switched on a light. The brooding, back-stabbing machinations of each district fell away like a tarantula shedding its skin to expose a sparkling new version of itself. To Quill, the change was bittersweet. She liked Dr Novack so shared in the collective relief that he'd returned relatively unharmed, but too many unanswered questions remained. Novack was safe, but Mordecai Templar most definitely was not. A circumstance that readily slipped the councillors' minds. Luna likewise seemed troubled, whimpering and whining and refusing her food. Quill hated shutting the little dog inside the laundry, but the master insisted he didn't want her antics ruining the festivity. Last and most concerning, a nagging, gnawing terror threatened to engulf her whenever she thought of her father.

Was he still alive? Can I get to him in time? Can I even secure passage to Asteria with nothing of any value to my name? Argh, stop, over-thinking serves no useful purpose.

While grabbing armfuls of crumb covered plates and napkins, she piled the tea trolley as high as she dared before heading to the kitchen. Determined to keep busy, she filled her mind with any random picture except the image of her father's kind eyes and soft whiskers, however mundane.

With her hip, she drove the heavy double doors free, dragged the tea-cart inside, squeaking and groaning under the sheer weight of dirty dishes. The second that a narrow gap appeared between the cart's wheels and the open doorway, a flash of fur surprised her as Luna made a daring escape. Provoked into flinging her arms above her shoulders, Quill knocked over a teetering tower of cups and saucers. Dregs of tea and coffee splashed over the sides and across the front of her brown tunic until it dripped from the hem like a dishrag. "Luna!" She stamped a moccasin in frustration, crushing a nearby saucer into a million pieces for good measure. Stood at the epicentre of a canine hurricane, it was no wonder the master considered the animal a nuisance. Then the realisation struck. If the bundle of trouble infiltrated the feast, she'd get the blame. Torn between cleaning the mess or preventing something far worse, Quill leapt from foot-to-foot over the white crockery landmines, hoping she could intercept the dog before anybody discovered what had happened.

Shoulders turned battering ram, barging through the exit she soon wished she hadn't, as a shooting pain tore the length of her spine as if lightning had struck. While grunting through gritted teeth, Quill was relieved to discover tiny paw prints on the stone flagons. For once the drinks' spillage came to her rescue, as Luna's padded furry feet soaked up the liquid, leaving a precise trail for her to follow. Remarkably, the tracks led in the opposing direction to the gregarious hubbub coming from the Judgement Chamber, headed toward the residential block. While following the perfect, damp doggy stamps, Quill rooted through her brain, trying to think where the puppy could go, but turned up nothing.

As she rounded a corner, she paused, peering over her shoulder. With a dry mouth and thumping in her skull, Quill weighed the options. Protocol reserved these rooms for the most senior protectors, the leading men of each region, including Dr Novack. They were off limits to anyone except their chosen defectos. If anyone witnessed her entering the corridor, there'd be much worse than a pile of broken crockery to explain. Typically, the paw marks continued into the passageway, so either she gave up tracking the puppy or she took her chances.

In the circumstances, there wasn't much else to lose, so Quill crept forward. With taut neck tendons, she was alert to any sound, ready to duck into any of the shadowy alcoves between each chamber. But nobody roused as the dignitaries enjoyed themselves at the celebration, unaware of the four-legged intruder. As she edged along the passage, she hopped between the shadows cast by the enormous oak tree, which watched from the quadrangle in the block's centre. Its gargantuan trunk and leaf clad branches barred entry to the joint forces of the sun and supernova, blocking their rays from transforming the walkway into a steaming hot house.

Passed the first two doors, Quill released a breath and gulped in air, a deepening sense of dread washing over her as a sudden draught caressed her ankles. Confused by the sensation, she scanned ahead, noticing an entrance into the wild quad.

It can't be coming from there. There's a huge padlock hanging from the handle.

While creeping closer, the pounding in her ears crescendoed as she spied that, despite the robust ironmongery, the door stood ajar. Enough space for an inquisitive dual coloured body. Scanning the floor, the incriminating stream of dog prints ended at the doorway.

Luna's escaped into the jungle, but who opened the locked door?

As she stepped into the lush meadow, barely able to see a few centimetres ahead, the stalks towered over her petite stature. Left to nature, the unloved zone flourished despite the lack of human attention. Wild flowers fought for light with fat grass spears, both climbing to new heights in an unceasing battle. Stout hairy borage, star-shaped endive, poppies and beaked parsley, the glorious results surrounded her in a mantle of green and pink and yellow and white and blue, all hues of the rainbow. Bees and insects buzzed and hummed, flying from one bloom to the next. Punch drunk on nectar and a spicy fragrance reminiscent of cloves and cinnamon, their legs were heavy in voluminous golden pollen trousers.

With no clue where she was heading and the train of doggy footprints impossible to follow, Quill circumnavigated the rectangular meadow. To avoid getting lost, she kept the ancient oak to her left and the residential suite on the right. She hadn't walked far when she noticed an opening in the foliage. Surprised, peering ahead, flattened plants created a thin corridor that stretched into the centre, toward the tree. As she weighed up the likelihood of becoming disoriented if she strayed from the margin, Quill battled the anxious thoughts that filled her brain. Resolved to find her four-footed friend, she took a deep breath, striding into the unknown.

The narrow path snaked its way through the grasses, a long winding route that doubled back on itself on multiple occasions. Whenever she thought the track would end at the oak, it turned away. At those junctures, Quill paused, contemplating making her own pathway, striking out to the tree to save precious seconds. Frequently, she changed her mind, concerned that if Luna was following the track, and it led somewhere else, they might not meet. So she pressed on, traipsing through the oppressive heat, unable to avoid the bloodsucking creatures she dislodged when brushing against the dusty stalks. After what felt like hours of walking in a circle, batting, swatting, and slapping the air, Quill stepped out from the undergrowth into a wide flattened elliptical area encircling the thick gnarled stem.

How didn't I see this immense space from the block?

As she guessed where she'd started, it was clear the mass of greenery hid the lot. "Luna, Loona," she called, exasperated, tired, hot and hungry, but nothing stirred on the flat plane. She felt like she'd stepped into another world. A hidden dimension where she existed alone. While pacing the tree's circumference, she determined that human hands, no feet, had formed the clearing. She searched for a plausible insight into *who* and *why*, but failed. The enormous girth of the trunk meant it was impractical to view all sides from any position. With every step Quill hoped to discover Lunar's sleeping body beneath the cool shade of the outstretched verdant canopy, but that moment never arrived.

Distracted, estimating she'd inspected half the clearing, she noticed a misshapen foliage covered lump protruding from the ground, three metres from the trunk. Quill froze, studying the lush hump, unable to guess what it was. Then she heard a faint, haunting, whining howl, strangled, as if miles away. While scratching her scalp, she approached the leafy mass, reaching out to touch fleshy tendrils, pulling them off to expose a hunk of rock. A monolith skewed at an angle, it toppled under the strangling ivy. As she stepped around the slab, unexpectedly, one foot no longer contacted solid ground. Aware she was falling, Quill threw her hands toward the stone, fingers grabbing at thin air, slinging her frame forward to arrest the downward motion. Despite snagging a handful of thick vines, she landed with a thud. Flat on her chest, chin colliding with the earth and ricocheting upwards, her leg dangled precariously over a gap in the floor. The vibration of her heartbeat flooded her ears as

Quill panted, clenching her eyelids. As she spat the grit and dirt from her mouth, wiping her lips on the sleeve of her tunic, she clung on with her right hand, too afraid to let go.

While the shock subsided, she found the courage to peek, determining she was intact and one solitary leg hung into the void. With her neck stiffening in response to the whiplash effect of the fall, she rolled onto her side and felt the comforting security of the stable ground beneath her. Millimetre by millimetre releasing her grip, she forced her upper torso off the dirt and stared into the gloom beneath her. The contrast between the brilliance above and the blackness below rendered it impossible to see inside further than a few centimetres, compounded by turf growing across the edges of what she assumed was a rabbit hole.

No wonder I didn't notice it.

Dirty and grass stained, she pushed onto her knees, flexing the pain from her stiff neck. Quill resigned herself to accepting that her fruitless search for the pet was over. Lamenting her misfortune, suddenly she thought she picked it up again, a muffled whining tone that seemed to get further away. Except now it was below her. Convinced now that Luna had darted into the rabbit hole, she muttered under her breath, cursing the animal's inquisitive nature. She grasped the thick blades of vegetation overhanging the rim and pulled, tearing off fistfuls as she travelled in a semicircle at the base of the slab. Handful after handful ripped under her, urgent tugging and yanking until she'd uncovered the biggest burrow she'd ever seen. On her stomach, she dropped her chin over the side and peered into the darkness, waiting forever for her pupils to adjust to the inky blackness. Alert, hearing the whimpering again, convinced her that Luna was down there somewhere beneath the ground, crying for help. The notion of the helpless creature lost and alone in the darkness threatened to overwhelm her. Hot tears pricked her eyes, but she brushed them aside, wiping soil into her eyeball, a move which made them water even more. As she blinked the dirt away, her father's bright voice came to mind. "Blink, blink, little bird. Don't rub, you'll make it worse," and the comforting kindness of the recollection hardened her resolve as Quill lowered herself into the unknown.

Chapter Thirty-Seven

Dr Fox was less than impressed by Red reporting a further suspicious death, but by the time he arrived at Flat 98, a cursory search of the premises uncovered copious letters from a Dr Chen about Olga Blackwood's pancreatic cancer diagnosis. The most recent selection urged her to return to his clinic for treatment. A faded photograph stashed away in a drawer showed a youthful Olga on her wedding day. An innocent joy lit up her plump face and that of an earnest young man, presumably Victor Blackwood. Laughter shone in their smiles as they faced each other, ignorant of the sadness yet to come. The picture was hard to take in, worse than dealing with the body, facing the pain of those left behind to grieve. Finding no trace of a gentleman in the house, together with the discovery that someone had hidden the photo, Red surmised that bridegroom and bride had parted company, and he resolved to track down Mr Blackwood. Not simply to break the sad news of his wife's demise, but to shed further light on the allegations against Novack.

When Fox arrived and Red showed him the physician's letters, the forensics man nodded, agreeing that Olga's emaciated state pointed to her having succumbed to the invading cancer. Though Red couldn't forget the scientist's remark that arguably the woman took her own life, refusing treatment to surround herself with the heartbreak of a dead child. For a nanosecond, he'd envied the boy, despite a brief existence his mother doted on him. Loved him fiercely to the point it broke her when he died, sealing her own tragic fate.

Frustrated to find himself at yet another impasse, the guardsman examined the scant information he'd gathered. On the one hand, multiple unexplained drug deaths, unidentified males, missing their clothes and personal items, and left at random locations around the city. Mr Vaughn, an engineer, victim of an overdose too, fitted the profile of the rest—middle-aged, no family. On the other, Dr Novack's disappearance with no direct evidence of anything sinister occurring, except that nobody had seen him in two days. Coupled with Olga Blackwood's allegation that Novack caused her son's death, the records of which were sketchy, including an autopsy report signed by Tedesko. A protector who, by admission, wasn't qualified to carry out the examination. Then there was Mordecai Templar's murder at the grove, rock salt on the soles of his shoes despite no-one being able to leave. Not forgetting that Mr Vaughn wore salty boots, too, the single tentative link between both investigations. He suspected there was a connection as he pondered the details. If only he could work out how.

Yet again, finding himself at Jim Ross's crimson front door, he hammered the paintwork, wondering if two visits in a week were too much. Ross soon appeared, beckoning him inside with a grunt and a wave of his hand as he headed into the kitchen. This time at least his former boss had dressed, his grey trousers and plain white shirt, a nod to smart work attire. Though closer inspection revealed tired frayed edges on the collar and cuffs and the slack's pockets. A lot like the man himself, the garments had seen better days. The kitchen looked tidier than when he'd visited last. Stacks of waste bulged from tied up orange rubbish sacks piled high in the corner behind the dinner table, the arrangement of dirty dishes in the sink reduced to half the size.

Red sat while Jim boiled the kettle and made the coffee. A ritual which neither man disturbed by talking.

"I love what you've done with the place," said Red after three enormous swigs of steaming hot liquid, scalding the roof of his mouth for the second time in as many days.

"Ha, funny." Jim's trademark grouchy manner appeared less intimidating than Red remembered.

It was curious how your perspective of a person changed when they were no longer giving orders.

Perhaps I jumped to unfair conclusions during the short period we worked together?

"I wondered when you'd be back?"

"Am I that predictable?" Red rubbed a brown stain from the mug handle. Nose wrinkling as it rolled into a sticky miniature cigar under his thumb and dropped onto the table. "What do you think of Mr Tedesko?"

"No small talk today, then? Do you want the politically correct response, or the say-it-as-it-is Jim Ross special?" The former chief smirked, a twinkle in his eye.

"The truth will do."

"Blimey, that's the tough part. When you're young, like you, your idea of the truth is simple, but as you get older and more experienced, you learn there are no black-and-whites, only shades of grey. So I'll tell you what I think, but as for the truth, you must decide."

"I'm not sure I understand what you mean, but okay?"

"Omari's ambitious, ruthlessly so, and he's inexperienced for someone in charge of Law and Order. Much like Dr Novack's young for a head of the Protectorate. They both rose rapidly, almost in sync. If you listen to rumours, that's no coincidence. In my world of jaded truths, I assume there's a grain of truth in every snippet of idle talk, if you can tease it out. Now I'm not saying that either of them has done anything illegal to get ahead, but giving their friends a leg up the ladder won't have hurt their prospects. While we're discussing sudden rises to power, Dorian Paine's done alright too. It pays to align yourself with powerful friends."

"What if their close association includes breaking the law? Then what?"

Ross sighed, clasped hands stretched above his skull before dropping them into his lap, swigging his drink with a lusty smack of his lips. "Now, that's trickier. The individual making such allegations better have proof, because that's triple jeopardy, three powerful state leaders for the price of one. If they're wrong, the consequences would be catastrophic, for those reckless enough to gamble their entire future on a hunch and the city. A city famed for its pursuit of a higher purpose."

"Is the Protectorate built on a lie?"

"Have you never heard of a white lie, son?"

Startled by the term of endearment, Red spluttered, chugged caffeine, irritating his throat as he coughed. "Of course I have. But they're for small things, for kids, you know?"

"Ah, see? Now we're back to the start of this conversation. Your version of truth and mine. In mine, white lies are sometimes the biggest of all, and often they're not so white."

"Come in, come in, join our celebration of *Feast*. It is a wonderful day to be thankful." Master Wittgenstein ushered Red into the Judgement Chamber. The hall looked less like a venue for making important decisions, and more like a gentleman's club way beyond closing time. The room stank of acrid cigar smoke and stale beer, the floor tacky underfoot as the protectors sat, or slumped, and even slept in varying degrees of upright, their suits dishevelled, ties loosened and buttons gaping. A long buffet table decimated by inebriated scavengers resembled a war zone. Sandwich crusts discarded on top of the few that remained uneaten. Limp lettuce leaves wilting in the heat, draped over the sides of bowls which disgorged their contents onto white linen. Tablecloths spattered with red beetroot juice and yellow mustard festering wounds. Red never drank, and the tableaux explained why. He told himself it was because he didn't enjoy the taste and his duty as a guardsman was to take care of his body, but it wasn't that simple. He'd tried alcohol once, as a recruit, trying to fit in with the group, but didn't like the way it made him feel, his self-control deserting him, not to mention the hours spent emptying his gut. Followed by a gruelling ten mile training run the next morning, during which he thought he might die. Secretly, a part of him craved the sweet spot of oblivion before the drink too far, and that frightened him. Because maybe, if he allowed it to happen, he might never return.

Unable to square the circle between the hedonistic scene and the events of the past couple of days—a missing leader and a murdered colleague—speechless, Red scratched his chin. He searched for tactful words before opting for a banal response. "Err, thanks, but I'm on duty."

"Cheer up, chief, it might never happen."

Bemused once more at the usually taciturn scholar's jovial manner, Red questioned whether he'd also yielded to the temptations of alcohol. "Am I missing something? Dr Novack's vanished, and Mordecai Templar is dead. I'm struggling to see a reason to be cheerful and am surprised at people's short memories."

The pained expression on the scholar's face suggested he'd taken the remark as a personal insult. His wrinkled cheeks sank, eyes pinched as if he was sucking on a lime. "You haven't heard?"

"Heard what?"

"Silly me, of course you haven't. The grove's locked up like a prison. Today's your lucky day. One of your problems vanished in a puff of smoke a few hours ago. Dr Novack is safe. Tired, and a little bruised, but alive, and returned to the fold. See, over there, on the dais." The scholar pointed through the gathering of revellers toward the seat of power, where Novack had been sitting quietly throughout the feast. Red craned his neck, twisting and turning, struggling to glimpse the elusive fellow through the crowds. Then cursed his lack of height and the billowing clouds of tobacco smoke hampering the view. When the partying masses separated, leaving an unobstructed line of sight, the master frowned. "Oh, he was there a second ago. He must've gone to lie down. Understandable in the circumstances, he was a bit bruised and battered, shell-shocked even."

"You're certain he was here?"

"Of course I'm sure. I may be old, but I'm not a pea-brain. Here's the steward if you don't believe me." The stoic warden approached, supporting a comatose individual on one arm. Wittgenstein grasped the other. "Tell the chief here that Dr Novack has returned to us. He thinks I'm talking nonsense or I'm drunk, or both." The scholar's right eyebrow arched vertically across his forehead.

Struggling to support the drunken man's weight now they'd ground to a halt, the porter grunted through gritted teeth. "You are eminently sensible master and anyone who suggests the contrary is illogical. To answer your question, yes, Dr Novack's back where he belongs. If you're wondering where he is, he retired to his room, asked me to pass on his apologies for not staying until the end. He's exhausted."

"Did he say where he's been?" Red asked, the heady atmosphere churning his stomach as he grappled with the doctor's unexplained reappearance.

"No. And before you ask, I didn't interrogate him. He's been through enough, and honestly, it doesn't really matter. He's home and life can return to normal." With that neat summary, the steward gave a curt nod and continued outside, dragging his charge like a sack of rocks.

Chapter Thirty-Eight

Quill crept forward in the darkness, using her fingertips to find a path through the tight, low tunnel. The sound of her breathing intensified in the pitch black, damp earthiness filling her nostrils as her pulse raced. Her mind played tricks as she imagined being buried alive in the cramped space. Unable to see anything, she tuned into the signals firing from her remaining senses, the angle of her feet hinting that the hole was leading her further beneath the earth. As the minutes passed, she fell into a monotonous flow—left hand grazing the side wall a metre ahead, followed by her corresponding foot, then repeated on the right. Now and then, as she shuffled, the murmur of whimpering pierced the gloom, spurring her onwards, despite every instinct telling her this was madness, to turn back before she got hurt, or worse.

Time had no reference point in the underground depths, but the plummeting temperature suggested that the corridor descended deeper and deeper with each footstep. Hypnotised by the repetitive shuffling, she stepped straight into the tunnel wall, which was now in front of her. Disoriented and frustrated, she spun, panting, until her spine hugged the spot she'd collided with seconds earlier. Paused, taking stock, Quill exhaled. Then, keeping her left hand in contact with the surface behind her, she groped into thin air with the other until her fingertips touched solid rock. The channel dog-legged ninety-degrees to the right, she realised, repositioning herself before continuing her painful shuffle. As the narrow pit widened, an infinitely more dangerous proposition in the blackness, she lurched from side to side. Until, ahead, a faint orange glow flickered, a beacon calling her onward in the gloom.

The soft gleam of the lantern pulled her like a magnet towards the end of the duct, from which she stepped into a broad tubular chamber. With a gaping mouth, incredulous, she peered up, then over the edge of the ledge beneath her. Stunned, she was two-thirds of the way up a wide shaft which stretched high above and plummeted below her moccasin feet.

What is this place?

Perpendicular to the vertical tube, at regular intervals, above and below, were the openings to crosscut channels, each shored up with wooden struts, levels joined by ramps and spiral steps.

Perhaps the torch was a trap, drawing unsuspecting victims like me into the open with its magnetic glow. This would be the perfect hunting ground for an underground beast, stalking its prey in the tunnels.

Despite the sound of hammering in her rib cage, nothing moved apart from the incessant *drip, drip, plop, splosh, splash* of water seeping through the walls.

Stop being so over-dramatic.

The simple but ingenious wooden engineering pointed to a less fantastical explanation of the scene. Human hands had built this mysterious structure, and the lantern proved that at least one person had visited recently. Unsure where to venture next, it occurred to her she hadn't heard the mournful whimpering in a while. As she scratched her scalp, a sudden blast of briny air from the shaft below took her by surprise, sending her scuttling from the edge as the world spun violently. Panicked by the attack of vertigo, Quill clamped her eyelids shut, grounding her body against the rock-face. She gripped the floor, toes curling through damp moccasins, waiting for the moment to pass.

Thankful to still be alive, she accepted the universe's sign to go down. After unhooking the lamp at the top of the stairs, her shadow distended, and she whipped around, convinced the monstrous creature from her imagination had joined her. But nothing was there. So, taking each rickety step one at a time, Quill headed deeper into the shaft.

※ ※ ※ ※ ※ ※ ※

"301, 302, 303, and 304." Quill counted under her breath, then returned to solid earth. With tunnels stretching in both directions, she dithered, unsure which way to turn. Then, deciding to leave things to fate, she scooped up a strange pebble—one half grey, the rest green.

Grey means left, green go right.

Tossing it into the air, she watched it fly. Over and over it tumbled before gravity won, pulling it onto the dirt where it rolled, settling grey side up.

Left it is, then.

Along the shaft in that direction, she strode. Quill hadn't got far when the hole widened, opening into a vast chamber. Hewn and sculpted, a space excavated from the clay with silver-grey banded veins running in all directions. From this cavern, there were nine fresh corridors, fanning out like sunflower petals, rendering the pebble trick ineffective. She recalled an old bedtime story, a favourite she'd begged her father to retell countless times. The tale of an intrepid explorer lost in a deadly maze hunting for treasure. She nibbled her fingertips, seeking a solid approach to avoid the same fate. With thoughts of the stone still percolating, she chose the farthest left tunnel.

At the edge of this passage was a fresh dizzying flight of stairs, as she walked onto the top step, she froze, focusing her attention on her ears, convinced she'd picked up a sound below her, but there was nothing, so she continued her spiralling journey.

As she reached the next level, she heard it again—faint, a hum, a rumble, something unidentifiable. Spurred on, ignoring the tiredness in her legs, Quill followed the noise, which crescendoed, swelling and rolling in waves as the tunnel twisted and turned. Suddenly the confusion unravelled, no longer an indistinct buzz. She heard voices, chattering and laughing, and something else. A hypnotic rhythm, edgy, dark as treacle, the tumultuous sound swelled as she rounded a corner. Heart hammering, lost for words, Quill froze to the spot, unable to believe her eyes.

🐾 🐾 🐾 🐾 🐾 🐾 🐾

Practised in the art of invisibility, Quill slipped into the shadows at the chamber's boundary, trying to take in the view. The place itself was a geological wonder. It simulated the tectonic plates of a gargantuan mythical creature. Each scale resembled a stained glass window framed in grey stone. Though touching their translucent, shining surfaces, they weren't glass—mineral, perhaps, but unique.

Brass lanterns attached to pure white stalactites hung from the ceiling. Each deadly pointed arrow grew like fungus to form a spellbinding, glittering mop of hairlike rocks. Though nothing compared to the sound, which hypnotised her into submission. The haunting song of the Lilith bird paling into insignificance in comparison, as she realised it was music.

Despite the enormity of the space, the cave was full of men in black dinner suits. A veritable army of masculinity of various ages, shapes and sizes, and all breaking a fundamental rule of Scolarian society. Though she couldn't escape a simple truth, her presence meant she was complicit in the crime. Torn between behaving like a good citizen and revelling in the new experience, she did nothing. Rooted to the spot, absorbing the excitement and danger through her pores, she was a sponge soaking up a lake. Keen to learn more, she skirted the perimeter to find a better vantage point, creeping to the business end of the room, toward the blaring music. Oblivious to anything except the sound, stunned, she hummed a tune she didn't know but seemed instinctively to get. With a life of their own, the notes swept from her nose and throat.

Like breathing.

Effortless, filling her with rapturous joy, sweeping aside misgivings and fear, she closed her eyelids and submitted to the mind-bending experience. With her spirits soaring, a voice, thick as syrup, expertly weaved through the music like an adder in the grass and though the sound's creator wasn't speaking any language she understood, the words hit distinct tones in a colourful tapestry which complemented the tune. Quill edged closer still, the crowd thinning as she approached the source of the melodic magic. As soon as she found an unobstructed view, she recognised the intriguing tableau as if someone had lifted it from the little black book's pages. A group of women strummed or blew into odd contraptions that emitted the glorious refrain. Stood in their midst, a singer, curvaceous with long, languid limbs. A shimmering mane of silver hair coiled around her from crown to toe was the singular thing separating her from total nakedness.

For a second, their eyes met through the mass of onlookers, a jolt of pleasure and terror hurtling through Quill's body, wrapped in one confusing sensation. Bewildered, hoping she'd imagined the moment, she couldn't help thinking she recognised the enigmatic woman from somewhere.

Chapter Thirty-Nine

The boy examined his shoes. Awkward as he stood in the doorway in his brown uniform, watching Red's careful but comprehensive search of Dorian Paine's study. "Please don't tell him I let you in here. No-one's allowed in this room," said the defecto, his squeaky voice quavering.

"Well, I won't mention it if you don't, and anyway, you had no choice. So if there's any trouble, send Mr Paine my way."

"That's easy for you to say. You haven't got to serve him."

"Why? Is a bad employer?"

"Not exactly. I'm lucky to have the job, 'specially as I get to live here, which gets me out of the DAQ, but sometimes, he gets angry over little things, then he's scary."

"Does he harm you?" Red paused his finger-tipped exploration of the handful of technical drawings laying in a neat pile on Paine's drawing board. The boy's nervous tone piqued his interest. He was young, twelve, thirteen at a push, slim built with curly brown hair and a smattering of freckles across a snub nose. A child, yet he was living with someone who frightened him.

I know what that feels like.

"No, not so far, but he's a big man. When he's yelling at you for bringing the wrong cigar, his face all pink and sweaty like it's about to burst, it's as if he's waiting for any excuse. He calls me terrible names. No-one would care if he hurt me, and who would know? I'm alone in this house."

"What about your family?"

"We only meet once a year, during the Ortus."

At the mention of the celebration, the child's features lit up, caramel coloured eyes twinkling under the lamplight, a radiant smile spreading across his angular cheekbones.

"So you'll be seeing them soon, then?" asked Red, throwing an emotional lifeline into the midst of the difficult conversation.

"Yes. My mother's in science. Her protector loves cake, chocolate flavour and lets her bake two for the Ortus, as it's a special occasion. One for him, the other for us. I can't wait."

It was impossible not to feel guilty as the young defecto gushed over sweet treats, something Red took for granted. A poignant reminder of the divide between the defectos and society. It wasn't a great sensation, and knowing nothing he did could change things, multiplied his discomfort. "I know you think you're alone, and I understand you're separated from your parents, but I hear how much they mean to you. I'm sure they think the same. That doesn't change because you don't live in the same place. If you're ever in trouble, reach me at Guard HQ. You know how to do that, correct?"

"Yes, thanks."

"Is there any coffee in the house?" Red needed a few moments alone, but chose not to hurt the boy's feelings.

Nodding, the boy said, "Yes, sir."

"It's chief, but you can call me Red."

🐾 🐾 🐾 🐾 🐾 🐾 🐾

To be frank, not knowing what you were looking for rendered the act of searching through someone's possessions difficult. Skills learned in theory were never quite the same in practice, but he refused to let it hold him back. The key to success lay in nurturing a receptive mind, making connections between what you saw, and linking that to your knowledge of a person of interest. The books, pens, instruments and drawings made sense for Dorian Paine's job. Nothing out of the ordinary raised any suspicion. Though that wasn't at all surprising, anyone with secrets rarely left incriminating objects on display.

With his attention on the trio of drawers beneath the drawing board, Red's heart sank, disappointed to discover they were unlocked. Either Paine assumed that nobody would rifle through his desk, or he had nothing to hide. Disappointment grew as he opened each individually. The top two rammed to bursting with a vast assortment of coloured pencils, which, without exception, were sharpened into piercing points. Pencil clips and rubbers, elastic bands and business cards lived in the middle compartment, each occupying their own quadrant. Still hoping the deepest bottom drawer might prove more fruitful, Red groaned inside as he slid it open to find a row of empty cardboard hanging folders.

After slamming the drawer shut, he rubbed his elbow, irritated but not yet ready to give up trying.

If I needed to stash something, where would I put it?

As he surveyed the room for inspiration, the lack of options struck him, and he wondered if this was a massive waste of energy.

Maybe it's time to shift to the rest of the building.

Then he remembered the break-in at Mordecai Templar's residence and scrutinised the impressive collection of books behind Dorian's desk. Weighing up whether it might make greater sense to start on the bedroom, he decided it was worth a look. He began with the top shelf in the case nearest to the door. Working methodically, he slid out each title, rotating the volumes through ninety-degrees until the pages faced down. Followed by vigorous shaking, searching for anything hidden between the sheets. The monotonous task lulled him into a rhythm—slide, turn, shake, replace, slide, turn, shake, replace—until cramp set into his wrist and fingers from the repetitive motion, forcing him to take a rest.

Once he'd flexed his digits to ease the discomfort, he returned to work, finishing the lowest ledge before shifting anti-clockwise to the next unit and starting again.

"What are you doing? No-one touches his books."

The unexpected squeak startled him, interrupting the conveyor belt system. "Don't sneak up on people. You made me jump," said Red, index finger poised above the spine of a leather-bound book. The rattle of china and a bitter earthy aroma assaulting his nostrils faded into the environment as he continued his efforts.

"Cream? Sugar?"

"Huh?" Red mumbled, his clumsy refreshment ruse forgotten for a split-second. "Oh, for the coffee, I almost forgot, black, lots of sugar, thanks." With his back to the boy, he pulled the next text. "I suppose you see all the visitors to the household?"

"Mostly, yes. Important men like Mr Paine don't open their own doors."

"Of course, ridiculous question. What about recently? Any unusual callers?"

"Nope, the same people, protectors, colleagues from this district."

"Mordecai Templar?"

"Here's the coffee. Mr Templar has been here a lot over the last couple of weeks."

"Any idea why?"

"Work, I assume, but I'm not sure."

"How about Dr Novack?" The silence that followed prompted Red to stop mid-flow and confront the boy, who was biting his bottom lip, a crimson flush rising to his forehead.

"Sorry, it's weird talking about this, especially as the doctor is such a powerful man. I can't afford to lose this job."

"Understood, but whatever you tell me is confidential. I won't share the source of any information you give me. Okay?"

The boy nodded, cocking his head to the side, hesitating. "I thought they were friends. Mr Paine regularly visits Montague Hall, but last week, Dr Novack came here. He's never done that before. Mr Paine got angry I'd answered the door, said to leave them to it, didn't want me upsetting such an important visitor. It was late by the time he left, after 10 pm. I heard the front door close, then—" The youngster faltered, wrapping both arms around his body. "Mr Paine said, 'One day, you'll get what you deserve.' He didn't see me. I was at the far end of the hallway and the lights were off. That's how he gets, nasty and rude, probably drank too much brandy. It's his favourite."

"What did he mean?"

"Dunno, possibly nothing. Like I said, he's horrible when he drinks. The next morning he was fine, like a different person. It's what scares me the most. You don't know who you'll get. I guess I'll leave you to it. I've got chores to do."

"No problem." The chief paid no attention until something fell out of the book that he was shaking. With lightning reflexes, he grabbed at it with his free hand, catching it between his fingertips. The gloss white paper and the size told him it was a photograph and turning it over the image of a young girl surprised him. "Hang on," he said to the boy's rear before he slipped out with the tray. "Who's this?"

The boy spun, squinting, the picture too small to detect at a distance. Red held the photo at arm's length, crossing the room. "Have you ever seen this girl?"

"No. I think I'd have remembered her."

You and me both.

The adolescent female was striking. Onyx eyes fringed with sweeping brown lashes stared out from rosy, flawless skin. A prominent forehead complimented an oval face. Her luscious lips parted, sufficient to disclose a gap between her front teeth. Although there was no obvious familial resemblance, he wanted to be sure. "Mr Paine's wife? Daughter?"

"No, Mr Paine never married. He always says he's too busy for a family."

"What about a cousin or a niece?"

"It's possible, but I've never heard him talking about relatives. Perhaps if he did, it might cheer him up."

Dorian Paine was another example of a powerful representative of Scolarian society who'd chosen duty over family. *Much like my father.* "That's an interesting theory and you're probably right."

The compliment elicited a smile as the boy took off with the empties, while Red pondered the picture. After several minutes, during which he realised that staring at the portrait couldn't help him discover who she was, he laid it on the design board. Then slotted the volume into position on the rack, ready for the next. Suddenly, the title on the spine jumped at him, *Dressmaking for the Modern Woman*, a pastel green hard cover which sat next to two related titles: *How to Crotchet for Beginners* and *How to Run a Household*. As he pulled them out together, their pristine spines suggested they'd hardly, if ever, been touched. Although it wasn't beyond the bounds of possibility that Paine had a penchant for handicrafts, Red thought it unlikely, particularly since the man was a workaholic who devoted his life to architecture. A theory formed, connecting the unidentified girl and the trilogy of texts, which otherwise were odd additions to the library. A cursory glance at the covers explained nothing.

About to return them to the shelf, he cursed himself for getting sidetracked on irrelevant details. In his haste, the housekeeping guide fell from his grasp, landing open to reveal an inscription on the inside cover. Words written in small lettering, crammed in tight, which he recognised as Paine's from the paperwork.

To my darling Elena,

On the occasion of our engagement. Let us bless our household with love and happiness.

Forever yours

Dorian

Chapter Forty

"Just try a slug. You won't regret it. This stuff's like nothing you've ever experienced. I mean, this place is amazing, and it's hard to imagine living without it, but this lifts things to a whole new level. Here, have some. It's free. They're so generous here."

Quill overheard snippets of conversation, replicating the same topic in varying degrees at most of the tables. She'd slipped away from the magnetic pull of the singer, the enigmatic woman escaping after her mesmerising performance. Now, nothing but the music and chatter remained. She was invisible amongst the frivolity as she was in the city, though she should have stuck out like a blood-red dress among the black suits and bow ties. Nobody challenged her or registered her presence and she'd almost relegated the electric sensation of catching the singer's eye to nothing greater than anxiety.

Eager to uncover what the seated gentlemen were recommending to their companions, raving about its mind blowing effects, she loitered, spine pressed against a stunning example of the rare stained glass rock. It wasn't difficult to wait. The melody swayed, notes dancing end-to-end through a tune and onto the next. She tapped her foot, her body compelled to mimic the rhythm, a subconscious primal instinct to move. An unquenchable thirst which reminded her of how she felt when reading books. Lost in the pages, oblivious to life around her, a perfect location to escape to, where she wasn't alone or unloved. Unlike her literary pastime, music was illegal, considered dangerous by the Protectorate, leading hearts and minds off the enlightened path. In her late night discussions with the master, when the library was silent and sombre, he'd explained that the arts spawned selfish men who desired beauty and pleasure for themselves at the expense of working for humanity. It made sense then, black-and-white logic, laws justified. The Meraki's existence, those who worshipped creativity, expunged from history. Yet experiencing the sound, Quill knew nothing would ever be the same.

Tuned into the conversations, a man seated at the table ahead, moustache curled at the tips and shining with wax, spoke to his companion opposite. "Have you seen Mordecai tonight?"

"No. Nor last night either."

"Maybe he's decided it's too dangerous after all. He's been taking an enormous risk leaving the grove while they're all holed up there. He's braver than me."

"Or he's reckless. A brash show-off who'll get us all caught. It scares the life out of me thinking about it. I nearly didn't come myself."

"Relax." The gentleman twirled the point of his whiskers with a stubby fingertip. "You worry too much. No-one will find us. It's not like anyone's going to reveal this location. We've got a lot to lose and nothing to gain by doing so."

The observation that Mordecai Templar frequented the place, whatever it was, was a surprising but crucial piece of information. Quill surmised that he, too, had discovered the entrance tunnel leading from Guidance Grove to the labyrinth under the city. A detail which explained the damp soil caked on the soles of his shoes. That his death didn't appear to be public knowledge suggested that perhaps he was the only escapee from the grove. Still, she couldn't shift the voice nagging her that a connection existed between his murder and this illegal gathering, though she wasn't planning to ask questions and draw attention to herself. Then the chap with the groomed facial hair slid a hand into his jacket, retrieving an item from the inner pocket, an object too small to see enclosed within his palm. Then he placed it on the tabletop between them, leaning in close. "Here, you need to relax. There's more where that came from."

"I'm not sure. Do you know what's in it?"

"Nope, can't say I do, but I know how it makes me feel. Look at me, I'm fine. All these rules and regulations, telling people how to live their lives. How is this hurting anybody? The Protectorate's been controlling us for too long. We work, we sleep, we work some more. Is that really all there is? It grinds you down, day after day, this joyless reality."

"I didn't realise you felt that way. It's not so bad. I love my practice, knowing that I'm contributing to the science community. My latest study of sunspots is yielding amazing results."

"You always were a book nerd, no offence. If I'm honest, I envy you. Engineering is okay. It puts food on the plate, but it's hardly going to change the world. Will you try this or not?"

"Thanks, but no, I think I'll pass."

"Suit yourself." The whiskered fellow reached for the miniature vial, lifting it above the counter while removing the glass stopper. In the lamplight, Quill saw an iridescent shimmer of multicoloured luminescence. As he set the vessel to his lips, tipping his chin and pouring the contents into his mouth, she glimpsed a G on the bottom. Quill's mind filled with unwanted images: Professor Hawkin face down, naked in the reading room, Ivy Penrose, his murderer, delirious and unpredictable, and the poor forgotten defectos, Bill and Finn and Val, the girl's tear-drop scar forever burned into her memory.

Unable to stop, Quill shot forward, striking the man's fist, swatting the flask from his jaws. The blow sent the vial flying until it landed perilously near to an adjacent group of men, smashing into thousands of tiny razor-sharp pieces, the liquid remnants splattered across the floor. "No! Don't drink it. It's deadly."

Quill confronted her mistake. Her violent intervention attracting precisely the scrutiny she'd planned to avoid, as the patrons closest suddenly noticed her as if she'd painted herself bright orange. The smashed bottle created a ripple effect, like a tiny pebble dropped in water, a wave of judging eyes turning toward her at the epicentre, until they all noticed her. Unsure how they'd react, she didn't have to wait long for a signal as a disembodied, menacing cry came from somewhere in the crowd. "Get her!"

Then the chamber erupted.

Chapter Forty-One

Although extra security at Guidance Grove was a good thing, Red found the delay frustrating as he waited in the oppressive heat. When the steward finally arrived, the chief had roasted in his own skin for at least twenty minutes. Thermal energy pulsing from the supernova made the temperature unrelenting, even as the sun dipped behind the trees which dominated the grounds.

Relieved, following the administrator inside, male bodies littered the turf below the entrance, proof that the festival was producing its fair share of casualties.

"Apologies for the wait. As you can see, we have our hands somewhat full with the feast." The steward gesticulated toward the prone figures, many of whom were snoring like grunting pigs.

"Rather you than me," said Red, wiping the sweat from his forehead with the back of his hand. "I need to speak to Dorian Paine at once. Take me to him, please."

The warden stalled, using his person as a barrier, his arms crossed over his chest in an obvious show of authority. "*Feast* is pivotal to Scolarian society. I don't expect a guard to understand, but I will allow no-one to spoil the celebration. I think it might be best if you visited tomorrow."

It was plain from the body language that he meant every word, but Red had a case to solve and wasn't willing to be waylaid any longer. The dilemma to consider, and quickly, was whether the problem required brains or brawn? He was sure he'd have the edge over the steward if things turned physical, but that wasn't his style. Instead, he opted for stealth. "Can I trust you to keep a secret?"

The steward's shrewd eyes lit up, shoulders relaxing, arms falling to his side as he leaned in closer, excited by the prospect of an alliance. "Have no fear, chief. You've come to the right man."

Brushing aside the fact he'd told a white lie, questions of morality forgotten, Red was relieved to bypass the steward and enter the building. If the scene on the front grass was hard to stomach, the interior view was positively vomit inducing. Dishevelled heaps of flesh littered the Judgement Chamber and the smell of cigar smoke and stale beer assaulted him. Most protectors showed no sign of stopping, despite listing precariously like newborn deer and talking unintelligible gibberish at a raucous volume, behaviour which served as a reminder of why he didn't drink.

Dorian Paine sat with his back to the door, conversing with a tall, gawky fellow who sported a striking hooked nose. The architect gesticulated with a brandy glass, unaware he was subjecting his companion to a complete body wash in the caramel coloured liquor.

"Mr Paine, sorry to interrupt, but I need to have a word with you."

"Eh?" The designer twisted his head. Cross-eyed from trying to focus, the inebriated specimen squinted, screwing up his features while he tried to reply, the words catching around his tongue. "Can't you see we're busy?" Although the question sounded more like a snake being strangled as he slurred through it.

"It can't wait, no. Can we talk in private?"

"I'm not leaving the feast and you can't make me. I have nothing to hide, so say what you want, then leave."

The malice in the man's voice was palpable and Red recalled the defecto boy's fear, the architect's mask of propriety ripped off by the brandy coursing through his veins, revealing a sneering, angry soul.

"Okay, if you're sure."

Red was about to ask a question when Paine's colleague interjected, jumping out of his seat, wringing his hands. "Please excuse me, I'm tired. I guess I'll go to bed."

"Don't be ridiculous Felix. We're just getting started. Stay and have a drink," said the architect, tugging his colleague's jacket sleeve.

The poor harangued gentleman stared at Red, then at Paine, an apologetic look in his eye. "No, thank you. I'll leave you to it."

Then Dorian turned ugly, a belittling scowl invading his cheeks as he yanked harder. The slight victim toppled into his chair with a thud as spit flew from the corners of Paine's mouth. "Sit. You're not going anywhere."

In that single act, Red recognised the man's calibre—he was a bully—it made the next part much easier. "If you insist on doing this in public, I'm happy to oblige. Where is Elena?"

At the mention of the girl's name, Paine's complexion bleached. His lower lip quivered, and tears welled in his eyes. It wasn't the reaction Red expected, but the strength of the response confirmed he needed to keep digging. This obscure investigation technique proved useful where you had no concrete evidence, yanking on a single loose thread, following it as it unravelled, hoping it might lead somewhere important. The probability of it working was slim to none, but it was worth a shot.

With the now empty glass discarded, Paine stood, wiping his lips on a sleeve, then rubbing his palms on his trousers, steadier on his feet than expected. Red's query seemed to have broken through Dorian's alcohol induced brain fog. "Perhaps you're right. Let's visit Wittgenstein's office."

Chapter Forty-Two

The black-suited owner of the moustache lurched forward, grabbing a handful of Quill's tunic. Acting on adrenaline and instinct, she jerked right, an unforeseen motion which took him by surprise as she broke free. Encircled by angry revellers, hyperventilating with fear, she weighed her options, such as they were. Desperate to disappear, Quill wagered on the assembled crowd's less than sober state. "Oh no, the guard's here." She jabbed a finger toward the exit tunnel and remarkably, the farcical ruse worked, as dozens of terrified patrons turned away. In those few precious seconds, she ran, keeping low, an easy feat for someone so short. By the time the throng realised the trick, Quill had a slight advantage, but the pounding footsteps over her shoulder signalled that the deadly race had barely just begun.

With her heart thumping, Quill dodged and weaved, threading her way through the seething mass of bodies in the lamp-lit grotto, heading for the entrance shaft. The second it came into view, the blank void suddenly overflowed with a tight bank of black-clad legs. A mob had answered the alarm call, darting around the vacant edge of the cavern to cut her off—they'd succeeded. The surrounding sounds changed, the noise muffled as if she were underwater. While her lungs screamed for oxygen, her gaze darted from side-to-side, searching for a fresh escape route. Confused, seeing nothing but enemies, Quill ducked. Hunched, sprinting left, she hoped to find an alternative duct somewhere along the outer wall.

"Grab her."

"Don't let her go."

"Where is she?"

"There, she's there."

"This way, here."

Anxious shrieks and dissonant tones called over each other, mingling with the soaring music, overloading her senses until she wanted to scream at them to stop. But Quill had to keep going, so she battled onward, clamping her palms to her ears while running for her life.

Eventually the vibration of feet receded, but she was too afraid to turn and check, in case it slowed her progress. As she was losing hope, Quill's spirits soared as a new hole appeared and she bolted inside, grateful to be swallowed whole by the darkness.

Soon after her daring breakout, she knew she'd lost her way. She'd assumed the alternative path would loop back to the start, enabling her to retrace her steps by consistently turning right, the opposite of the choice dictated by the pebble. She was wrong. The substitute course reminded her of the squat, cramped rabbit-hole at the start of her underground odyssey. As she crouched, still trying to run, no-one followed.

Do they know something I don't?

Presently, the floor's elevation dropped further, leading her deeper. The muted sound of voices and the occasional thudding footfall startled her. She jumped, waiting to be caught by the pursuing horde, but she soon learned she was hearing the echo of noises elsewhere in the labyrinth of tunnels. As each minute passed, the cries sounded further and further in the distance. Her panic subsiding as her racing gait diminished to a trot until finally she was strolling again.

Without warning, the narrow tube opened into a further gigantic cavern. Silent and empty, an underground lake occupied the centre, surrounded by a glittering crystalline shore. White spongy growths like cauliflowers littered the ceiling and an overpowering smell burned her throat as her eyes streamed. A foul sulphurous odour of brine devouring rock and a crunching beach suggested that the remarkable cave system was some type of prehistoric geological salt deposit, the shafts proving that humans had at some point exploited it. Probing her mind for a reference to such an enterprise in any of the thousands of books she'd read proved fruitless.

How could such a structure vanish from history?

The sudden plaintive note of the dog's whimpering froze her legs, reminding her why she was there. Except now, the chilling howl was close—close enough to follow. Spurred on, she raced, circling the glassy, stinking lagoon until she reached a tunnel on the opposite side and plunged head-first into blackness.

Chapter Forty-Three

"I don't know anyone called Elena." Paine lowered himself into a chair, calm and emotionless, the colour returning to his cheeks.

Worried that the short walk to Wittgenstein's office had given the man a chance to sober up and straighten out his story, Red understood the need to keep up the pressure. "You didn't say that a minute ago. Anyway, I think you're lying. I found the housekeeping book you gave her to mark your engagement. It's a serious offence, misleading the guard."

The architect launched forwards, his cheeks crimson, unable to keep his usual poise. "What were you doing rummaging through my house without my permission? I'll be making a complaint about this to Tedesko. You'll be sorry."

With the bully returned to the surface, Red said nothing, choosing to respond to the threat with nonchalant silence.

Dorian bit his bottom lip, waiting for a reaction that never came. "Well, don't just sit there. I don't have all day."

"It's interesting that you mention Tedesko. We'll get to him in a second." Paine met Red's remark by frantically running his fingers through his sparse hair. "Let's start again, shall we? Who is Elena?"

The architect paced back and forth before throwing himself into his and perching on his hands, tapping his heels together as his legs wobbled like pistons. "An acquaintance from a long while. I haven't seen her in years. Why is this important?"

Electing to ignore the question on the basis he had no clue, Red said, "She was more than an acquaintance, Mr Paine. You were engaged to be married according to the inscription. Stop wasting my time."

"It was a lifetime ago. A period in my life I choose to forget. If you must know, she broke off the engagement. She did me a favour. I wouldn't be where I am today if I'd shackled myself to a wife and family."

"Where is she?"

"I've told you. No idea."

Paine's story sounded plausible to a degree, but Red still couldn't shift the feeling there were details the designer wasn't prepared to admit. For now, he moved on to the next topic. "Where were you on the morning of Mordecai Templar's death?"

"What? Surely you don't think I was involved?"

"It's routine. Please, answer the question."

Paine kneaded his forehead with his knuckles. "Much like everyone else, I got up early. Ate breakfast in my room, then went straight to the Judgement Chamber to meet the master. We were together from that moment onwards."

"And your bedroom is in the same wing as Templar's?"

"Now look here. I don't appreciate what you're insinuating."

"I'm not insinuating, merely stating the facts. Let's move on. Why did Dr Novack visit your house the evening before he disappeared?"

"What's the relevance of that? Novack's back, poor fellow, seems a bit off colour, if you ask me. I wonder if he's had a blow to the head. Anyway, I've answered this already. We're old friends, and he came for a drink."

"My understanding is that he never visits you at home. You always go to Montague Hall. What was different that night?"

"Who said that? Who have you been talking to? Was it that disgusting boy?"

Paine's rage simmered again, threatening to boil over at any second, and Red's conscience twinged. "I'm not at liberty to say. Can you give me an answer, please?"

"Honestly, I don't understand what you want from me. Yes, usually I go to him. Novack's a busy fellow. As for why he accepted an invitation to my place, you'd have to ask him."

"How do you know Olga Blackwood?"

Dorian paused, staring into space, a vein throbbing above his left temple, apparently derailed by the total change of direction.

"Mr Paine, how did you meet Mrs Blackwood?"

After a brief interlude of utter silence, the architect flinched, a sheen of sweat glistening on his top lip as he whispered. "Who?"

"Tell me about your relationship with Omari Tedesko?"

"What's his connection to this? You're confusing me with all these questions."

"It's a simple question."

"It's an inane thing to ask. We're protectors. We serve the city, nothing more, nothing less."

Exasperated by the designer's ability to dodge his questioning, Red felt sure he was on to something. Somehow there was a link between Paine, Tedesko and Novack and the death of Blackwood's son. He longed to put the allegation to the fellow, but there wasn't sufficient evidence to tie the events together, and he knew it. Once again, he remembered Jim Ross's nuggets of wisdom and decided against career suicide. The clearest avenue of attack had to be Mordecai's death, so he pivoted. It was still a gamble, but he reckoned the odds of success were higher.

"Dorian Paine, I'm arresting you on suspicion of the murder of Mordecai Templar under Section 1 (b) of the Scolarian justice code. I'm also placing you into secure custody until we release the council from Guidance Grove, pursuant to emergency power 26. You have the right to notify a protector of your arrest. Would you like me to contact someone?"

The horrified bug-eyed expression on Paine's face was enough to terrify small children, mouth gaping to reveal remnants of macerated lunch in his teeth.

"Mr Paine, do you need somebody with you?"

After several painful seconds, during which saliva dribbled from the corner of his slack lips, the architect stammered. "Wittgenstein, get me Wit."

The door opened to the sight of Master William Wittgenstein in full flight, barging past the crimson-faced steward, throwing his arms in the air. "Explain this intrusion at once. There's no time for games, chief. We're in the middle of *Feast*, and I have to organise the Ortus."

Stepping aside, Red cleared the path for the venerable scholar who took up position behind his desk, grabbing a handful of robe and twisting it across his thighs as he sat.

"No-one is playing games. Murder is not a joke, sir."

"Of course not, that's not what I meant, and you know it. I assume you're referring to Mr Templar's unfortunate death."

"His murder, yes."

"But you can't honestly believe Mr Paine's involved? He was with me all morning, trying to secure the city's future."

"Not *all* morning."

"Are you calling me a liar?" asked the scholar, sounding indignant.

"No, sir, but maybe you're forgetting the period before you met in the chamber. Mr Paine admits he had breakfast alone, in his bedroom, and he had to pass Templar's accommodation on his way through, and I'm sure there's something else he's not telling me." The guardsman flicked his head in the architect's direction, causing the designer to shift like he'd sat on a pine cone. "I expect between us, we can figure out whatever this is all really about."

While rubbing his chin, the ancient academic went cross-eyed as he stared at the chief down his nose. "Sorry, you've lost me. Understand about what?"

"That's what I'm hoping to find out, but we're missing one important piece of the puzzle."

"Huh? What's that then?"

"Not what, who."

"Oh, for goodness' sake, please stop talking in riddles. You're giving me a diabolical headache."

"All will become clear. The steward is fetching him as we speak."

"Who? Fetching who?" asked Wittgenstein, the tendons taut in his neck like string.

Red paused, glancing between the scholar and Dorian Paine, the latter handcuffed to the chair, a furious scowl plastered on his mouth. With his attention focused on the architect's reaction, the guardsman finally broke the tension. "Dr Novack."

Chapter Forty-Four

Too late to prevent the inevitable, Quill fell, the narrow shaft absorbing her descent. She spun like dregs in a pipe whose walls were slick and impossible to grab. For the first few metres, she screamed for help, a lone moccasin slapping her cheek as it jettisoned skyward. Arms flailing, she tried to stop her descent, bile rising in her throat as her stomach churned. But nothing worked. As she remembered the angry mob, she clamped a hand over her mouth, dampening the sound of her desperate cries. The further she tumbled, the tighter the space became and Quill hoped that eventually it might break her fall, but the occasion never materialised.

Unexpectedly sighting a glimmer below her feet, she braced herself for impact. Instead, gathering momentum, she sensed her torso travelling upward, until at last she saw light at the end of the cylinder. Ejected like water from an upturned spout, she flew before gravity sent her hurtling downward. With her eyelids clenched shut, she curled into a foetal position and waited for what felt like an age to hit the ground.

Instead, the splash was a tremendous relief, the realisation that she hadn't broken all the bones in her body, convincing her to relax and uncurl. The sense of security was short-lived. As her skull sank, the freezing temperature sucked the air from her lungs, multiplying the force of the impact on her chest. It took all her mental strength not to inhale, brain screaming as water shot up her nose and the tang of salt filled her throat.

I'm drowning.

The words repeated over and over in her mind as each molecule of oxygen exited her airways, forming a perfect stream of bubbles to the surface.

Down she sank, further and deeper, until abruptly her survival instincts took charge. Cautiously opening her eyelids, she glimpsed light above and darkness below, confirmation at least that she wasn't upside down. Then, with every scrap of fortitude, she kicked with both legs, hands by her sides, forging a streamlined shape as she propelled her way to the top, unsure how much longer she could hold her breath before passing out. Finally, her head cleared the surface, and she gasped, sucking in huge, lusty gulps of air.

After several minutes of choking and spluttering, saline liquid poured from every orifice. Thankful to be alive, Quill circled a full three-hundred-and-sixty degrees, searching for a way out. What she discovered made her spirit sink. The shaft filling with water had sheer walls. Her own personal swimming bath. Dotted above were countless holes, like the one she'd dropped into before feeding into the pool, but they were out of reach.

It didn't take long for the frigid chill to take effect. Her teeth chattered uncontrollably as the thin brown tunic clung to her like a second skin, frosty briny fog escaping from her mouth and nostrils. The irony of not drowning simply to die of hypothermia inspired a chuckle, the vibration echoing macabrely around the spot. Lethargic, her body shutting down, Quill's eyes closed, her shaking toes erratic as she drifted in and out of consciousness. As she was about to slip under again, a crisp bark from above jolted her awake, feet mobilising as she flung her arms in circles, struggling to work out the sound's origin.

The sight of Luna's pink nose followed by the rest of her fluffy head and a hint of the white circle on her neck sent Quill's heart soaring. An injection of energy and determination she desperately needed. "Luna, you are here, girl. I've been hunting for you everywhere and now look at me. No idea how to escape this mess. I need help, particularly as I'm talking to a dog as if you can understand me."

The puppy barked, turning in tight circles in the duct so that Quill's view alternated between a furry black skull and a wagging tail, and she couldn't stop giggling, for a moment forgetting her predicament. Without warning, the puppy's excited yaps morphed into a low menacing growl as she disappeared from view.

Quill slapped her palms on top of the water in frustration. "Wait. Luna. Loona. Come back. Silly animal." Then she heard it. A faint rumbling in the distance, growing louder and louder as liquid dribbled from each of the openings above her. As the flow increased to a trickle, glassy-eyed, her whole body convulsing from the intense wet chill invading her bones, Quill suddenly understood where she was.

This isn't a random shaft, it's a drain, and from the number of gaps, not any drain.

She'd fallen into the main pipe, fed into by the innumerable others, and the burgeoning noise meant one terrifying thing. Someone somewhere had pulled out a plug, and she was about to drown all over again.

Chapter Forty-Five

The thundering uproar of multiple waterfalls ejecting thousands of gallons of frothing, salty brine drowned out Quill's screams as the gushing overflows battered her skull, forcing her repeatedly under the surface. With each fresh barrage came another full throttle ducking and a gut load of saline swept up her nose. It was relentless. Faced with the unmitigated terror of the realisation she was about to die, all logic deserted her as she tried to fight her way out of her plight. Helpless, waving her arms overhead, her efforts to divert the torrent did nothing to stem the tide, as it forced her under the lagoon.

Think brain, think!

But time and oxygen were in short supply. As she returned to the top, Quill hunted for a break in the endless streams as they blasted her from all directions. Between the spray and constant bobbing up and down, the task appeared impossible. By this point, she'd been in the pool far too long already. Numb, crinkled hands turned blue in the freezing temperatures as she lost all feeling in her lower limbs. Resigned to her fate, Quill stopped fighting, conserving the final molecules of energy as she slipped under one last time.

Downward, drifting like seaweed, leaving the pummelling chaos behind, tranquillity wrapped her in a deathly embrace as she slipped into a state of unconsciousness. Drawn once more into the black hole inhabiting her dreams, Quill let go, relinquishing hope, and with it, fear—a tiny insignificant speck in an ever-expanding universe. The ambition she'd prioritised, the anger and frustration of unfulfilled desires, vanished. The second that doubts crept in, there he was—father—his blood-red lips calling her to his side in his lilting voice. A sound reserved for her imagination over the last fifteen years. At peace, surrendering to the comforting sensation, nobody else mattered.

Father.

A jolt of reality shot through her like lightning, eyes wide, horrified at the expanse of brine above her.

If I don't act now, they won't just be digging my grave.

Energised by the need to save him from an unknown future, Quill kicked, struggling against the immense pressure exerted by the sheer volume of liquid. Blowing bubbles through her nostrils, battling against the overwhelming instinct to inhale, she ascended. A slow and painful process that felt like swimming through glue. Each time it seemed she was about to reach the surface, it didn't come, the depth perception under water working on parameters her brain couldn't compute.

Then she saw a shadow.

No, a change in colour in the wall of rock above my left ear.

Her spirits lifted, the slim prospect injecting a dose of much needed adrenalin into her legs. Ankles flicking like flippers, she reached above her shoulders with outstretched fingers, searching for the anomaly in the stone. With her heart hammering, her fingertips grasped the bedrock, curling over a hand-hold as she co-ordinated her feet and palms, hauling herself skyward, until her face burst clear with a triumphant outcry, sucking in oxygen in enormous juddering gulps.

With her chin resting in the air pocket, Quill clung to the lip of stone, the rest of her still submerged. She waited for her breathing to recover, eyelids closed as the brine dripped from her pert nose.

After several minutes' recuperation, she opened her eyes, understanding she wasn't out of danger yet. As far as she could tell, there were at most two viable choices. The first involved returning to the ice cold drain and gambling that she had sufficient strength to make it to the surface. It was impossible to know how much further she'd have to swim, nor whether the shaft continued to fill from the outlets. The thought of all those unknowns was enough to spike her pulse rate once again, her stomach churning as anxiety bit deep. The alternative option was to haul herself upward, into the airlock, hoping it might lead her out of the drainage system. As she peered into the blackness, Quill had no clue if it led anywhere. For all she knew, it was simply a random hole. Frozen and quivering, teeth chattering uncontrollably, she dithered, weighing the options, neither of which was appealing.

In the end, breathing seemed the most palatable consequence of two less than attractive propositions. Still clinging on with her wrinkled fingers, Quill let fly with her right hand, swinging her arm over her shoulder, settling her entire forearm into the opening, then repeated with the other. Hopeful, feeling more secure, she pressed on her forearms, driving her torso into the void in a rocking motion. With momentum building, after five repetitions of the exercise, Quill reckoned she was ready to move. On the next push, she bore down with all her strength, crying out in anguish as her joints endured the manoeuvre. The effort paid off as her face lurched toward the wall, above her waistline landing inside the gap, rib cage smashing into jagged stone, winding her. Black caterpillars crawled across her vision as she lay in the vent like a beached whale, waiting to rally from the agony.

Unsure how long she'd laid out to dry, Quill groaned, wondering if she'd passed out. As she shifted onto her elbows, pain shot through her forelimbs to her neck and skull. Then she hauled herself forwards. Forearm over agonising forearm, dragging her lower extremities free, her knees scraped along the rough rocky surface, which sandpapered through her skin. Swallowed by the eerie murk like a worm, the effort required multiplying with each passing second.

It didn't take long to regret the choice she'd made. The opening was free of water because the borehole climbed at an acute angle, and that wasn't her only problem. With each passing centimetre, the surrounding clay hugged tighter, the shaft narrowing, gripping her shoulders, followed by her hips and waist, flanks and legs. Until she was stuck, wedged tight between the bedrock.

Devastated, she planted her cheek on the damp rock, silent tears mingling with the salt water dripping from her sodden wavy hair.

Chapter Forty-Six

"He's not in his room," said the steward, flushed and gasping for breath, his usual unflappable demeanour deserting him. "I've checked the usual places, nothing, and no-one's seen him. I'm sorry, I don't understand it."

"Oh, for pity's sake, not again. He must be somewhere. Are you sure you searched properly?" Wittgenstein spat the knotted hair from his lips.

"Of course, master. We've looked in the bathrooms and outside in the grove. I even considered the kitchen and the laundry. He's nowhere to be seen."

Standing, throwing his arms into the air, the scholar said, "Typical. If you want a job doing well, do it yourself."

With a growing sense of unease, Red stepped forward, raising his palm at the agitated fellow. "It might be better if you stayed. I may need these cuffs, so I'm relying on you. Do not let Mr Paine leave under any circumstances. Agreed?"

With his hands on his hips, the master asked, "Do we have a choice?"

While wishing he'd insisted on speaking to Dr Novack sooner, Red jogged through the corridors. The steward's rapid fire directions took him to the side of the residential block reserved for the most senior protectors. Novack's chamber was spacious, functional, but not luxurious by any stretch of the imagination. Inside appeared normal. Even the plain white covers were still tight on all sides, the corners folded in perfect crisp lines by an expert hand.

If the doctor was tired, why didn't he lie on the bed?

Eager not to waste any further time, Red threw on the gloves always stashed in his jacket pocket. Then, yanked open the four drawers in the tall chest opposite the bedstead.

They were empty, as was the wardrobe. It made sense. To be frank, the physician's arrival hadn't exactly been conventional. All hope of immediately finding a clue to his whereabouts vanished, much like the man himself.

Think. Where would someone go to escape from the crowds when no-one can leave?

As he discounted the places checked by the warden—the wash-rooms, kitchen and laundry—Red hurried along the outer hallway, out of ideas and hoping for inspiration to strike. The sun slumped, slipping behind the outstretched arms of a majestic oak tree which dwarfed the jungle of wild flowers and grass. The meadow flourished beyond a padlocked door and the windows spanning the corridor. Hues of burnished orange, deep russet red, and fuchsia pink swept in bold strokes across the horizon like the layers of an exquisite cake. But the glorious panorama paled into insignificance compared to the guest star.

Iridescent, it flashed, dying with every pulse of energy, hurling a last desperate signal into the silent, impotent universe.

What was that?

A ripple spread through the thicket, barely visible in the creeping dusk, snaking through the thick grass, toward him at speed.

There's nobody there. It's only the wind.

Tired, hot, and hungry, Red turned away. Resigned, although searching each room might take hours, it was necessary. Headed for the next bedroom, he froze, convinced there was a sound outside. Certain he'd heard it again, the past few minutes fell into place. "Luna," he muttered, retracing his steps to the door. As he glanced down, the chief smiled, spotting the tip of a damp doggy nose poking through a gap between the door and its frame. The huge iron lock had deceived him.

"Where have you been, girl?" he said, pushing the entrance to let her in, crouching to ruffle the fur between her ears.

Luna barked, a sharp insistent alarm call repeated over and over, trotting into the wild meadow, ears pricked, then returning to repeat the cycle.

"Okay. I can hear you. There's something in there, right?" To which the puppy snarled, her muzzle sinking between her forepaws, tail thrashing like a whip. Then she was off, bounding, a hare disappearing into the undergrowth. "Wait," he called, trailing in the dog's wake as he sprinted after her, plunging into the unknown.

Though it was impossible to spot the black-and-tan bundle of vitality in the overrun meadow, it was enough to follow the yapping. Within minutes, he burst through the towering stalks onto a trodden pathway hidden from view. Free of obstacles, Red picked up the pace, revelling in the physical exertion, adrenalin coursing through his veins as he pounded the earth, pulverising his frustrations into the track.

Suddenly, he charged into a clearing, the ancient oak silently watching as he almost collided with the gnarled trunk. Red veered to the right, palms thrown in front of his face in a defensive manoeuvre as he tried to stop, but his forward momentum propelled him onward like an avalanche. On a collision course with the petite cavalier spaniel, she sat patiently, looking up at him with huge doleful eyes. "Argh," he said, waving his arms in her direction, "move, daft dog." But the pup stood her ground, staring at him as if she didn't know why he was making such a commotion. Centimetres from the dog's position, he leapt two-footed, leap-frogging the animal before landing in an unceremonious heap, knees collapsing under the weight as he skidded to a halt.

Stretched out in the dirt, the guardsman groaned, his muscles burning from the exertion. As he stared into the night sky, shielding his view from the fierce flashing supernova, a rough, wet slab of flesh slathered his cheek. Exuberant, panting, tongue drooping from the side of her mouth, Luna licked him until he laughed, submitting to the hilarity of the situation.

As he recovered, she trotted a short distance away, then turned to face him, her gaze fixed on his, long enough to secure his full attention.

Then Luna vanished.

🐾 🐾 🐾 🐾 🐾 🐾 🐾

"Luna. Luna?" Red searched in all directions for the errant pup. Suddenly her crown appeared, sticking out of the ground as if severed from her torso. Toward the animal, he crawled on his stomach, still nursing his injuries. The chief struggled to understand what he was seeing in the gloom, but as he crept nearer, the knot in his stomach expanded until it felt as if he'd ingested a rock. Sweat poured from his forehead, finding its way under his chin, and beneath his shirt, hugging his muscular frame. With a dry mouth, the guardsman swallowed, frequently licking his lips to produce some moisture, generating nothing but a mouthful of muck for his trouble. The earthy taste of soil and grit crunching between his teeth added to the discomfort as he spat sticky globules, which refused to move. No sooner had he reached her, the comforting sensation of her warm body soaking through his fingertips, than he faced his ultimate torment, realisation smacking him in the gut with a brick.

Luna's underground.

Even the thought was unbearable. A war broke out within him, fear screaming in one ear, drowning the voice of reason and public service in the other. As usual, terror transported him, hurtling through time to his childhood, to the hours spent locked in that cupboard under the stairs, the dark, tight space suffocating, squeezing the oxygen from his chest.

I can't go down there.

Red pushed onto his knees, wiping dust and sweat from his cheeks with the lining of his coat, removing the article of clothing. Moisture evaporated in the humid night time heat, and he shivered as the magic of his body worked on autopilot to regulate his core temperature. Luna yapped, skull darting into the hole and up and out on repeat. "I can't do it." He hung his head in shame, dizzy, acrid bile in the back of his throat as he fought the urge to retch.

Luna growled, a deep rumbling warning, to which he couldn't help a wry smile.

I'm a disappointment to my parents and now I can add a small dog to the list.

"Come on, girl, you've had your fun. You must be hungry. Let's find you some dinner." Patting his palms on the tops of his thighs, he called the pet to him, but Luna ignored the summons, growling as her furry head disappeared into the gap once more. Reluctantly peering over the edge, inside was pitch dark, which provoked an instant reaction. As if someone had stabbed a spear through his chest, flattening his lungs like popping a balloon.

Then, to his utter horror, the little animal reappeared, gripping an object between her sharp puppy teeth. After depositing the item in front of his knees, the pet lay flat on her belly behind it, staring up at him with mournful eyes. There was no mistaking the article—soaked through, exuding a strong, overpowering aroma of salty brine—a misshapen brown moccasin. As he dragged his gaze over the pitiful shoe, duty and responsibility hammered a hairline crack in the all-consuming terror.

There was no choice. Red had to face his worst nightmare.

Chapter Forty-Seven

"Quill. Quill, is that you?"

The smouldering, disembodied voice startled her, puncturing the unconscious bubble she'd drifted into inside the rock tomb. Wedged fast, a bloated cork in a bottle, she dismissed the sound as a figment of her imagination, simply the embodiment of a desperate desire to be rescued. She slipped back under, succumbing to utter despair.

"Wake up. Quill, you must wake up. I can't quite reach you. Give me your hand."

The faintest feather touch of skin on skin roused her from a fatal slumber, a flicker of promise in the gloom. Not convinced she wasn't hallucinating, the jagged fingernail scraping the tip of her middle finger suggested otherwise, and she welcomed the jolt of pain. Arm stretching as far as it could, she reached in desperation for the unknown palm as her voice cracked. "Please, I'm stuck, help me. Don't leave me here."

"Come towards me. There's not much farther to go."

"I can't." She swallowed the sob attempting to escape her throat. "I'm trapped."

"Try again."

Quill gripped the rock with her ragged and torn fingernails, discomfort ricocheting through both arms, travelling to her feet. Tendons straining on her neck, she pulled, her scraped knees driving into the dirt. She groaned with the effort, gritting her teeth to quash the screams that threatened to overcome her, but it made no difference. She was stuck. Panting from the exhaustion, she slumped, stammering between each laboured breath. "It's—no good. Can't—move."

The silence that followed stretched on interminably until the quiet convinced her that her unknown saviour had left. "Hello. Are you still there?"

"Of course, sorry, just thinking. See if you can roll onto your side. Maybe that will help. I'm so close to reaching you."

With the words of encouragement on repeat in her brain, Quill exhaled. Each molecule of air expelling from her breast in the vain hope she might shrink enough to pull clear. Then, twisting her torso, leading with her right shoulder in an upward arc, she rested on one forearm. Once set, she focused on the major obstacle, her lower half. While flicking her hip forwards and backwards, the bone scraped agonisingly across the rock face, snagging at regular intervals as she tried to complete the turn. The additional pain barely registered as an extra injury. Little by little, she worked her joint through ninety-degrees. Occasionally catching her breath, she focused on her father's image, which she conjured behind her eyelids. At last, her pelvis swung free, and she rolled on to her side, provoking awkward hysterical laughing as she leaned against the duct.

"Are you okay?" The voice reminded her she was not alone, and Quill ended the hysteria with three simple words.

"Yes. I did it."

"Good. I knew you could. Now, shimmy toward me. Then I'll try to haul you out."

Quill lay her tired head between her outstretched arms as she pushed off with the edge of her foot, mimicking an undulating worm. A ripple fired from the tips of her toes to her fingertips. Inching upward, finally she felt the welcome grip of another human. Exhausted, battered, bruised and unable to advance a millimetre further, her body went limp. Relieved, she succumbed to the delicious thrill of sliding effortlessly out of the deadly shaft.

When the motion stopped, and she mustered the courage to open her eyelids, she flinched, the features staring at her filling her field of vision. Confused, wiping the rear of a bruised and bloodied fist across her eyes, the face pulled away, shrinking as it came into focus.

While Quill didn't know who to expect, the identity of her rescuer was an extraordinary surprise. "What are you doing here?"

"Let's not talk about that yet. There are people searching for you. It's not safe. Come, let me help you up."

The prospect of moving made Quill sick to her stomach. Every part of her physique throbbed through to her bones, and now she was free of the tight shaft, her core temperature plummeted. The frigid underground air magnified the effect of the damp clothes that clung like melted wax. Tentative, afraid to move, she levered herself into a seated position, drawing her knees to her chest and hugging herself to control the shivering. The gallant rescuer laid his thick coat across her shoulders, pulling it closed, enveloping her entire body in a deep pressure hug. The enormous garment swallowed her petite frame whole, as she felt him lifting her upright. "Here, lean on me. You're in a dreadful state. We must get you out of here." With one arm thrown around and under her armpits, he supported her weight. "I'm pretty sure if we follow this channel, it leads to the main tunnel that returns to the grove."

"Okay," she said, leaning against her guardian's enormous chest, his protruding gut pressed against her flank as she limped along the path. Anxious, she tried to ignore the thought of managing the next step, let alone a climb to the surface.

After several minutes of silence, their progress slow and painful, her thoughts drifted, returning to wondering how he'd found her. There were many questions to ask, but the comments kept snagging under her plump, dehydrated tongue. In the end, all she could manage was, "How? What?" before giving up, defeated.

"If you mean how did I find you, what am I doing here? An embarrassing confession, to be honest. I watched you walking out to the oak tree, so I followed. I needed a rest from making polite conversation. Some folk think it's all glamour, being a special envoy, but it gets tiresome after a while, and it plays havoc with my belly." He patted his pregnant stomach. "Still, if I hadn't seen you I'd never have found that marvellous club. The music's divine. It made me feel quite at home. Then I realised this entire set-up is illegal in Scolaris, though who knows why? Music hurts no-one."

"Do you have clubs like this in Asteria?" she asked, through a thick tongue, her curiosity piqued.

"Many. Asteria's raised on creativity. It's the lifeblood of our nation. Painting, sculpting, dancing, song, you name it. If you make something beautiful, everybody loves you for it."

"Isn't that vanity? What about serving society? A legacy of knowledge built for future generations so that each era is better than the last?"

"I admire your philanthropic view, young lady. But why not both? Is it wrong to fill the world with joy? There's beauty all around us, even here in the dark. Take these rock formations—who would have thought they're folded and layered from something so simple as salt?"

So I'm right about this place, and it explains the smell and the white substance on the soles of Mordecai Templar's shoes.

Knowledge and creativity combined wasn't a prospect she'd considered, but once planted as a seed, the idea germinated, throwing out minuscule roots, altering her perspective forever.

With her intellect focused on the fascinating philosophical debate, Quill didn't notice their route. Time vanished like a puff of air as they navigated the labyrinth's twists and turns. "Why are we going down? We have to climb to get out."

"Yes, yes, I understand, but those people you upset, they're looking for you. This passage connects to the opposite side of the shaft, away from the club. We travel down and around before climbing. Trust me, I know what I'm doing."

Sapped of energy, hungry and dehydrated, Quill relinquished control of the situation to her knight in shining armour.

He's got us this far. I should rely on him to do the rest.

Ten minutes later, they rounded a sharp bend where, up ahead, to her immense relief, the tunnel opened into a wide cavern. As she stepped over the threshold and peered up, she saw they'd reached the bottom of the central shaft, her original entry point. Dread replaced momentary happiness at the thought of the climb facing them. As if reading her mind, her companion interrupted her fear. "It's a long way up. We'll take a break before we start. Recover your strength. There's an abandoned blacksmith there," he said, pointing to their left. "We should be safe inside."

Relieved, Quill hobbled, re-using him as a crutch while they wandered inside the forge. Dimly lit by the glow of lamps illuminating the vent outside, a magnificent fire pit dominated the space, iron tools long since discarded around its edge. A huge anvil pointed to where the flames once roared, licking the brick chimney and lining it in dense black soot.

Her liberator eased her onto the ground, propping her against the rear wall, far from prying eyes. "What's the history of this place?"

Quill's head lolled, sleep dragging her from consciousness like a slab of meat. "Huh?" she said, opening one eye. Utter blackness filled her vision, raising the possibility she was asleep. Then she noticed a picture, familiar somehow, if she could only move.

Where have I seen it before? What is it?

The information was just out of reach. Then her trusted saviour came back into view. He'd been stood over her, checking she was alive. Immensely thankful but helpless to articulate it, Quill grinned, flaunting her teeth, hoping he'd understand her silent message.

"Here, drink this," he said, pouring liquid into her grateful mouth as she gulped.

While she quenched a tremendous thirst, he exposed his chest as he leaned over, saving her life. Groggy, she studied close-up the inked images decorating his skin. In particular, the figure of a curvy woman, dressed in nothing but a mane of floor-length hair. With expanding pupils, she turned aside from the trickle of liquid, shunting her fat tongue to the roof of her mouth to block the path to her windpipe. Quill choked. Knowing she'd made a terrible mistake, she spat out the substance with every ounce of strength she could muster.

Before slipping into darkness again, she heard Uriah Crisp's voice, "Sorry, nothing personal."

Chapter Forty-Eight

Breath fast and ragged, lowering himself into the hole, panic closed around Red, swallowing him whole like a malevolent storm. His feet hadn't even touched the floor of the underground passage before he was a quivering wreck. The voice in his brain screaming.

Escape. Run. You're going to die. I'm going to die. Can't breathe. Can't see. Get out. Get out.

A cacophony of terror squatted inside his brain, waiting to pounce, given half a chance, but he daren't ignore the saturated, misshapen shoe. Unless he was mistaken, it belonged to Quill, which meant she was down there somewhere, in who knew what state, and it was his duty to find her. To preserve life, whatever the personal cost. The rasping of his own hyperventilating lungs echoed around the tunnel. Amplified, reverberating through his eardrums, overloading his already overworked senses. With his arms stretched ahead of him, Red groped the walls and ceiling, conjuring the image fed through his fingertips and wishing he hadn't. For a short man, space was scarce, though searching for a positive at least he wasn't smashing his skull on the roof. The chief swallowed, his mouth dry, sweat gushing down his spine in rivulets, soaking his shirt.

He could either go on or go back—neither of which was palatable—but he had to try. Creeping forward in the darkness, feeling his way along the cramped low tunnel, his pulse raced, the rampaging claustrophobia squeezing him in its vice-grip. Damp earthiness and ripe, rotting plant matter filled his nostrils as aimlessly he edged forth, tuning into the wild signals arriving from his body. The receptors in his soles registered the pit was drawing him deeper and deeper beneath the earth. As he battled his deepest, darkest fear, the prospect of being buried alive landed hammer blows in the battle raging within him. The horror came in waves, building and rushing at him from all sides. Swollen to a monstrous unstoppable peak, terror paralysed him to the spot, unable to put one foot in front of the other. When he thought he couldn't continue, the welcome sensation of Luna's warm body, tight against his left calf, grounded him. A reminder that here, unlike his childhood experience, he wasn't alone. A simple gesture of companionship delivered at the perfect moment. An instant hit of serotonin spurring him onward as he shuffled in the dark.

Navigating a dogleg to the right, the void on either side of his outstretched limbs suddenly widened, relieving the tension between his shoulder blades. While stretching his knotted neck muscles, he could barely see the white circle of fur on the dog's breast as she peered at him from guard duty at his feet. "Thanks, little lady. I owe you." Then, much to his relief, up ahead, a faint orange glow illuminated the trail, and he picked up the pace, desperate to free himself from the tunnel's claustrophobic clutches.

Amazed, emerging into a wide cylindrical chamber, Red peered over the side of a rocky platform. He marvelled at the sheer scale of the shaft, which dropped at least six levels below him.

What trouble has she found now?

Above were further ledges, the entire chimney dotted with tunnels, joined by ingeniously constructed wooden ramps and steps. Whoever had built the place deserved the utmost respect. It was a masterpiece of engineering. What it was for and why it remained hidden were the most intriguing questions.

"So, up or down?" he asked the puppy, scratching his scalp. "What am I doing? I'm talking to a dog." Then his faithful companion trotted to the staircase, dropping onto the first step before turning to him, signalling to follow. "Okay, if you say so. What could go wrong?" As he reached the dog, he noticed an empty hook embedded in the rock face, a match for one on the rear wall only minus a lantern.

Someone's been here.

"Let's do this." Red bounded down the steps like a mountain goat, happy to track Luna's path.

🐾 🐾 🐾 🐾 🐾 🐾 🐾

Red heard the music long before he arrived at the club and recognised it immediately, the melody provoking the few fond memories of his infanthood. Old Nan, his parent's defecto when he was a lad, kept a dangerous secret. That she'd shared it with him made him love her even more. Nan's grandfather, a man he'd never met, taught her the craft. The skill passed through generations of her family, the generous surrogate mother hoping to share it with the world, but that would never happen. He'd always remember her words from the day she disappeared. "Behave for your parents and never forget that you're my boy, too, so I'm leaving the responsibility to you, understand?"

He never saw her again. It was the one moment in his history where he welcomed the punishment. It must have been his fault they'd sent her away. Everything was his fault, so he clung to the pact, his birth mother oblivious to the true meaning of those parting remarks, and for once, he felt powerful.

Nan sang. A song to melt the hardest heart, if only anyone could hear it. A rich, comforting sound penetrating the isolating locked cupboard as she pressed her lips against the door. The tune forced as loudly as she dared through the unforgiving surface to inhabit the space alongside him—a light in the darkness. After she'd gone, while he was inside, alone and terrified, hugging his scraped knees to his chest, he'd hum the refrain, the heavy weight of her secret borne on his young shoulders.

While wiping a fat tear from the corner of one eye, the nostalgia provoking a flood of emotions, Red followed his ears and his heart with a suspicion he'd found the source of the unusual match-books.

Chapter Forty-Nine

While drifting in and out of consciousness, Quill heard thudding footsteps as if a herd of stampeding cows were ready to trample her to death. Curled into a foetal position, protecting her skull from the onslaught, she whimpered, expecting the inevitable, but it never appeared. The noise ebbed and flowed, rising and falling like a Lilith bird catching a thermal, soaring and swooping with effortless ease. Sounds which signalled danger, club patrons desperate to prevent their secret from becoming public knowledge. Logic urged her to move, but her body had other ideas, broken from the multiple rounds of near death she'd endured in fewer than twenty-four hours. Somewhere in the depths of semi-consciousness came an understanding that Uriah Crisp hadn't rescued her at all—the ultimate betrayal—he'd saved her from one disaster to inflict his own. Whatever he'd given her to drink had done its work as Quill lay in the redundant smithy, soaked through to the skin. Filthy dirty, her clothes shredded, bleeding and blackened and now incapacitated.

The groan came from nearby, and in her bewildered, drugged state, she assumed it emanated from her. She laughed, an intense feeling of elation sweeping her along on a wild ride. Images of long-limbed curvaceous figures with glorious manes of hair danced behind her eyelids, morphing into the murderer Ivy Penrose. The phantoms' fluid rhythmical movements were enchanting, seductive, and deadly, while the hypnotic club music played, her pulse providing the bass as the spectacle raced toward a heart-stopping climax. Deep in her psyche, Quill understood she'd drunk Professor Hawkin's murderous butterfly toxin, and she glimpsed what Ivy must have experienced in the moments before her death. The mind-blowing beauty of nature's intricacies magnified—snowflakes, honeycomb, dandelions and pine cones, whirlpools and galaxies spiralling. Their mathematical perfection filling her with joy as the soft sheen of downy skin morphed into lustrous black locks which fell in slow motion. Hair which tumbled in waves, over and over, slower and slower, in time with her failing heartbeat, and nothing else mattered.

Surprised to be alive, she woke, her guttural groans mingled with another's. Head in her palms, pummelled by a pounding headache hangover, Quill peered into the gloom, trying not to move, but it was no use. She couldn't see a thing. The note, like a wounded animal, continued unabated while she shuffled sideways on her bottom to investigate. As she passed the forge's entrance, a full height wrought-iron pair of gates fastened with an enormous padlock barred the exit.

I don't remember seeing those.

Crisp had drugged her, locked her in and left her to die, and that was enough to convince her—he'd murdered Mordecai Templar. The same motive for both acts: to protect the secret club's existence and the identity of the sultry singer tattooed on Crisp's heart.

Suddenly remembering that she'd been following Luna's trail, imagining that the whimpering was the little dog injured, Quill discovered an untapped reserve of energy. Spurred on by the horrendous notion that the pet was dying, she shuffled faster, closing in on the vibrations as she chewed her lip, afraid of what she might discover.

A misshapen lump of cloth spread on the floor a couple of metres ahead. Timid, edging closer, she grew in confidence that the brown mass was the source of the dreadful noise. "Hello," she said, her voice thick, raspy and unrecognisable. No-one replied. With the drug leaving her bloodstream, feeling stronger, Quill drew her knees into her chest, pushed off with her feet, slipping her shoulder blades upward against the rock-face until she stood. Wobbly still, she paced towards the heap, keeping her distance until she could decide what it was. Then it moved, making her flinch, sending her off balance as she flailed her arms out to the sides, struggling to find her grip on the stone wall. As she waited for the moment to subside, breathing shallow quick breaths, four digits and a thumb appeared among the folds. Filthy and bruised like her own, but identifiable. Pity overcame fear, driving her on, supplying the strength to lift her legs, until at last she settled in front of the stricken individual. Confused and afraid, she gasped, sliding to the ground again. Then, crouched on all fours, she made a beeline for the body. Almost unrecognisable under the dense crust of salt and filth, she stroked his white hair, sweeping it from right to left, and whispered. "Dr Novack. It's me, Quill. Don't worry, you're safe now."

"Quill? What are you doing here?" His voice sounded thin and hoarse, a victim of the ordeal he'd endured. She leaned in closer, the delicate caress of his breath brushing her cheekbone as he strained to talk. "You need to get out of here. It's not safe. He'll be back and if he finds you here, there'll be trouble."

"Don't worry about me. I can take care of myself. Anyway, it's too late. Mr Crisp did his worst and I'm still standing, just about. I believe he thinks I'm dead already."

"Uriah? The Asterian envoy?" The injured man's eyebrows furrowed. "What's he got to do with anything?" Pain etched on his cheeks as he tried to change positions.

Flummoxed by the unexpected remark, Quill's mind whirred, mulling over recent events to make sense of what had taken place. When, out of nowhere, a single question formed.

If Novack's here, who's enjoying the feast?

Terrified by the possibilities, Quill quivered. "Doctor, who did this to you?" Though she waited, the shell of a man didn't answer.

🐾 🐾 🐾 🐾 🐾 🐾 🐾

However much she tried to rouse him, shaking an arm, speaking his name into his ear, Novack remained out of reach, and Quill's suspicions mounted that if she couldn't get them out, he might not survive to see another day.

Painstakingly, she dragged herself toward the fence securing the entrance to the forge, spying a shiny new padlock which mocked her, glistening in the glow of the lit shaft. Sounds of movement in the surrounding tunnels ebbed, giving her the confidence to emerge from the darkness, hoping to discover a way out. With a gate grasped in each fist, she rattled them. Leant forwards and backwards with her entire body weight, in the vain hope that the solid lock might miraculously pop open. Of course, that didn't happen, and the best she could manage was hurling useless insults at the bars, infuriated by her own trusting naivety and lack of insight into human nature, the traits she blamed for her current predicament.

Using the fretted ironwork as a ladder, she lowered herself to the ground, laying in a pool of brine collecting in a dip where the two frames met. Head to one side, Quill squeezed beneath the bars, pulling herself forward on torn fingertips, barely reaching as far as her earlobes before she was stuck. With the heel of her hands, she pushed, driving her body backwards, angrily accepting that the route wouldn't work. Next, she considered climbing over the top, the opposite approach, but the sheer height of the doors and her current physical state ended that idea after less than a few seconds' thought.

Quill sat, resting her spine against the chilled metal, pressed into the vertical struts, massaging her tired muscles on the framework, as she watched Novack's chest, the faint rise and fall of breathing almost imperceptible. Resigned to being out of ideas, curling up next to him was tempting. But unable to forget her father's plight, she persevered, hoping for inspiration. Then she remembered where she was.

There should be tools in a smithy.

The furnace clearly hadn't operated for decades, but it had to be worth a try. The prospect injected her with adrenaline, launching her brain and body like someone had struck a match, lit the forge and pumped the bellows to feed the flames. Quill rose, waddling over to the fire-pit, peering over the brick ledge, imaginary fingers crossed behind her as she placed her palms on top of the oven wall. Discarded at the base, covered in dirt and soot and tangled in thick cobwebs, lay two iron punches—one round, one square. Relief flooded her senses, intellect firing, as she scrabbled around in her brain, probing for useful material she thought she'd seen in a book borrowed for her late-night study sessions. The process was remarkably straightforward, like searching the library itself, if you knew how the books were organised. Alphabetised in sections for every elementary subject, her mind operated in the same way. Each text read, knowledge gathered, filed and stored logically, ready when needed. The right information for the right occasion—*that* moment had come.

Chapter Fifty

The planned reconnaissance of the underground club started well, as Chief Red snuck into the entrance unnoticed. The music throbbed, mimicking his heartbeat as it pounded in his ears. Captivated by the sound and the sheer scale and beauty of the unusual rock formations forming the chamber, it took a supreme effort not to stand and gawp, unwittingly revealing his existence. Hiding from view in the dark recesses at the edge, Red observed, calculating his next move. Divided into zones of activity, patrons congregated in distinct areas. Furthest from his entry point, the musicians held court. Male revellers in black formal dress swayed in unison, drink in one hand, cigar in the other. Whenever the soundtrack paused, rapturous applause accompanied by shouts of, "More," elicited instant gratification as a new tune began. The one thing missing was a singer, so Red couldn't stop thinking about Nan, imagining her voice as the perfect accompaniment.

As he travelled further from the musicians, the focus was on groups socialising. Some stood, waving their drinks in the air as they discussed whatever it was men liked to talk about after work. The one simple difference between clubs approved by the

Protectorate and this version was the music. All the remaining details he recognised from the few times his father had dragged him along to the gatherings in Law and Order, back when the old man still clung to the expectation of Red joining the legal profession. He hated the place. Gentlemen postured, feigning interest in their competitor's achievements, with the sole purpose of exploiting a weakness, storing up titbits of information to leverage an advantage, any advantage, however small.

The most intriguing zone inhabited a space that was mostly in darkness. Tables reserved for sitting and perhaps engaging in secretive, risky behaviours. The club was busy, but not rammed, and Red wondered if there were breakout spaces he couldn't see. In particular, he noted a hole which led out behind the performers, access blocked by a distinctive character, a fellow no-one should forget in a hurry. Ink tattoos covered his face and extended onto his chest, much of which was on show. The gentleman sported a flamboyant neon pink and orange shirt open to the naval, which protruded from the unadulterated expanse of his gut.

After making a mental note to navigate through to whatever lay beyond the shocking garment, Red prioritised whatever was going on at those tables. He had his suspicions, but he needed to prove them with hard evidence. Spurred on by the tingle of excitement, he plotted the best route, picturing the elation of locating the source of the drug responsible for so many deaths.

No-one could have predicted the unfortunate sequence of events that followed. Red edged toward the entryway, keeping to the shadows as he manoeuvred closer to the seated area. On arrival at the entry tunnel, he wavered, searching for a route across that didn't involve stepping into the light.

There's no way through without someone seeing me.

Even circling in the opposite direction didn't solve the problem. That entailed passing the tattooed gentleman, and judging by his size, the chances of emerging unscathed were slim. Deciding the key to success was simply a matter of timing, he watched, primed and ready to act. Seconds, then minutes, ticked by as his gaze flicked between the different factions, waiting impatiently for an opportunity. Yet each time he mentally crossed off a zone, he discovered that the rest didn't match the winning criteria. So it continued, a circle of irritation multiplying with each disappointment. Until he accepted the ideal moment might never present itself.

Instead, electing to lower his expectations, the guard focused on the groups gathered closest to the entrance, hoping that those further behind wouldn't notice him. With his plan set, he waited until no-one looked his way, striding into danger as he crossed the tunnel. The scheme should have worked, but the second he moved, the passage filled with patrons. Red heard them a second before seeing them, but it was too late to react as he stepped into their path, an act that silenced the crowd, as the guardsman confronted the mob alone.

"Nobody move," he said, trying to project the maximum authority possible for a lone man facing so many. A ripple of anxious voices swept through the party-goers as they considered their options.

From somewhere over his shoulder, a deep booming tone shouted. "Run!" Then utter pandemonium broke out. Most of the throng turned on their heels, sprinting through the underpass without glancing back, bulldozing through a handful of fellows who'd chosen to stand their ground. The brave contingent were fighting a losing battle as they called to their fellow revellers. "Stop, he's just one guard."

"Wait, this is ridiculous."

"Cowards."

Followed by a fresh tsunami of panicked customers exiting the cavern at once, converging on Red in a maelstrom of erratic limbs and bodies. Buffeted from side to side, a seed pod in a hurricane, he protected his skull with his arms. His body anchored by widening his stance, grounding himself as he softened at the knees. Until the vibration of stampeding shoes subsided and he dared to peek beneath his forearms. As soon as he did, the chief understood the predicament he faced and, while swallowing the bile flooding his throat, he prepared to fight.

Chapter Fifty-One

Quill slotted both metal punches into the gap in the padlock's handle, unsure if she had the strength to carry out the plan. Inserted into the hole until their wide ends butted together, she wiped the dirt and sweat from each palm, knowing the manoeuvre required a firm grasp to work. With a round punch in one hand, square in the other, Quill pushed both toward the gate, leaning into the forward motion with her whole body. She strained as the widest points of both tools acted as fulcrums, magnifying the pressure to separate the loop from the lock. Grunting, neck tendons taut, chin tucked to her chest, she shoved and heaved. Feet slipping on the wet floor as she overbalanced, Quill cursed under her breath, losing momentum and having to change grip as she grew weaker with each failed effort. Until, at length, a padlock shard flew through the fence, clattering to the ground as the handle popped open while the implements whirled free, bouncing off the gates, narrowly missing her rib cage on the return journey.

Unable to comprehend that the idea had worked, Quill stood, staring at the broken bolt hanging loose. Tentatively, she prodded the right gate with her middle finger and watched, amazed, as it swung free, screeching alarmingly. The harsh sound galvanised a response, grounding her in the present moment as she remembered her location and that Crisp could re-appear at any second. After hobbling to Novack as fast as her physical state allowed, she shook him. "Doctor, we need to go now. Get up, please. I can't lift you."

The stricken man groaned, groggy with sleep and pain. "Quill? What are you doing here?" Their recent conversation forgotten.

"That's not important. Let me help you up."

"You're wasting your time, my dear. I can't move. You can see that?"

However much she wanted him to be wrong, Quill knew it was true. Which left one choice: leaving him behind to fetch reinforcements and hoping he'd survive in the meantime. It was a terrible idea with a low chance of success, but it was the last thing left to try.

"Don't worry about me," he said, as if reading her doubts. "What is meant to be will always come to pass."

Quill crouched, laying a palm on his arm. "I'm going to bring help, okay? Sit tight, don't move, I'll be back, I promise."

Novack grinned, his lips contorting into a grimace. "Ha, I don't think I could go anywhere, even if I wished to."

Quill took a deep breath, mentally preparing to climb the hundreds of steps on her way to the surface. With a deep sigh, she scanned her surroundings, memorising the details to safeguard her prospects of finding the forge on the return journey.

Just as she was ready to leave, a clarion voice made her flinch. "No-one's going anywhere."

※ ※ ※ ※ ※ ※ ※

Red faced a trio of men who'd apparently decided they'd stacked the odds in their favour. He didn't recognise them, but suspected he wasn't likely to forget their faces in the future. With his palms up in a gesture of conciliation, he stalled for time. "Let's talk."

"We've got nothing to say." The middle man, who was at least six feet tall, replied before glaring at his companions, who nodded their agreement at break-neck speed.

"I don't care what you do with your spare time, but I *am* interested in tracking down whoever's peddling the drug responsible for the deaths of several individuals. Anything you can tell me about that?"

The lanky man's sidekicks—one of whom was shorter than him, with a bright orange beard down to his midriff—turned to their mouthpiece, who obliged. "Nope."

An invisible signal passed between the trio, who spread out, circling Red as he twisted from side-to-side, struggling to keep them in his peripheral vision. "So here's what happens next." The chief bent his knees as he circled anti-clockwise, against their direction of travel. "You're leaving, like your friends, and I'll choose to forget you whilst finding the answers to my questions." As the last word slipped from his lips, he stopped, stunned by the sight of a neon pink and orange shirt. The garish cloth encased the enormous girth of the tattooed man he'd spotted earlier. It took him a nanosecond to compute that the prospect of escaping unscathed had gone from unlikely to impossible. Remembering his training, he took a deep breath and plastered on a mask of confidence. "Okay, well, don't say I didn't warn you."

Then the bearded fellow charged, head down like a raging bull, aiming for Red's waist, crying out as he did so with a strangled, "Argh."

To counter the movement, the guard took a large step forward, feeling the draught as his misguided opponent sped past. Unable to see the hazard before it was too late, the hirsute chap plunged head-first into a section of stained glass rock, which splintered with an ear-splitting crack.

One down, three to go.

The prospect was exhausting even as the vandal dropped like a sack of bones. Cagey, circling one another again, nobody wanting to make the first move, Red repeated his offer of peace. "Are you sure you wouldn't prefer to chat?"

Goaded into action, the tallest of the group swung out a rangy arm, fist balled as his unexpected attack connected with Red's jaw. Coppery blood seeped into the guard's mouth as he stumbled backward, reeling from the jab. With no chance to recover, rough hands shoved him in the back, thrusting him into range. Fortunately, as Red tripped, the next punch didn't connect, the lanky fellow's long reach swiping thin air above the chief's skull. Inspired by the unshaven chap's manoeuvre, the guard harnessed his forward momentum to barrel into the tall man, cutting him off at the legs as he crumpled in half, winded by the body blow.

As the chance of success increased once more, Red stepped over the groaning heap, blood dripping from his lip onto his shirt. "Who's next?"

The survivor of the original trio, a skinny forgettable fellow in a dinner suit two sizes too big, responded, squealing like a piglet and sprinting away like his shoes were on fire.

Red confronted the inked man. "Then there were two."

"Shame there can only be one."

The unmistakable threat hung between them as both men stalked, searching for a weakness. Red's brain churned, desperate to find a strategy in the endless hours of drill he'd never used in real life.

※ ※ ※ ※ ※ ※ ※

Quill could hardly believe her eyes, staring at Novack mark two, and all at once insignificant details fell into place. "That's why Luna growled at you. She knew you weren't Dr Novack. I should've paid attention, but you're so alike." She noticed the olive-green suit was baggy on him and a white carnation drooped in his lapel. "The flower. How could I have missed it? The doctor's hay fever." As her mind purged itself, a tight band formed across her forehead, the dull throb of a tension headache. The clothes confirmed that whoever the mystery man was, he'd played an integral part in the doctor's disappearance. "You did this to him, didn't you? Why? He'd never hurt anyone."

"Ha!" The stranger's pitch was higher than the real Novack, now that she scrutinised the finer details. "Shows how little you know about our dear leader. Doesn't it, brother dearest?" he asked, shouting the last part at the physician's prone figure.

Brother? Dr Novack's an only child.

"He doesn't have any brothers or sisters. Tell the truth. Who are you?"

"Ask him, go on, I dare you."

Quill tried to catch the doctor's eye, keeping her frame as a barrier between the men. Novack dodged her gaze, pain washing his face. "Meet Henry. Says he's my half-brother, but I merely have his word for that."

Henry kicked the floor with the toe of his brown boot and Quill kicked her brain for not noticing sooner. The imposter wore a *pair* of boots, an added detail that should have set off alarm bells, knowing that Sterling had lost one of his in the flower bed. The doppelgänger's undisguised fury erupted into a jet of spewing volcanic ash. "You see? I have to put up with this. Anyone else would be thrilled to discover they have a brother, but not him. I threaten his perfect world, apparently. It's not my fault our father had a wandering eye."

"Don't talk about him like that. You're not worthy to lick his shoe leather." Surprised by the physician's venomous outburst, which he followed with a deep hacking cough from the effort, Quill stooped to make sure Sterling was breathing. Seen in a new light, the halo of his exalted position in Scolaris slipped, revealing a glimpse of the flawed human beneath the glow. After all, he was simply a man.

"Shut up!" Henry stormed the gap between them, bristling with rage. "I should've dealt with you permanently from the beginning. You and your worthless vows of support. Lies, all of it. Well, now's the day to claim my birthright, and this girl has a point—one Novack is better than two."

With that declaration, the threat level sky-rocketed, so Quill's intellect raced, planning her next move.

What if I leave them to it? It's a family drama that doesn't concern me.

She soon dismissed that idea. She wasn't about to surrender a defenceless man to an even worse fate. The alternative, getting physical, didn't seem like a practical choice, mainly because she had zero skills in that department and Henry was much bigger than her. She needed time to figure a way out for them both, so she improvised. "How's your mum?"

The offbeat question stopped Henry in his tracks, furrowed brows showing his mind was working overtime to figure out her motives. "None of your business. Now get out of my way."

"It must've been difficult, growing up without your dad," she said, a lump in her throat as she pictured her own. "How did she manage?"

Henry sized her up, but his smirk suggested he'd written her off as *just a girl* like the rest, and Quill knew that might prove crucial. "She worked for our dad. A defecto lured in by the riches of their master. She won't be the first nor the last to be taken advantage of by a protector. As soon as mother declared her pregnancy, the Novacks sent her packing, and nobody else would take her on. We lived on the charity of our neighbours, people who have insufficient themselves but still share it. I grew up watching her struggle to set food on the table, and when she died, I swore I'd find justice. I watched brother-dear for a long time. He seemed to be a good person, but when I introduced myself, it was obvious he was exactly like father, a man of lavish promises, none of which he intended to keep."

"And you're a gentleman of your word, correct?"

"Of course, now move or I won't be responsible for my actions."

"But that's the point, isn't it?"

"Eh?" Henry threw his hands upward, puffing air out of his mouth.

"If you're searching for justice, then harming either of us won't deliver on your promise. You *are* responsible for your actions, and from what you've said about your mum, I can't imagine her approving of your methods."

Henry's slack-mouthed vacuous stare proved her comments had stalled his violent intentions, which gave her enough time to retrieve the square punch from the dirt at Novack's feet, where it had landed after her padlock breaking exploits.

As Quill shielded Sterling's dying carcass, weapon in hand, Henry's vacant expression morphed into absolute fury as he understood she'd duped him. Quill swallowed the acrid bile flooding her throat, adopting a broad stance, acknowledging that with this move she'd unequivocally declared war.

"Interesting designs you have there." Red pointed to his opponent's chest as they faced off, shuffling like crabs from side-to-side. "Particularly that one. Who is she?"

The pot-bellied fellow laughed, a deep throaty chuckle which made his gut wobble. "I could tell you, but then I'd have to kill you. Oh, wait, I'm going to do that, anyway." With that revelation, he lunged at Red, huge plump palms clutching for a piece of his shirt, but the guard changed direction, his nimble toes keeping him out of harm's way. The tattooed warrior roared like a bear, throwing his arms in the air with frustration that he'd missed.

With first points to the young chief, he strategised, planning to wear out the heavy man before making his own move. In this manner, they performed a brand of balletic chess. The fit youngster tempted the inked stranger forward by edging closer with his guard down, only to raise his fists, jumping out of reach just in time. Not without its close shaves, this game endured for over five minutes, during which the decorated chap's breathing grew louder and increasingly ragged until his face resembled a beetroot. The neon top plastered on to his upper torso like badly hung wallpaper.

As soon as Red's adversary ignored the bait, instead grimacing with his hands on his hips as he gulped oxygen, the guardsman capitalised, jabbing a knock-out punch straight to the chin.

Much to his dismay, the chief's aim failed as the battle-weary opponent ducked at the last second. Then, on the upward trajectory, his foe took his chance, grabbing the guard's arm as it recoiled. With one limb under control, the rotund specimen yanked his rival tight to his gut, grinning wildly, a stomach churning stink of stale booze and cigar smoke on his breath. "Gotcha."

Red winked, staring into the tattooed features. "I wouldn't be so sure," he said, stealing a glance at his enemy's wrists. Following the guardsman's lead, the stranger's eyes darted to where he thought he had hold of Red's arm. To discover the opposite was true—the Chief of the City Guard had deployed his pair of iron cuffs in the confusion. Resigned to the defeat, his conquest slumped to the floor, crestfallen, hands clamped together and useless.

As Red smoothed his blood-stained uniform, panting after the prolonged exertion, he knew there was work still to be done. He had to find the drugs, and he figured the neon-shirt could tell him what he needed to know. Before he could question the suspect, the sound of barking, followed by a streak of black-and-tan fur, flew through the tunnel toward him.

"Luna, what is it?" he asked, as the spaniel skidded to a halt at his feet. She growled at the tattooed individual, barked again, then returned through the hole at speed. "Don't move." Red jabbed a finger at his captive and charged after the dog.

"You'd better know how to use that, girl." Henry's eyebrow arched as he raised his arms, spreading his fingers and looking menacing.

Quill gulped, the cold solid tool in her right fist weighing her down, sapping her confidence, which was the exact opposite of what she'd intended. Then the fraudster lunged, aiming straight for the weapon, which he grabbed, taking her by surprise. As he yanked, she stumbled forward; the punch slithering from her grasp. Quill tightened her grip, leaning back and digging her heels into the ground to offset his manoeuvre. The tug-of-war ebbed and flowed, as the pair fought for supremacy over the object, assuming it held the key to success. Unfortunately, the power imbalance between herself and Henry quickly gave him the edge as the impact of her injuries and his superior size loosened her control. Until, with a triumphant howl, he ripped the iron from her clutches and set it above his head like a trophy.

"Don't say I didn't warn you." Henry pulled back the metal pole behind his ear, poised to strike.

Quill fought her instincts, rushing forward as she closed in on Henry instead of running. Despite figuring she'd never outrun him, the daring step was a risk, but his shocked expression suggested she'd given him something unexpected to consider. Still frowning, he swung the weapon in a descending arc, but the brave young woman had already stepped inside and his attack missed the mark.

As she gritted her teeth through the pain, Quill jumped, throwing herself at him, wrapping her arms and legs around his collar and waist. Like a dead weight hanging, she mimicked a toddler. Henry yelled, rotating like a spinning top, trying to dislodge her. "Get off me, get off." But locking her forearms and squeezing her thighs, she gripped harder, clenching her eyelids to counteract the dizziness as he increased speed. Furious at the tenacious move, her nemesis swatted at her continually with the implement. Unable to co-ordinate a winning blow, more often than not he pounded himself with his fist.

The clanging of iron hitting the rock floor was a glorious sound as she revelled in a minor victory, but it was short-lived. With both hands free, the imposter clawed at her arms, coughing and spluttering, choked by her strangulating embrace. Terrified, sweating from the exertion, she felt herself sliding. Focused on gripping tighter with her hips, climbing his torso with her feet like a monkey, Quill clung on. Henry scrabbled behind his neck, prising her digits away, bending them backward as she shrieked in agony, heart pounding as her grip loosened, sending her slipping downward.

Just when she thought she couldn't hang on a second longer, he stiffened. Eyeballs rolling in their sockets, hands and arms falling slack at his sides, he slumped to the ground with Quill on top. Then she heard Luna growling and barking, sniffing Henry's carcass and licking her bruised arm. Tears of relief fell silently onto her feather-marked cheek as she rolled off the fake man's chest and gathered the little dog into a tight embrace. Nuzzling Luna's warm body, inhaling her damp doggy smell, she lifted her gaze to discover Chief Red of the City Guard with the round punch in his hand and she'd never been so grateful to see anyone.

Chapter Fifty-Two

The Ortus

The torrid gale blasted the assembled scholars as they swayed, battling to hold their position in the precise semi-circular formation. With bowed heads, they gathered on the roof of the Great Library of Scolaris, awaiting the next crop of students. Below, tens of thousands of Scolarians stood in silence, waiting for the Ortus to begin.

Distant thunder rumbled, menacing as dense black clouds invaded the city from below the horizon. The dazzling glare of the supernova flared and vanished in a diminishing cycle of light and dark as the residents witnessed a miracle of the cosmos. Quill watched from her usual position in the shadows at the rear of the stage.

Master Godwin struck a man-sized brass gong. A pure bass note vibrating outward as the first shaved head appeared through the narrow opening in the roof's base, signifying that the ceremony had begun. A week ago, she'd have seethed at the injustice of seeing others begin the life she dreamed of living. Strangely, as a cooling shower soaked the city, a blessed downpour after the stifling heat, Quill felt calm. Novack had offered to make her dream come true as thanks for saving him. But she'd declined, preferring her status as a defecto to the idea of her integrity being bought.

With a sideways glance, she spotted the Head of the Protectorate. Still nursing his fractured ribs and broken legs, reams of white bandages had replaced Sterling's customary green suit. The monumental scale of Dr Novack's deception was shocking. As an inexperienced junior physician, he'd failed to record the recommended quantity of pain medication for his patient. This terrible error led to Otto Blackwood's tragic death from an overdose. From that single mistake grew a web of deceit. Novack, Paine and Tedesko made a pact. Men who shared the same social circle and the same ambitions. Between them, they'd worked behind the scenes, promoting each other into lofty positions until they were untouchable. At least they thought they were. Nobody could have foreseen Henry's arrival and he was unaware his actions would end with the destruction of the most powerful gentlemen in Scolaris.

Scholar Godwin hit the cymbal again, the vibrato dong calling the student scholars forth, stepping to a clanging, steady rhythm, one at a time in a continuous line. Master Wittgenstein strode forward holding a flaming torch, which he raised aloft to rapturous applause from the attending crowd. Grey straggly mane flapping as he confronted the wind and driving rain, while his robes billowed about his legs like unruly sails. Quill's spirit soared, swollen with pride as she witnessed the ancient academic hurling the beacon into a rectangular fire pit. Flames surrounded the platform in heat and light to defy the deluge. Relieved she was alive, Wit had confessed to a desire to keep her by his side, afraid to tell her about the letter from her father, scared she might leave. The revelation made her smile, an intermittent respite from the fears for her father's safety, as the howling squall distorted her jowls, whipping the soft curls around her ears. In response, she'd capitulated, forgiving and seeking forgiveness, confessing to the disloyal act of telling Bran of Novack's disappearance. With a clean conscience, she was leaving Scolaris after the rite to find her dad and wasn't sure she'd ever return.

How ironic that love possesses the power to heal and to destroy.

When Elena Deverall broke Dorian Paine's heart, changing her mind about marriage, the ambitious young man told himself it was for the best. He'd poured his energies into furthering his career as an architect. With the support of Tedesko and Novack, he'd risen fast, their clique benefiting them all. Years later, he discovered his sweetheart had jilted him for Sterling, taking her own life when the doctor didn't return her affections. With this knowledge, the designer found himself chained to the one person responsible for his unending despair. A truth he couldn't evade, no matter how much he drank and plotted his revenge.

As Cecil Sheppard approached, symbolically crossing the wall of fire through a narrow gap, Quill stepped forth. While her cheeks glowed through the battle scars, she bent low to her master. Then, dipping the metallic disc into the magnificent golden ewer, she filled it with cool clean water and placed it at her feet. As it cascaded over the sides, mingling with the rainfall, she glimpsed Red in his distinctive uniform hovering behind the main event, standing by to deliver justice in private. The guardsman chewed his fingernails, awkward and out of place. He'd reluctantly agreed to Novack's participation in the show for the sake of appearances, but she knew he hated the compromise. Still fuming over Uriah Crisp's escape despite the handcuffs, he'd recovered a vast quantity of Euphoria in a cave accessed from a tunnel behind the club's stage. Exploration of the tunnels revealed a myriad of long forgotten entrances, like the hole hidden in the undergrowth at Guidance Grove. Cross-checking with the drug deaths, someone had been stripping bodies of their dignity and dumping them a short distance from a concealed shaft. An ingenious scheme which disguised the macabre finds as random unconnected incidents. The details brought Quill circling back to Novack's half-sibling, Henry. An imposter who now languished in the lock-up at Guard HQ, expecting to be re-united with his brother after the ritual.

None of the lies might have surfaced without Crisp's devotion to his stomach. Uriah's search for an early morning snack meant he witnessed Henry's brutal attack on his brother. A fortunate coincidence for the diplomat. With his own agenda, Crisp surprised the Sterling lookalike then persuaded him to join forces. With the Protectorate's leader of action in the forge, the pair schemed to replace him with his half-sibling. Henry swore there'd been a woman in charge. A curvaceous lady with floor-length silver hair, though he'd never caught sight of her face. Quill recognised the singer from the description which also explained Uriah's risqué tattoo, a blatant declaration of passion if ever she'd seen one. Red unearthed no evidence to corroborate that such a person existed, and the patrons were unlikely to incriminate themselves by volunteering any information.

The Chief discovered a pair of walking sticks, a thick black wool coat and a grey fake beard among the drug vials. The items confused them all until Kai reported Professor Moore missing the day after Quill's daring exploits. Reminded that you should never judge a book by its cover, she'd made her own connections between the mysterious woman and Kai once again finding himself without an employer.

The master nodded, the sign to douse Sheppard in the water she'd collected. A symbolic gesture which washed away his old existence as he embraced the new. Followed by a procession of youthful, expectant faces, each trod through the blaze; Prosper Foley, Jacob Dowling and the Leitch brothers. Aric humbled as she purged him in the same fashion as the rest. The inexperienced students chastised and detached from the hideous Norris on Wittgenstein's orders.

As the sky blackened, a thunderclap boomed overhead. Rain spears stung them as the remaining scholars received their blessing. Until at last Quill encountered the sole barb threatening to pierce her soul—Bran, his imposing and irresistible nature difficult to stomach in the face of his betrayal. So they faced each other, unrepentant as the tempest raged around them.

"Scholar Harland, you have proved yourself the brightest and most capable student and worthy of special recognition." The storm muffled Dr Novack's speech as Quill radiated superiority, smiling like a silent assassin knowing that this honour arose from her diligent teaching. "You will travel, studying across the continent of Neorah and reporting your discoveries as you go. Be reborn and start at once."

Master Godwin beat the final gong. A deep vibrating tone amplified a tremendous thunder roll, while Quill loaded the concluding dish with water from the gleaming vessel, raising it above Bran's shining bald scalp.

Then the nova imploded. A dazzling white flare, blinding in its ferocity. Neorah and everything in it bleached of colour, replaced by utter darkness as the star perished. The death of light above Scolaris generated a collective gasp from the multitude of spectators. With everybody's eyes trained on the skies, a jagged spear of lightning ripped through the atmosphere. A clamorous crackle accompanied an earth shattering sonic boom as the indiscriminate power of nature struck a target. Startled, Quill flinched, throwing liquid far and wide as the salver flew from her grasp, time slowing as she watched it fall. Rolling and tumbling, it clattered to the ground, spinning on its shiny edge until it rested against a naked skull.

In the darkness and confusion, Quill sank to her knees, wailing into the wind as she clutched Harland in her arms. As Bran's pulse ebbed, she cradled him as Olga Blackwood had once held her beloved son Otto. In that moment, hatred, love and life drained unchecked like pulverised ash through her powerless fingers.

Thank you so much for reading *The Death of Light,* Book 2 in the Scolaris Mystery Series.

Would you like to discover more about Master Wittgenstein? Delve into his past? The truth might surprise you!

Sign up to my mailing list and I'll send *The Death of Hope*, Book 0.5, a prequel short mystery in the series, straight to your inbox.

Get the FREE eBook at loulovesbooks.com/hopebk2 and be the first to hear about new releases.

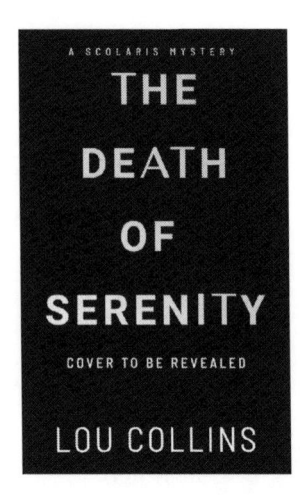

Coming next...

As the Serene Maiden departs for Asteria, Quill embarks on an exciting journey aboard the magnificent ship. But as the tranquil waters give way to dark secrets and hidden dangers, she finds herself facing her most challenging mystery yet...

Enjoy the Story?

I want to share the magic of stories with as many readers as possible. But, here's the problem—have you ever felt like finding your next great read is like looking for a single strand of hair in an ocean of DNA? Well, for a new author, multiply the size of that ocean by a bazillion (not sure that's actually a number?!), and that's the probability of readers finding my books (eek).

Before I lose all hope, if you enjoyed the story, you can help other readers find the book by leaving a review on Amazon, Apple Books, Kobo, Google Play, BookBub and Goodreads. Or anywhere else you can think of!

Thank you so much for your review <3.

Also By Lou Collins

<u>Chloe Essex Cozy Mysteries</u>
The Only Way is Larceny, a prequel short mystery
The Only Way is Murder, Book 1
The Only Way is Forgery, Book 2 coming soon
The Only Way is Burglary, Book 3 coming soon

<u>The Scolaris Mystery Series (not-so-cozy)</u>
The Death of Hope, a prequel novelette
The Death of Knowledge, Book 1
The Death of Light, Book 2
The Death of Serenity, Book 3

About Lou Collins

Lou grew up in Essex, England, reading Swallows and Amazons, the Chronicles of Narnia and the Lord of the Rings. Tales which sparked a passion for mystery and adventure.

Uniquely influenced by a touch of legal wizardry, her writing also weaves together the echoes of classic mystery writers like Agatha Christie and Sir Arthur Conan Doyle.

In Lou's cozy and not-so-cozy mysteries, you'll encounter a vibrant cast of quirky characters, cunning puzzles, and unexpected twists that will keep you on the edge of your seat. Prepare to be swept away by Lou's wicked sense of humour as her tales unfold at a thrilling pace, leaving you grinning from ear to ear.

When Lou isn't immersed in the world of storytelling, she finds joy in ballet and theatre trips. And, in a spirited plea against the pointless and mundane, she invites you to join her one-woman-crusade to defeat ironing!

Don't miss out!

To learn more, find Lou online: loulovesbooks.com or follow her in all the places:

- facebook.com/loulovesb00ks
- instagram.com/loulovesb00ks
- tiktok.com/@loucollinsauthor/
- amazon.com/author/loucollins/
- goodreads.com/author/show/5231961.Lou_Collins/
- bookbub.com/profile/lou-collins?follow=true

Printed in Great Britain
by Amazon